He couldn't believe his eyes!

Every muscle in Jabarie's body froze. He knew her. Even from the distance he could see her perpetually pouting lips and those large hazel eyes, or was it because he had those features committed to memory? After the way his pride had been badly stomped, he wasn't likely to ever forget.

As he tried to reclaim his breathing, he continued to watch the woman rearrange the front display in the small bookstore across the street.

She was barely five-four yet packed a lot of curves onto her small frame. Curves he remembered holding in his arms all too well. Open at the top, her clinging pink blouse revealed smooth caramel skin and cleavage that sent his libido into overdrive. It had been a long time since any woman had gotten to him like this. Why'd it have to be Brenna Gathers? Jabarie let out a deep sigh. It took a lot of guts for her to come back to Sheraton Beach after what she had done…

Books by Angie Daniels

Kimani Romance

The Second Time Around

ANGIE DANIELS

is an award-winning author of twelve works of romance and fiction. A chronic daydreamer, she knew early on that someday she wanted to create page-turning stories of love and adventure. Born in Chicago, Angie has spent the last twenty years residing in and around Missouri and considers the state her home. Angie holds a master's in human resource management. For more on this author you can visit her Web site at www.angiedaniels.com.

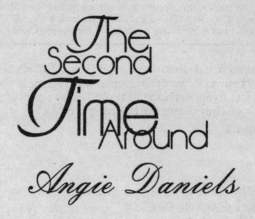

The Second Time Around

Angie Daniels

KIMANI
ROMANCE

This book is dedicated to my girls Tonya Hill (Gross)
and Latoyia Edwards for keeping me laughing while
I was trying to finish this book. The next glass of
Grey Goose and cranberry is on me!

KIMANI PRESS™

ISBN-13: 978-0-373-86023-4
ISBN-10: 0-373-86023-4

THE SECOND TIME AROUND

Copyright © 2007 by Angie Daniels

www.kimanipress.com

Printed in U.S.A.

Dear Reader,

Well it appears that after years of heartache and pain, love has prevailed, and Brenna and Jabarie are back together again. I wish them a life filled with happiness and little Beaumonts running underfoot.

I spent four years living in Delaware and fell in love with the beaches. While lying out on the sand, listening to the ocean, I came up with the idea to create a beach town of my own. Sorry, folks, Sheraton Beach doesn't really exist; however, I hope you enjoyed your visit enough to come back. After all, Bianca is ready to give love a second chance and of course we can't forget about Jace. Just how long is it going to take before he realizes that love has always been standing right in front of him? Hmm…
I guess we'll have to wait and see.

Until next time!

Angie Daniels

Chapter 1

Jabarie Beaumont had a feeling that something was about to happen.

He had felt it last night and again earlier this morning. Even now while on his way to work, the strong sensation still hadn't gone away. As he turned his silver Lincoln Navigator onto Main Street, he scowled. Whatever it was, he hoped it hurried up and happened.

While obeying the twenty-mile-an-hour speed limit, his eyes traveled up and down the wide cobblestone street that was lined with single story buildings and mom and pop stores. Summer was a busy time for the merchants of Sheraton Beach. Inside, store clerks were waiting anxiously for tourists to arrive. The Main Street Café was already crowded with people dying to taste Carla's infamous pecan waffles.

At the end of the block, Jabarie eased to a complete stop and waited for the light to change. Tapping his fingers lightly against the steering wheel, he gazed over at the Cornerstone Bookstore. The quaint little store had been a prominent fixture on the busy corner for over two decades. Dozens of books of all genres were proudly displayed on one side of the window and at the other end…was a woman. Pursing his lips thoughtfully, Jabarie wondered who she was. He knew she wasn't the owner. Ever since she had twisted her ankle three days ago, Ms. Nellie had been at home with strict instructions to stay off her feet. The store had been closed ever since.

Jabarie lowered his sunglasses and rolled down the window so he could get a closer look. The woman turned slightly and removed a book from the display shelf. Her honey brown hair tumbled across her shoulders, glistening in the sunlight. White shorts that were barely legal clung to her hips and showed off shapely long legs.

Every muscle in his body froze. He knew her. Even from the distance he could see her pouty raised lips and those large hazel eyes, or was it because he had them embedded to memory? After the way his pride had been badly stomped, he wasn't likely to ever forget.

The driver behind him blew his horn. Startled, Jabarie put his foot on the gas and moved through the light then eased to a complete stop directly across from the bookstore. As he tried to reclaim his breathing, he continued to watch the woman rearrange the front display.

She was barely five-four yet packed a lot of curves onto that small frame. Curves he remembered holding in his arms all too well. Open at the top, her clinging pink blouse revealed smooth caramel skin and cleavage that sent his libido into overdrive. Damn, it had been a long time since any woman had gotten to him like this. Why'd it have to be Brenna Gathers? Jabarie let out a deep sigh. It took a lot of guts for her to come back to Sheraton Beach after what she had done.

"Don't even go there," he told himself firmly, but it was too late, his mind had already delivered detailed memories he'd rather forget. Details of the night she'd walked out on him.

Shaking his head, he still couldn't believe she was back. After she skipped town the night before their wedding, he never thought he'd see her again. The recollection brought along with it a flash of anger he quickly pushed aside. It no longer mattered, he told himself. That was five long years ago.

"So what are you going to do?" he heard himself say. If he had any sense, he would have put his Navigator into Drive and sped towards work. But he'd never been able to think straight when Brenna was involved. After a long thoughtful moment, Jabarie decided he couldn't sit outside forever. He climbed out of the SUV and moved across the cobblestone street. But instead of going straight to the door, he stopped on the sidewalk, directly in front of the window.

After all these years, what did he possibly have to say to her? Brenna walked out on him, not the other way around. His hand stilled over his heart, the one she'd torn to shreds years ago. He'd gone on to build a life without her and regretted the feelings that just looking at her could still bring forth. Gazing through the window, he scowled. It wasn't fair that she still looked

amazing. Her curvy body was exactly the same as he
remembered. It just wasn't fair. Their reunion would
be so much easier if she had gained weight. Instead,
she looked better than ever.

Brenna Gathers was still nothing short of gorgeous. She was the kind of woman that with a single
smile could get a man to do anything she wanted. He
always wondered if she knew she had that type of
effect on people. Obviously, she had. Otherwise she
would have never had the guts to ask his mother for
one-hundred-thousand dollars.

He sighed deeply, and as if she'd heard, Brenna
shifted in the window and her gaze came up to meet his.
He knew the moment she recognized him. Her jaw
dropped and her body went slack and a half a dozen
books fell from her cradled arms. Her cheeks were
flushed and she blinked rapidly. His surprise at seeing
her again was nothing compared to her reaction.

Good.

Turning on his heels, Jabarie headed toward the
door.

Brenna had known it was only a matter of time.

There was no way she could have returned to a small
town like Sheraton Beach and not run into Jabarie Beaumont, although she had prayed for a miracle.

In the meantime, she had tried to prepare for this exact moment. She had even memorized what she would
say. The tilt of her head even practiced a mechanical
smile. But now that the moment had finally arrived, she
scrambled her brain, and for the life of her she couldn't
remember any of it. Instead she closed her eyes and

took a deep breath just as the bell over the door jingled, letting her know Jabarie had entered.

"Hello, Bren."

The heat from his words radiated her body. Just as it did every time she dreamed about him. How ridiculous she had been to think that she could have prepared for this exact moment.

Brenna swung away from the window and forced herself to finally face the man who five years ago had broken her heart. Looking up into his piercing dark eyes, her breath caught in her throat. They were so intense, she felt like she had been hit over the head. She had to force herself to speak. "Jabarie," she said breathlessly.

"I didn't know you were back in town."

His voice sounded cool and controlled while his eyes studied her reactions. Needing to free herself of his intense stare, she dropped her gaze and stepped away from the window. Her knees were shaking, and it angered her that after all these years he still had that kind of affect on her. Moving behind the counter, she looked up at him again and tried to keep her emotions in check. "I got in last night," she said, struggling to find her voice. "As soon as Aunt Nellie told me she'd twisted her ankle, I tied up some loose ends and came back to help run the store until she's back on her feet."

Jabarie's brow furrowed. "I just saw your aunt. She never mentioned that you were coming."

Brenna simply shrugged. "Maybe it slipped her mind. Anyway, she's at home on bed rest."

He let out a slow breath. "I know. I'm the one who drove her home from the clinic."

"You did?" Brenna found it equally strange that her aunt had forgotten to mention that Jabarie had brought her home. Then again, the way she cut her aunt off at any mention of her former fiancé, she couldn't blame her.

"I even called and checked on her this morning and Ms. Nellie never mentioned you were back."

"Someone has to run the store," Brenna replied as she continued to look across at the man she had loved since the fourth grade and gave him her full attention. Good Lord. He was still fine as ever. His large dark eyes were still mesmerizing, his dimples irresistible, and his mouth still just as delectable looking as ever. It had been five years yet right now it felt like she had just left. The pain had resurrected and panged her heart. She had hoped with time and distance she would have gotten over him. But sadly she hadn't. She had never forgotten a single detail. Realizing her thoughts were heading down the wrong road, she busied herself straightening a stack of bookmarks. Next thing she knew, Jabarie had moved behind the counter. Goodness, she hadn't even heard him move.

"How long are you staying?" Jabarie asked, leaning in closer, caging her in behind the counter.

"Uh…until Aunt Nellie's back on her feet." She took a deep breath. His cologne hadn't changed in five years, or was that just his natural scent?

"Then what?" he asked silkily.

"I go back to my life," she replied barely above a whisper.

Brenna noticed his eyes darkened dangerously before he stepped away and moved over to gaze out the large floor-to-ceiling window. She took that moment to try and pull herself together as she stared at his strong profile.

After doing a complete sweep of his body, she noticed Jabarie had packed on the muscles over the years. He had always taken care of himself and the solid body standing before her was definitely proof of that. Jabarie still wore his thick curly hair low on top and faded on the sides. Above his right brow was a scar that he'd gotten while the two were skateboarding. She had to have been ten. Jabarie hadn't noticed the rock that jammed one of the wheels of his board and had sent him landing face first onto the hot asphalt. She had never seen so much blood in her life. Yet, thirteen stitches later, they were back racing up and down the street.

"How have you been?" She knew that question sounded stupid but at the moment she didn't know what else to say.

Jabarie turned away from the window, hands buried in the pockets of his pleated slacks and nodded. "I've been well, and what about you?"

Still trying to get over you. She swallowed. "I've been busy."

"So I've heard," he said, his voice dripping with sarcasm.

"What's that supposed to mean?" she countered.

He raked a hand across his face. As she stared up at his intense gaze she realized one thing hadn't changed. He still managed to make her heart flutter with a single look.

"That means I heard you opened your own bookstore." His voice had softened considerably.

Brenna simply nodded.

"I'm glad to hear your dream finally came true."

Her dream had been to be his wife and have a couple of babies. Just thinking about it caused anger to brew to the surface, but she wasn't about to go there. "Thank you." She didn't know what else to say.

"Have dinner with me tonight?"

Brenna gasped. Sharing time together was the last thing she had expected to hear from him. Jabarie moved toward her then lifted one hand and caressed the side of her face. She tried to stay still and fought the urge to close her eyes and lean into his hand.

"Why would you want to have dinner?"

He cocked his head to the side and frowned. "Why not?"

She backed away from the heat of his hand and sucked in some much needed air. Afraid he might see how badly her hands were shaking, she moved over to the coffeepot brewing in the corner and shook her head. "I don't think that's a good idea."

"And I asked you why not?"

Before she could come up with a plausible answer, the sound of the bell jingled over the door, shaking Brenna out of the private place she'd gone too. A woman with identical twins moved to the children's section of the store. Brenna sent a smile their way then looked back over at Jabarie again. "I need to get back to work," she said and turned on her heels.

"Shall I take that as a no?"

She stopped and turned around. He stood before her trying to hide his anger but Brenna had always been able to look into his eyes and see beneath the surface.

"I think it's best if we leave the past behind us."

Chapter 2

For the rest of the afternoon, Brenna was a nervous wreck. She spent half the day thinking about Jabarie, and the other half on pins and needles expecting him to walk through the door at any moment. The younger Jabarie would have, she thought as she shut off the coffeepot. Stubborn and used to getting what he wanted, he was never one to accept no for an answer. Five years ago, he would have kissed her senseless until she'd agreed to have dinner. But as she moved to make sure everything was locked up tight for the night, she realized a lot of time had passed. She was no longer naive and twenty-one. She was a different woman and apparently Jabarie was a different man.

With a sigh, Brenna turned out the last light in the store then armed the alarm on the way out. It had been

a long and tiring day. Nevertheless, Aunt Nellie would
be quite pleased. The store had had a good day.

While moving out to her aunt's Toyota Corolla, she
inhaled the salted air and allowed the feeling of home
to wrap around her. Despite her reason for leaving in
the first place, it felt good to be back, even if it was
only temporary.

Brenna climbed behind the driver's seat and started
the car. If it hadn't been for a box of used books she
needed to bring into the store this morning, she would
have walked into town like she had done for as long as
she could remember.

Driving slowly down Main Street, she noted how
little the ocean-view town had changed in the last five
years. She was pleased to discover it had preserved its
small-town charm. Annie's Antiques was still to her left
and the Sheraton Gift Shop to her right. One thing she
noticed was that Gabe's Candy Store was gone. Her lips
curled upward as she remembered dashing there every
Friday only seconds after receiving her weekly allow-
ance. The store with the bright red awning out front was
now a video store. From the crowd of young kids standing out front, Video Adventure was the happening place
to be.

As she turned onto Palmer Road, she allowed her
mind to travel back to the good times. Chasing ice
cream trucks, flying kites, and of course hours of
swimming. Feelings of warmth flooded through her
chest. Yep, it was good to be back even if it was just for
a short time. In three weeks she would return to her new
life and once again leave the past behind.

Brenna pulled in front of her aunt's small, ranch-style

home and turned off the car. As she climbed out, she exchanged waves with Ms. Lucy next door, who was sitting out on her porch swing.

"It's nice to have you back," the seventy-year-old widow said in a low raspy voice.

As Brenna moved up the sidewalk, she gave the woman who made the best peach cobbler in town a friendly smile. "It's nice to be back, Ms. Lucy." Then with a nod, she hurried through the front door before the old lady could strike up a conversation. Once she did, there was no escaping.

Brenna tossed her purse onto the couch then glanced around the small uncluttered room. Everything was handmade, from the Afghans draped across the aging furniture, to the crochet tablecloth and homemade drapes. The thing she loved the most about the house she had grown up in, was the abundance of windows overlooking the smooth, sandy Atlantic shore where as a child she had spent hours playing.

Removing her tennis shoes, Brenna padded across the hardwood floor and entered the first room on the right where her Aunt Nellie was sitting up in a full-size bed with her ankle propped up on a pillow.

"There you are," she replied, chestnut eyes dancing with excitement. "I was wondering when you'd get in."

Brenna flopped down onto the rocking chair beside her bed. "Busy afternoon. Where in the world did all these people come from?"

Her aunt chuckled lightly. "It's gotten really popular around here since you left. I think tourists have discovered that by traveling just a little farther south from

Rehoboth Beach they can find a small town more
charming than any other resort on the east coast."

Brenna nodded in agreement. In the last several
years several families had converted their homes into
a bed and breakfast. No sky rises. Nothing commercial-
ized. Sheraton Beach offered their visitors beautiful
blue waters, friendly local merchants, and old fash-
ioned hospitality. It was some of the things she missed
most about this place.

"How did you get along today?"

Aunt Nellie gave her a dismissive wave. "Don't
worry. I was fine. Lucy came over and made me lunch
and then rolled my hair while we watched the soaps."
At fifty-five, her thick shoulder-length hair still didn't
have a strand of gray.

Brenna crossed her ankles and smiled. It had always
eased her mind to know that the small close-knit community always knew how to pull together when a resi-
dent was in need. It was one of the advantages of living
in a small town. The disadvantage was that everyone
knew everyone else and gossip spread fast. She could
bet word had already spread of her return to Sheraton
Beach.

"You see anybody in particular today?"

"Anyone like who?" Brenna asked, suddenly becoming suspicious.

Aunt Nellie shrugged. "Oh, I don't know…like
maybe Jabarie perhaps?"

Just as she'd suspected, someone had already
blabbed about him coming into the bookstore.

"Who told you that?"

Her aunt turned to her with an amused look on her

face. "Gavin Holmes said Jabarie stopped in the middle of Main Street and almost caused a traffic jam when he spotted you standing in the window."

"What?" she cried at the ridiculous story. Mr. Holmes was practically ninety and blind in one eye. "Aunt Nellie, you don't actually believe that do you?"

"When it comes to you and Jabarie, yes I do."

At one time she would have thought the same but not anymore. She shook her head. "It was nothing like that, believe me."

"What did the two of you talk about?" she asked, eyes wide with curiosity.

"Nothing really," Brenna said trying to sound bored. "He asked how long I was going to be here. I told him then went to help a customer."

Aunt Nellie's brow arched. "You sure he didn't ask you to dinner?"

"How did…" she paused and gave her aunt a long suspicious look. She was fishing and she wasn't about to bite her hook. "No, he didn't, and even if he had, I would have told him no. He had his chance five years ago and blew it."

Aunt Nellie looked disappointed by her response. "I really wish the two of you would take the time to talk."

"What's there to talk about? He betrayed me. End of story. There is really no point in reliving that time again. Besides, I'm leaving as soon as you're back on your feet." With that she rose. "You need anything?"

Her aunt gave her a long hard look then finally shook her head. "No. I'm going to sit here and watch *Deal or No Deal*. Why don't you sit back down and join me?"

"Maybe later," Brenna replied with a weary sigh.

"I'm going to go shower and fix myself something to eat."

"Mabel brought by some fried chicken."

At the mention of Ms. Butler's famous southern fried chicken, her stomach growled. "Sounds scrumptious." With a finger wave, she moved toward the door.

"Brenna?"

She stopped and turned. "Yes, Aunt Nellie?"

"I'm glad you're here," she said with a wink.

Brenna couldn't resist a smile. "So am I."

Showered and dressed in an oversized orange T-shirt, Brenna leaned back against the long wooden bench and propped her feet onto the porch railing. Staring out at the Atlantic Ocean, she couldn't imagine a view that was quite as breathtaking. A distance away, high on a hill overlooking the ocean, lights glittered from the Beaumont Hotel. Guests could utilize the hotel's lavish accommodations or stroll down onto a private beach. It was a luxurious structure with marble flooring, cathedral ceilings, sixteenth century furnishings and columns throughout the main lobby. She should know. By the age of twelve, Brenna had known every single corner of the hotel. Seeing it again after all these years brought back memories, some more painful than others. Dropping her forehead to the palm of her hand, she tried to brush the past aside but it was too late. The memories had already pushed to the surface.

Her mother Shaunda Gathers had once been the hotel's housekeeping supervisor. She was a beautiful woman who'd always believed there was something better out there waiting for her. She despised having to clean rooms up after rich folks. She wanted to be one of the guests arriving with Louis Vuitton luggage, dressed in Donna Karan suits and staying in the presidential suite. Brenna remembered her mother often saying how life was unfair.

And then Shaunda met a rich, married politician who swept her off her feet and promised her the life she had always dreamed of as his mistress. She took it, leaving her daughter behind along with a scandal that local folks talked about for years.

Brenna tried to push away the nauseating feeling she got every time she remembered the day her mother abandoned her. Thank goodness her mother's older sister welcomed her into her home, and smothered her with more love than she could ever imagine. During that time, Aunt Nellie was all she had in the world besides her dear friend Jabarie Beaumont.

The two of them had been friends since he had caught her running through the main lobby of the hotel. Heir to the Beaumont fortune, Jabarie was required to spend all his summers at the hotel learning everything there was to learn. When he started cleaning the guest rooms, Brenna was certain that wasn't what his father Roger Beaumont had meant by learning the business from the ground up, but Jabarie didn't seem to mind and neither did she. While her mother daydreamed, flirted, and tried on clothing that belonged to the hotel's wealthy guests, the two of them would change the linen and vacuum the rooms.

Brenna pulled a leg to her chest and couldn't help smiling. They used to have so much fun together. Then on her thirteenth birthday, Jabarie gave her a plastic ring from a Cracker Jack box, and promised that some day they would marry and run the hotel together. Although, both innocent at the time, he was her first love. However, after her mother ran off with the politician everything changed. His parents looked down on her more than ever before and Brenna was no longer allowed at the hotel. What was even worse, Jabarie was forbidden to ever see her again. She remembered crying for three days. It was bad enough her mother had abandoned her. Although as she had grown older, she realized that Shaunda Gathers had never really been much of a mother. She was too busy chasing after a dream. It was Aunt Nellie who had nurtured and cared for her since birth. No, what had hurt the most during that painful time was losing her best friend. Yes, as much as she hated to admit it, she had loved Jabarie Beaumont from as far back as she could remember.

Hours later, the shock of finding him standing outside the bookstore was still buzzing through her mind. Shifting on the bench, Brenna pushed the memory aside and focused on the boats in the distance. Moored to a pier, they bobbed. To the far left of the hotel was a long boardwalk lined with tourist shops and plenty of food, all starting to close up for the night. Her eyes shifted to the Beaumont Hotel again and with it more thoughts of Jabarie surfaced. Leaning back, she took a deep breath, trying again to wipe him from her thoughts. Seeing him today shouldn't have been so difficult. After all, five years had passed. Five long painful years, which as far as she was concerned, was long enough to have gotten him out of her heart.

She could still see him standing outside the bookstore window staring at her. Her breath had caught in her throat, startling her so, she had dropped a handful of books. He was the only man who had ever made her feel that way. Vulnerable, weak, and so madly in love. Brenna groaned inwardly. Oh, what a fool she had been. Young and so naive to have thought she could have had it all.

Nothing about their relationship had ever been easy, first her mother, then his uppity parents, and then the wedding that never happened. Brenna closed her eyes and tipped her face into the cool breeze while her hair blew about her face. This was exactly what she needed to calm her thoughts and cool the desire blazing within, only it wasn't working. She couldn't stop thinking about Jabarie, and what if things had been different.

She shook her head then convinced herself that things would have never worked between them. They were from two different worlds. Although to Jabarie that never seemed to matter, or at least that was what she had thought. It still pained her to think about the hurt, the betrayal. The night before her wedding was supposed to have been the happiest time of her life. And in a matter of seconds her heart had been torn from her chest.

Brenna took a deep breath of the crisp salted air and reminded herself that was all in the past. She now had a wonderful new life in Dallas and was the owner of her own Cornerstone Bookstore. If nothing else, she had Jabarie to thank for seeing her dream come true. The check he had pawned her off with had provided her the means to start over.

One thing she could say for sure, was that she had gotten over some of her anger. Even when she saw him today, being angry was the last thing on her mind. Let

bygones be bygones she'd always said. She had forgiven him years ago; her problem was forgetting. There
was still a small piece of her hurting from his betrayal
even after all these years. Because of him she had never
had another successful relationship. Because of him,
she was afraid to trust another man. Only she couldn't
keep going on like this. Not if she hoped to someday
have a family of her own.

It's time to let go.

Opening her eyes, she stared up at the starlit sky. The
salty air, the sandy shore, Sheraton Beach was home to
her past. It had been easy pushing Jabarie to the corner
of her mind while living in Dallas. The distance was a
perfect barrier. But being back was something altogether
different. Inside, a part of her was aching for him and
what could have been if they had gotten married. But
that time in her life was over and it was time for her to
let go and move on. If nothing else, she needed to find
closure so that when she left Sheraton Beach for good
this time, she could finally get on with her life.

Chapter 3

The following morning Brenna walked to work, glad for the opportunity to clear her head after a night of tossing and turning. Jabarie had invaded her dreams. Somehow she was going to have to find a way to close that chapter in her life before she returned to Dallas.

She arrived at the bookstore shortly after nine to find a pretty teenager waiting on the front steps. Since long before Brenna was even tall enough to reach the cash register, Aunt Nellie had offered part-time employment to students who had proved themselves academically during the school year.

"You must me Rachel," she greeted with a wide friendly smile.

The blonde pushed her glasses up over her nose and nodded. "Yes, ma'am."

Brenna frowned playfully as she stuck her key in the door. "We won't have any of that. I'm Brenna, and I'm so glad to see you. My aunt warned me we're in for a busy day." On Fridays the store offered buy one get one half priced and according to Aunt Nellie, the promotion was quite a hit.

Just as she promised, the bookstore was extremely busy. While Rachel handled story-time hour, and the dozen or so children that came to listen, Brenna assisted their customers and worked the register. By lunchtime she was hungry and exhausted. Where in the world did all these people come from she wondered. Not that she was complaining, but she never dreamed so many people read during their summer vacation. By two o'clock people were still coming through the door and Rachel, who had an appointment with her orthodontist, had already gone for the day. Brenna was trying to explain to a woman that half price was offered on the book of the lesser price when she spotted a tall handsome man moving toward her. Her heart raced. Jabarie was wearing an expensive navy blue suit including tie and wing-tip shoes. He had no business looking that good. No business at all, she thought as he moved closer. She released the breath she had been holding and watched as he headed in her direction. Desire rolled though her body. She hadn't felt like this in years and hated him for that. Hated him because she still wanted him.

"Looks like you could use some help," Jabarie said as he moved around behind the counter.

The deep sensual tone of his voice vibrated through her body and settled down low. She caught his scent.

His presence pulsed around her. Suddenly, panic gripped her. She shook her head. "I'm fine, really."

"No, you're not," he mumbled under his breath.

Glancing at the people standing and waiting patiently in line, she inhaled deeply and had no choice but to agree to his help. While she finished ringing up customers, she watched as Jabarie slipped out of his jacket and moved to help the next person in line.

For the next half hour she worked the counter while he assisted customers throughout the store. As soon as the last customer left through the door, Brenna moved over to the nearest chair and flopped down on the seat.

Jabarie leaned against the counter. "Looks like you've had a long day."

She gave a tired laugh. "Yes, I have." She gazed up at him towering over her and couldn't resist a smile. "Thanks for your help."

"No problem. Have you eaten yet?" he asked following a long pause.

Brenna pushed a wayward curl away from her face and shook her head just as the bell over the door jingled. With a groan, she slowly rose from the chair.

Pushing away from the counter, Jabarie replied, "Help your customer while I go up the street and grab you something to eat."

She was too hungry to argue.

Jabarie walked to the end of the block to Clarence's Chicken and Fish House. As he strolled through the door, the smell of fish floated to his nose. The lunch rush was over but there were still plenty of patrons filling the wooden tables. He moved up to the register and spotted Old Man Clarence behind the counter.

"Well, well, well, if it isn't Master Beaumont," he greeted with a hearty chuckle that jiggled his round belly.

"Hello, Clarence," he returned with a scowled. Since Beaumont Manor was on top of a hill, looking down on the small town, rumor had it that his family were descendants of royalty. There was no truth to the rumors but for decades no one seemed to care. The Beaumonts were prominent and important members of the community. Although the hotel was responsible for creating an abundance of jobs and for keeping food on so many tables in Sheraton Beach, Jabarie had always felt uncomfortable by the way so many people treated him.

"What can I do for you?"

After quickly glancing at the menu on the wall, Jabarie replied, "I'll take two of your fish specials."

Clarence's eyes lit up. "Two? One wouldn't be for a particular beauty who just recently returned to our small town, would it?"

Jabarie didn't even know why he was surprised. Word definitely had gotten around fast.

At his silence Clarence continued. "The reason I asked is because Ms. Brenna doesn't like catfish fillets. She only eats the nuggets."

Jabarie raked a hand across his face. How could he have forgotten? She preferred not having to deal with bones. He gave the sixty-year-old man a sheepish grin and said, "Then you better make one catfish nuggets."

Clarence winked. "Coming right up."

While he waited, Jabarie strolled over to the window and felt his cell phone vibrate at his hip. Glancing down

at his hip, he noticed it was his brother Jace calling, probably to remind him of his five-o'clock meeting. As the
hotel's general manager, his days were usually bom-
barded with meetings. Not in the mood to discuss
business, he ignored the call and allowed it to go into
voicemail.

Staring over at the bookstore, Jabarie asked himself
after several seconds, what in the world was he doing
spending the afternoon helping Brenna? After everything she had done why in the world was he having anything at all to do with her? That was something he was
unable to answer except to say he had done nothing but
think of her since seeing her standing in the window
yesterday. She dominated his thoughts, haunted his
dream last night, until he couldn't even draw a breath
without smelling her feminine scent. This morning he
had awakened with a hard-on and the burning need to
see her. A part of him still found it hard to believe that
she was back in Sheraton Beach and thought maybe it
had just been a dream. He had hurried out of his twelve
o'clock meeting just so he could drive down onto Main
Street. As soon as he had stepped into the bookstore his
heart hammered against his chest, and when he saw the
look of panic on her face he had rushed to her aid just
as he always had. For as long as he could remember,
he'd had this strong need to protect her.

Jabarie's gaze darted up and down the street but his
eyes were zeroed in on the bookstore. Now that he'd
seen her, he couldn't stay away and that was strange
considering he was supposed to hate her for having
chosen money over his love. For the last five years he
tried to hate her, but couldn't. He found that a part of

him had forgiven her for walking out on him with money he was certain his mother had been more than happy to give. The other part of him still loved her. He guessed everyone felt like that about their first love. However, for him, Brenna had been his only love.

Jabarie felt his body responding just thinking about her. He still wanted her. He could already taste her delicious mouth. Her thick honey-colored hair he longed to run his fingers through. He ached to touch her, to make love to her again. Desire tore through him, and Jabarie ran his hand over his face shaken by the depth of his need. It had been five years. Five long years, and in one day all the emotions and feelings he had felt then had come rushing back. He asked himself the same question he had asked himself so many times before, of all the women he had met, why Brenna?

Damn, he needed to stop thinking about her. *But I can't*, he thought as he reached up and loosened his collar. After everything they had been through, he knew it was ridiculous to still feel anything for her. Now that she was back, maybe if they spent enough time together whatever he thought he still felt for her would die. Maybe that was what they both needed to end what had started five years ago. Maybe during her visit they could both discover that it was really over between them. That there wasn't anything left to hold on to any longer.

Jabarie sighed deeply. One thing he knew for sure was that, no matter how short her visit may be, he planned to find a way to get her out of his system once and for all.

"I got your order ready."

He reached into his pocket for his billfold and moved toward the register. As soon as Clarence noticed the money in his hand, he shook his head. "It's on the house. Tell Brenna I made it just the way she likes it."

"I'll do that, thanks." He reached for the Styrofoam containers and headed out the door. Halfway down the street, Jabarie slowed his step when he realized he was practically running.

As soon as he returned, Brenna moved to the small office to the side of the store and dove into the food while Jabarie covered the floor. As she chewed, she made a mental note to thank Mr. Clarence for remembering she loved her catfish nuggets smothered in hot sauce. She took another bite and groaned out loud. Nobody's catfish came close to his. It was no wonder he'd been in business for over thirty years. One of the things she had missed most about Sheraton Beach was the food.

With a heavy sigh, she reached for the orange soda and took a long swig then glanced through the glass wall at Jabarie behind the counter. He had finally loosened his tie. His wide shoulders strained against the fabric of his shirt. At six-two, he looked like a giant standing over a pair of giggling teenage girls who were obviously infatuated by his good looks. Brenna couldn't blame them. She'd been just as mesmerized at their age. Watching his mouth as he spoke she couldn't help wondering what it would be like to kiss him again. She remembered his lips being soft and gentle while his kisses used to have the power to make her toes curl. She blinked and dragged her eyes away from the glass. What in the world was she doing? *Have you forgotten he ripped your heart in two?* There was no way she was going to fall for him a second time.

Yet she couldn't take her eyes off of him. A deep sigh escaped her lips as she concluded how attracted she still was to him. Watching him excited her and sent heat flowing down between her thighs, and made her yearn to have him hold her in his arms again. She breathed quietly, stunned by the physical need that had been dormant for five years.

Hearing a light rap on the door she glanced up to find Jabarie staring down at her. Her heart did a somersault as he turned the knob and opened it.

"All quiet," he said as he rested against the doorjamb.

She swung around in the chair and took a deep calming breath before speaking. The attraction between them was much too strong for her to ignore. "Thanks for everything. I owe you one."

His dimples deepened. "Good. I'm going to hold you to that."

"It's been a zoo today. My bookstore is twice this size and in a busy part of the city, but even when my partner's out I have never been this tired."

He nodded knowingly. "The growth of Main Street has been very good for the economy around here. You might want to talk to your aunt about getting some more summer help. Those girls were just asking if there were any openings."

She just bet they did. Probably thought they'd have the privilege of seeing Jabarie every day. Jealousy brewed in her little head, and for the life of her, Brenna couldn't understand why. Jabarie meant nothing to her.

She nodded and reached for the soda can. "I'll make sure to talk to her tonight."

Jabarie nodded in agreement then glanced down at his watch. "Well, I guess I better head back to the hotel."

"Oh, gosh, yes! You better hurry before someone tells the queen you've been mingling with the peasants," she teased. And when he groaned, she laughed. Brenna knew how much he hated the wisecracks.

"I see you haven't lost your sense of humor," he said when he stopped chuckling.

Crossing her legs, Brenna returned the smile. "No, I guess I haven't," she said, even though she hadn't had a lot to laugh about lately.

There was a long silence before Jabarie finally pushed away from the door and said, "See you around."

Brenna simply nodded and watched as he retrieved his jacket and headed out the door.

The rest of the evening was smooth sailing. With food in her stomach, she was able to handle just about anything. In between customers she finished working on the display in the front window, replacing the current books with several hot new releases. However, no matter what she was doing she still had time to think about Jabarie, and she found herself wondering why he was being so nice. She pondered the question until closing time and finally came up with one possible answer—guilt. He felt guilty about breaking her heart. Well, too bad, she scowled. There was no way she was going to willingly help ease his conscience. She was going to make him earn her forgiveness, although in her heart, Brenna knew she already had.

At seven o'clock, she punched in the security code then shut the door behind her and ran right smack into Jabarie. She staggered back a step or two before he caught her.

"Oops, sorry about that."

Feeling the heat flowing from his hands, her mouth went dry and her knees trembled. A voice inside screamed for her to move closer. Instead, she flinched and stepped out of his reach. "What are you doing here?" she asked, totally shaken by his touch.

He shrugged. "I spotted Nellie's car in front of her house so I thought I'd come by and walk you home."

"Why?" she asked, finally finding her equilibrium.

He paused long enough to give her an irresistible grin. "Because I'm a gentleman."

Gazing up and down the street she returned her eyes to him. "Where's your SUV?"

"I left it in front of your aunt's house." He gave her a puzzled look. "Is something wrong?"

She shook her head and tried not to notice how relaxed he looked. He had removed his jacket and tie and his shirt hung loose with his sleeves rolled up past his elbows. Finally she shrugged, as if to say, "suit yourself," and became quiet as he fell into step beside her.

The evening brought on a gentle warm breeze that she was thankful for after a long and tiring day. As they strolled down Main Street she spotted Ms. Pearl at the sunglass shop looking through the window waving in their direction. At the jewelry store it was the same thing. By the time they had made it halfway down the block, she heard Jabarie chuckle. Shaking her hair out of her face, Brenna turned to him and asked, "What's so funny?"

He lifted his brow in amusement. "I think we're going to be the talk of the town tomorrow."

He was right. At Milly's Tailor Shop, she noticed the redhead with the receiver to her ear, pointing in her direction. Obviously, she intended to be the first to spread the news. Brenna groaned inwardly. Aunt Nellie would know long before she set foot in the house.

"That's why I didn't need you walking me home," she snapped.

Jabarie was struggling to keep a straight face. "Sorry."

Brenna glared at him. He wasn't sorry. By the look on his face, he was getting a big kick out of the whole thing. And it angered her. What did he have to be embarrassed about? She was the one who had gotten dumped five years ago.

At the watch repair shop she cut around the building and walked heavily down towards the sandy beach. She kicked off her sandals and hopped across the hot sand down to the cool, wet shore. Why should she care that a few busybodies couldn't mind their own business? But she did. She'd always cared what others thought about her. Brenna took a deep breath and kept walking, ignoring Jabarie as he called her name.

Glancing over her shoulder, she spotted him kicking off his expensive shoes and tucking his socks inside.

"Can you please slow down?" he asked as he rolled his pants up just below his knees.

"Why should I?" she called after him.

"Because I'm supposed to be walking you home!"

Brenna didn't turn around, but she did slow down so that he would have an opportunity to catch up. As she neared a couple of kids frolicking around in the water, Jabarie fell into step beside her. The wind caught her curls, tossing them hopelessly as she strolled down the shore in silence.

Brenna knew he was watching her because the hairs on the back of her neck tingled, but she didn't dare look his way. Walking along the shoreline, she stared out at the rising ocean tide instead. Seagulls screeched overhead. Tourists were sailing and fishing along the pier, others were visiting the numerous shops.

"You're still attracted to me."

"What?" She halted and planted her hand on her hips.

Jabarie pinned her with a hard look then tossed his head back, his rich laughter rolling over the ocean waves. "That's why you won't go out to dinner with me. And that's why you're angry, because everyone in town has noticed that we're still attracted to each other."

Brenna stood with her legs braced apart and her sandals clutched tightly in her left hand. "Don't flatter yourself. I got over you a long time ago." With a roll of her eyes she turned on her heels and headed down the beach again. She could see her aunt's backyard and right now it wasn't nearly close enough.

Jabarie quickly moved up beside her. "Quit lying to yourself, Bren. I know I have. We still have some unfinished business to attend to."

Not bothering to stop, she glanced to her right and rolled her eyes. "You're a bigger fool than I thought," she stated boldly. Did he really think she'd admit to holding a torch for him after all these years?

Brenna picked up her step and hurried along the shore toward the house. Anger brewed inside. The sooner she got away from Jabarie the better.

"Hey, slow down," he suddenly said and grabbed her elbow.

As she turned around she felt the imprint of his fingers branding her with his heat. It took a second or two for her to pull her brain cells together so she could reply.

"Listen," she began between breaths. "I didn't come back to town for this." He didn't let go and for some insane reason she wasn't in any rush to move.

"Can we at least talk about it?"

Talk about what? she wanted to scream. *How much I miss lying in your arms?* "I'd rather not," she retorted then blew hair out of her face. "Now if you'd let my arm go, I would like to go home and take a long hot bath and relax for the rest of the evening."

He released her and she started towards the house again, only slower this time. Jabarie moved beside her with a wing tip shoe tucked underneath each arm and his hands buried deep inside his pockets. "Brenna, I would really like to talk about what happened."

"Jabarie…" she warned. She was seconds away from weakening if she didn't put a stop to this line of questioning right now. "I don't want to talk about what could have been. We were both young and stupid back then. I've moved on, started a new life, a better life, and I don't want to go back and revisit that time…it's over."

He was quiet for the duration of the walk although she could tell he was deep in thought. Brenna didn't look his way because she didn't trust herself if she did. Instead she stared ahead and allowed the wind to whip around her. By the time they reached Aunt Nellie's gate, the cool wet sand beneath her toes had calmed some of the fire that raged inside her.

Brenna reached down to open the gate, then paused and glanced up at Jabarie standing beside her. He tilted his head, studying her face in that quiet intense way that always made her throat dry and her nipples harden. Feeling a tingling at her breasts she quickly folded her arms across her chest and said, "Thanks for walking me home."

"You're welcome."

With nothing else to say, Brenna opened the gate and stepped into the backyard.

"Remember when you said you owed me one," Jabarie called after her.

She stopped and turned slowly. Something told her she wasn't going to like what he was about to say. "Yeah, so?"

Jabarie grinned. "So, I've figured out how you can pay me back."

Afraid to ask, Brenna waited for him to speak again.

"I want a kiss," he said as if thinking out loud.

She couldn't have heard him right. "A what?" she whispered her voice uneven.

"A kiss."

"No way," she said shaking her head.

Before she had a chance to react, Jabarie moved into the yard and closed the gate behind him. "You said you're not attracted to me. If that's true then a kiss won't matter, right?"

She stared up at him and felt the sweet slow pull of want rise up in her again. From the moment he'd arrived back at the store she'd felt it. Heck, she'd felt it since the moment she spotted him staring at her from the store window. A rush of desire that was so powerful she felt her knees buckle. It was as if the last five years hadn't happened. Five years of not seeing his face, not touching his skin, not feeling him buried deep inside her. Five long years without a single tantalizing kiss. She swallowed when she saw his eyes focus in on her mouth.

At her continued silence, Jabarie smiled and finally said, "I thought you'd agree."

Brenna tried to stop the heated desire racing through her body as he dropped his shoes in the grass and took a step closer. Before she realized what she was doing, she tipped her chin and her lips parted. "You probably shouldn't," she suggested softly.

"I know," he admitted as he brushed his lips across hers. "But I'm going to do it anyway."

Before she could even prepare, Jabarie tugged her to him and took her mouth with enough heat to make her forget everything but taking all that he had to offer. As his tongue traced her lips, it occurred to her that she might have lost her mind but she didn't do anything to stop him. Instead she dropped her sandals and enjoyed the feel of his tongue sliding inside her mouth. His lips were hard and hot, and so possessive that Brenna arched up to meet him. His hands came around her waist and held her closer. It had to be a dream. Yet everything that she had remembered about Jabarie was real and it was hers again at last. He explored, teased and tasted like no one else could compare. And that was exactly why she had to fight him. His passion was enough to burn away everything else.

Jabarie was making it hard for her to resist. Desire consumed her. She pushed him away slightly to see how much he truly wanted her, and Jabarie brought her closer just as she had hoped. She sank into the hunger, the taste, the need to meet him stroke for stroke.

He deepened the kiss, one hand cupped her head, the other slid down to her buttocks and pressed her against him. She could feel him growing long and hard. And for a moment she allowed herself to remember how good he had felt buried deep inside her wet core. A moan erupted from her throat. The kiss was glorious and wild. He was zapping her senses in a way only he could. Jabarie always had that kind of power over her and he knew it. Slowly snapping out of the dizzy haze he had created, Brenna realized how easily she had succumbed to him, and knew she needed to put a halt to what was happening immediately or risk losing everything she had worked so hard to build. With a firm push, Brenna broke off the kiss, but Jabarie continued to hold her against his beating heart.

"It's not over," he whispered roughly.

She could feel him smiling as he nibbled hungrily at her earlobe. Did he really think she would forget everything that had happened between them so easily? With renewed anger, she pressed her lips against the warmth of his throat, and bit him lightly on the neck.

"Ow!" he yelled as he jumped back and gave her a confused look. "What did you do that for?"

Brenna's hands were balled at her waist and defiance had tilted her lips. "Listen up, Jabarie Isaiah Beaumont, and listen good…" she began as she tried to catch her breath. "It's over between us, and if you think I'm stupid enough to give you a second chance you better think again." With that she swung around and stormed inside the house.

Chapter 4

With his hands inside his pockets, Jabarie stood there for the longest time wondering what in the world had just happened. *Fool. Did you really think you could just kiss her and that would make everything right between you two?*

Yeah, right. He scowled as his anger resurfaced. He wasn't that crazy, although as he shook his head, he had to admit he didn't know what he had been thinking. For a moment, he had indeed lost his head. While holding her soft, curved body against him, he had forgotten that five years had passed and was back to a time when everything in the world was right between them. All he could think about was tasting those lush lips again. But the instant Brenna sunk her teeth into him, his mind had zapped back to the present and his anger had returned.

Wiping a palm against the side of his neck, he looked down and was happy to see that she hadn't broken the skin. *Stupid.* What in the world had he been thinking? Jabarie scowled. That was the problem. He wasn't thinking. Instead his anger and resentment had been M.I.A since the moment he'd spotted her in the bookstore window.

Still standing in the middle of her backyard, he took several deep frustrated breaths and debated going in after her, but decided against it. For some reason he had a hard time remembering to be angry when Brenna was within several feet of him. Why was that, he wondered then shrugged. It no longer mattered because his anger was back and brewing darker and hotter than before. *Stupid, stupid.* He had no business kissing her.

Briefly lowering his eyelids, he could still see her eyes glaring and her nostrils flaring. Brenna was mad at him? Hell, if anyone had a right to be mad then it was him. What in the world was he doing letting his guard down? Brenna left him, not the other way around he scolded inwardly then opened his eyes and glanced once more at the back door.

Jabarie reached down and while he slipped his socks back onto his feet followed by his shoes, he tried to figure out what Brenna had done that angered him the most.

She still hasn't apologized.

Hell, yes. Yesterday and again today, Brenna had several opportunities since her return to apologize and still hadn't.

Maybe she didn't feel there was anything to apologize about.

His frown deepened. The hell there wasn't. She

walked out on him the night before their wedding with a check for one hundred thousand dollars. He still had a sneaky suspicion that his mother had initiated the transaction. However, if Brenna would apologize and explain her reason for taking the money then maybe, just maybe, it might make more sense. Then maybe he could get past that point in his life and move on.

Jabarie moved across the lush green yard and was careful not to brush against Ms. Nellie's massive rose bushes. As he closed the gate, memories of Brenna's deception raged through his mind. It was as if it was yesterday. The pain. The devastation. He remembered that even after his mother told him what Brenna had done, he still didn't want to believe it. Instead, he went searching for his fiancée at her aunt's house only to discover she had packed her things and left without any type of explanation. Completely devastated, he had hoped that in time Brenna would have called and said something so he could understand, yet she neither explained nor returned. It wasn't until his father showed him the canceled check with her signature that reality finally hit him. Brenna wasn't coming back. With enough money to start a new life, she had left him and Sheraton Beach behind. Then to drive the nail further through his chest, a week later, by certified mail, she had returned his engagement ring without bothering to enclose a note. The realization left him both confused and hurt, and to this day he still didn't understand why she left and instead he had come to his own conclusion that they had been too young. And maybe she, like her mother, really was all about the money. But that was the part that he refused to believe because his heart told

him it was something else, even though the evidence
said otherwise.

As he moved across the grass, Jabarie glanced over
at the small ranch-style house hoping that by the time
he reached his SUV, Brenna would have come out on
the porch to at least say goodbye. Reaching into his
pocket, Jabarie removed his keys and moved across the
sidewalk out to the curb. But by the time he climbed
behind the wheel, the porch was still empty. Growing
increasingly agitated by the second, he started his Navigator, and with a frown gave the front door one final
look before putting the SUV in Drive and heading to his
parents' for dinner.

Jabarie's fingers tightened around the steering wheel.
He was furious because after all these years Brenna still
managed to get to him. Kissing her again, it took everything he had not to scoop her into his arms and take her
home with him. As he turned the corner, he silently told
himself he was going to have to get it together. Even if
it meant finding a way to get her out of his head once
and for all.

Ten minutes later, Jabarie pulled in the drive of a
stone and stucco house hidden from the main road by
mature pear trees. As he drew near he took in the three
acres of well-tended lawn and the overabundance of
flowers that lined both sides of the house. Beaumont
Manor was massive. Some would call it a mansion. He
always thought of it as being more like a museum.
Filled with expensive things that one could look at but
never touch. Jabarie frowned. What was the point? That
was one thing he had loved about Ms. Nellie's house.
It was simply decorated with things that had been made

with tender loving care. Walls with framed photographs of Brenna and drawings she had done all the way back in grammar school.

With a quick shake of his head, he erased the thought of Brenna from his mind. He rose from the vehicle then moved over to the porch and climbed the stairs. Before he could knock an elderly black man opened the door.

"Good evening, Jabarie, sir," said the butler in greeting. He then moved aside while Jabarie stepped into the soaring, two-story foyer. Wayne had been working for his family forever and no matter how often he asked him to drop the formal greeting, he had not.

"The rest of your family is already in the formal dining room."

"Thanks, Wayne."

He strolled across a gleaming oak hardwood floor past the gallery of photographs that adorned the walls. Beaumonts, several generations. When Jabarie reached a sweeping turned staircase his younger sister Bianca appeared at the second-floor landing. He paused to wait for her and admired how elegant she looked in a green linen pants suit.

"There you are!" The nutmeg beauty raced down the stairs and launched herself at him. Her luminous eyes crinkled in a radiant smile. You would think they hadn't seen each other in the office earlier. Pulling back slightly, she gave him a long scolding look. "For a moment there I thought you weren't coming. Mother was having a hissy fit."

Leaning closer, Jabarie kissed his sister's silken cheek, her soft amber perfume lingering in his nostrils.

At twenty-two, Bianca could be overly dramatic at times. She had inherited that trait from their mother. He glanced down at her short brown hair, styled and cut into layers, and then to her wide walnut eyes that sparkled with excitement. She looped her arm through his and steered him toward the dining room.

"I heard Brenna's back in town."

Jabarie silently cursed. No wonder his sister was waiting for his arrival. "Word travels fast around here," he mumbled, while thinking about the busybodies who were watching them earlier.

"Have you spoken to her?"

"Yes," he replied as calmly as he could manage.

Bianca stopped walking and turned to meet his expression. "And?" she asked inquisitively. Jabarie had to resist a grin. Despite everything, his sister had always liked Brenna, and even though she was barely seventeen at the time, she had been one of the ones who had tried to convince him to go after her.

"We spoke. No big deal." He tried to keep his tone as nonchalant as possible but he should have known Bianca wasn't buying it.

She wrinkled her nose. "Who do you think you're fooling? Regardless of how hard you try to hide it I was here and I saw the way you fell apart when Brenna left. And you expect me to believe it's no big deal. I'm not buying it. You loved her since you were ten years old."

"And look what good it did me," he replied with a scowl.

"How long is she staying?"

"Until her aunt's ankle is better." Ready to change the subject, Jabarie glanced down at the Rolex on his wrist. "Enough about my personal life, we better get in to dinner before Mother has a stroke." He slipped his arm around her shoulder and steered her toward the dining area, but Bianca dug her heels into the long Persian wool runner that ran the length of the hallway.

"Wait!" she cried, stopping him in his tracks. "Are you going to at least talk to her?"

"Why?" Jabarie asked.

She slugged him in the arm and her frown intensified. "You know why. The two of you need to discuss what happened."

He raked a frustrated hand across his face. "I already know what happened."

Bianca narrowed her eyes at Jabarie. "Well at least try to find some kind of closure. You can't keep going on like this."

"Like what?"

"Non-existing. You need to love again."

Jabarie laughed bitterly. "Love is the last thing I need."

"Surely you're not totally against love and marriage?" she asked, apparently appalled by his answer.

"Love is a dangerous thing. And no one knows that better than me. You see what good it did me." With a wink he grabbed her hand and squeezed it as they moved past an old grandfather clock toward the dining room.

"But it's been five years."

His shoulders tensed and his jaw knotted. "And there'll be many more to follow. Marriage is not part of my future."

"Really?"

"Really," he replied then gave her a quizzical look. "Wasn't it a couple of months ago that you were preaching that love is a recipe for disaster?"

Bianca shrugged. "Actually I've had a lot of time to think and I now understand that college romances don't work. This time when the right man comes along, I'll be ready."

He gave her a skeptical look. "Does that mean you're seeing someone?"

"No-o-o," she said musically.

His lips curled in a slow smile. "Good, because I'd hate to have to break someone's legs."

Laughing, she slugged him playfully in the arm. "Oh, please. When I finally meet the right one there is nothing you or Jace can do about it." She gave him a dreamy-eyed smile. Jabarie shook his head. After a heartbreak, he didn't think she'd ever bounce back, but she had. If Bianca could, then what was stopping him from getting on with his life as well? The answer was simple.

Brenna Gathers.

Brenna lay across her bed, trying to read a mystery she'd been looking forward to for months. It was one of the pleasures she tried to indulge in on the weekends. However, tonight she was having a difficult time concentrating. Whenever her mind wandered, memories of Jabarie's kiss filled her thoughts. He was a man who knew exactly what to do with a woman. That hadn't changed. He knew how to kiss, how to touch, how to be gentle. Raising a hand to her mouth, she lightly traced her lips. The kiss had been far better than she had remembered it to be. It not only had shaken her, but it scared the hell out of her because it made her feel so much. It was also a mistake. One that couldn't happen again because she wouldn't allow it. But even as she finished that thought, she shuddered as the memory. That kiss had been fueled with five years of pent-up frustrations. Her lips still tingled and her hands shook. After all this time her mouth still knew his. She was amazed at how naturally her lips molded to his and the way her tongue remembered his slow determined strokes. The kiss had been so pleasurable she'd had no choice but to respond with a moan and a throbbing ache down below.

Running her fingers through her loose hair, she took a shaky breath and tried to forget how good it had felt being pressed against his body.

Damn him! How dare he kiss her after everything that had happened between them. Did he really think they could just continue on as if nothing had ever happened? What was even worse was that he thought that while she was in town they would spend time together, then as soon as her aunt's ankle was better, life would return to the way it was again. Taking a deep breath, she realized she was furious at her vulnerability to him. No way should she have allowed him to kiss her, yet she had and enjoyed every second of it. Somehow, she was going to have to find a way to stay strong around him.

Pushing the thought aside, she turned the page and started the next chapter. Brenna had read the same paragraph three times when the phone rang. Quickly, not to disturb her aunt, who was sleeping in her room,

Brenna reached over to the nightstand and brought the cordless phone to her ear.

"Hello."

"Bren."

It was Jabarie. She knew that deep baritone voice anywhere. It tickled her ear and reminded her of all of the years she spent with that same receiver to her ear talking to him as they drifted off to sleep. A whisper of a sigh escaped her lips. "What do you want, Jabarie?"

"I wanted to find out if you were still mad at me."

"Mad?" she repeated in a huff. "I'm not mad, just pissed that you think just because I'm back I'm ready to jump back into your bed for a fling."

"No, that's not what I was thinking."

"Then what?" she barked impatiently.

He sighed heavily into the mouthpiece before finally saying. "I don't know what I was thinking. And that's the problem. When I'm around you I can't think."

Neither could she but she'd be damned before she admitted that to him. "Then maybe if you'd stay away from me you won't have that problem."

"Sorry, but I can't do that."

His words startled her. "Why not?"

"Because I've never gotten over you, Bren. I don't know what it is, but there is something about you I just can't seem to let go of."

Neither could she. Her thoughts and dreams were still about him, holding her, kissing her. Loving her. That last thought caused her to frown. If he loved her the way he had claimed then there was no way she would have caught him in the arms of another woman. Just thinking about it caused her temper to flare. "We can't go back in the past. The best thing we can both do is find some way to get along until it's time for me to leave. Maybe it would be best if you stayed away from the store."

"I can't promise you that. I like being around you. Always have. Always will."

Brenna closed her eyes, fighting the emotions stirring inside her, and took a deep breath. "Listen, I'm not in the mood to talk about this."

"I didn't call to upset you."

She sighed. "Then why did you call?"

There was a noticeable pause. "I called because I needed to hear your voice."

His confession made her feel all queasy inside and immediately, she shook off the feeling. She thought about pretending there was static on the line the way she did whenever Aunt Nellie called and mentioned Jabarie by name. She tried to think of a snappy comeback but the only answer she could come up with was, "Oh."

Silence hummed on the line. Brenna heard a door shut and a jingling of keys. She blinked then focused on the clock by her bedside and noticed it was almost ten o'clock. "Did you have dinner with your parents this evening?"

He chuckled lightly. "You remembered."

"Yeah." Oh, how could she forget? She remembered when Jabarie had invited her to start joining his family on Fridays. She would be sitting across the table as his mother snubbed her nose down at her and said or did whatever it took to make her feel uncomfortable.

Moving over to the window, Brenna gazed out across the water to the grand house at the top of the hill.

Every detail of the manor was burned into her memory. She knew exactly how many windows were at the front of the structure; how far the driveway was from the main road. She knew the habits and routines of the staff and the layout of the entire interior of the house. She knew everything there was to know about Beaumont Manor, except one thing—how to feel welcomed.

"We had our usual dysfunctional dinner."

Hearing the despair in his voice, she couldn't help but sympathize. "Sorry, I see not much has changed. How are Jace, Jaden, and Bianca?"

"Jace is still trying to run a tight ship with the employees. Jaden is still living on the West Coast fixing cars, and Bianca is still a customer relations genius."

"Did she attend Morgan State like she had wanted?"

"Yep, and graduated with honors."

"That's fabulous." He went on to talk about his brothers and sister while she listened attentively and jumped in when appropriate. She'd always liked his siblings. Jace was three years older than Jabarie and reminded her so much of their father, Roger Beaumont. He was so consumed with work he rarely found time for relationships or fun. But underneath his tough demeanor was a puppy dog. Jaden, the black sheep of the family, and the younger brother, had taken off shortly after graduation to find his own way. He was the only one who'd ever stood up to their parents and she admired him for that. It had been at one of their family dinners with her in attendance, that Jaden rose from the table and told his father where he could shove his money. The look on his face was priceless. Bianca was more like

Jabarie than the rest of the family. Warm, with a wonderful sense of humor and a creativity about her that made her the perfect director of guest relations.

There was another long pause and Brenna moved over to a small white vanity and took a seat. "Well, I guess I better get ready for bed."

"Don't hang up…not yet. The night is still young."

She lowered her eyelids while the soft murmur of his voice vibrated through her. "Jabarie, what do you want?"

"What I've always wanted, Bren. You."

Then why didn't you come after me? Brushing the thought aside, she blew out an impatient breath.

"I want to apologize for kissing you."

Oh, great. Even though the kiss had been a mistake the last thing she wanted was for him to regret kissing her.

"I apologize for kissing you when I know that is not at all what you wanted to happen. However, I don't regret it," he added as if he could read her mind.

Brenna didn't say anything because she didn't trust herself. The best thing for both of them was to pretend it never happened and that was exactly what she had planned to do. "Look, I gotta go. I'm running bath water. When you see Jace and Bianca, tell them I said hello."

"Bren, wait a minute."

She didn't hang up although her instincts told her it would be the smartest move she would have made all day.

"Are you angry at me?"

"No. Should I be?" she asked softly.

"No."

"Then I'm not," she said trying not to sound as frustrated and she felt.

He chuckled lightly. "Okay. Then we're cool, right?"

"Yes, Jabarie," she said impatiently.

"Good, then how about dinner tomorrow?"

"You are so hardheaded."

"Yes. I am," he agreed with a hearty chuckle.

It was a trait she knew all too well, but not one she had ever held against him. "I already told you before, no."

"What's wrong with two friends sharing a meal?" he whispered, and the rumble of his voice warmed her blood.

"Nothing, but too much has happened for us to just pretend we're simply friends. Look, I've really got to go." With that, she ended the call and returned the phone to the cradle. An overwhelming level of emotion surged through her reminding her that she still cared way too much about Jabarie. Brenna released a heavy breath. She could see already that being around each other was not going to be easy.

She sat there for the longest time and realized that being in the same proximity would be a problem unless she got her head on straight.

Brenna pushed him from her mind and allowed her eyes to travel around her private domain. She smiled. Her room had remained unchanged from its state five years ago when she left home. It was decorated in two shades of yellow with angels stenciled on the walls. Moving over to the small vanity, she reached for a comb and ran the teeth through the thick mass. Within seconds she had wrapped her hair and secured it with a scarf.

She rose and didn't bother trying to read again. After hearing Jabarie's voice there was no way she would be able to think about anything but him. Too wired to go to bed, she rose and suddenly felt desperate to be outside so she could breath. She didn't bother putting on any shoes. She wanted to feel the earth beneath her feet.

She moved out the sliding glass door and stepped onto the deck across the yard and out onto the beach. She breathed in the cool air that raised goose bumps on her bare arms. Instead of being cold, the wind calmed her nerves. She didn't stop walking until she was at the water's edge. She then lowered onto the wet sand and drew her legs to her chest and wrapped her arms around her. Closing her eyes, Jabarie's face pushed to the front. They had spent so many nights lying out on the beach with her head on his chest and her fingers beneath his shirt, stroking the soft hairs that lightly covered his chest. Back then she loved everything about him. Now he was back stirring up emotions and feelings she hadn't felt in years.

A sob caught in her throat. She wished things could be the way it used to be, but it couldn't be and no matter how much she still cared about him there was no way she was going to fall victim to him again.

Sighing she realized she was letting her mind become cluttered with thoughts of him. It was her hormones dictating her actions. Nothing else. It was better than thinking she was going insane the way she couldn't get him off of her mind.

Her world had collapsed the day she walked into his apartment and found him lying on the couch with another woman. Anika Arnold. The vision of that night was still fresh in her mind. Anika's naked body straddling his lap. Her throaty laughter. Anger shot through her and tears filled her eyes. *Damn him!* She loved him with everything she had. How could he do that to her?

One thing for sure, she wasn't going to again fall for the only man she had ever loved. The only man with the power to break the wall she had built around her heart.

Chapter 5

Jabarie stood in front of the large window that took up an entire wall in his office and gazed down at the ocean below. The window was open, catching the sounds and smell of the water, moving onto the shore.

Looking to his far right, he gazed in the direction of Ms. Nellie's house. Even though he couldn't see her, he knew Brenna was sitting out on the deck with her bare feet on the railing, drinking a cup of Irish Cream flavored coffee. He knew her routine by heart because he, too, used to get up extremely early in the morning just so he could join her before going to work. They would sit together on the bench and plan their future while watching the sun rise.

Man, he thought with a tight lipped-smile, that was such a long time ago, but to him it still felt like it had just been yesterday. Those had been the times when he couldn't keep his hands off her, or his lips for that matter.

A whirlwind of emotions traveled through his chest as he remembered the taste of her sweet lips when he kissed her yesterday. What had got to him was that it was like no time had passed. He knew the way she tilted her head and the soft purrs that slipped from between her lips whenever he pressed her against his hardened length. When she had parted her lips and invited him inside her mouth, he had entered as if he and he alone had the right to be there.

Struggling to breathe, he turned away from the window. Jabarie felt every bit of his thirty years as he lowered into the large swivel chair and reached for the mug of coffee and brought it to his lips. Even now, just thinking about Brenna made his heart skip a beat. She was the only woman that had ever gotten under his skin. The only woman he'd ever loved. The only woman who had broken his heart.

He clenched his jaw and fought the unwanted need that snaked through his veins. While walking into work this morning he had found himself distracted by a woman in the lobby because she had been wearing the same perfume Brenna used to dab on her wrist and neck. But it was missing her sweet alluring scent that made him dizzy with an adrenaline rush. *I'm losing my mind.* Somehow he needed to get her off his mind, because last night he could not. After a painfully long, boring dinner with his parents and siblings, he had gone home to an empty condo and an even colder and lonelier bed. So he called her, needing to hear her voice, hoping that it would help him sleep, only instead, talking to her, confessing to her how she made him feel, had only made matters worse. Images of her honey-brown hair and large hazel eyes had dogged his sleep. He spent half the night tossing and turning, yearning for her warm body to be lying next to him. He dreamed of making love to her and wanted badly to bury himself so far inside her one wouldn't know where one began and the other ended.

Taking another sip of the lukewarm liquid, Jabarie scowled as he remembered somewhere between three and four this morning, he decided it was time to face the undeniable fact that for the last five years he had tortured himself night after night reliving the passion that only Brenna was able to extract from him. No other woman had ever come close. Sure he was a man with needs so celibacy had never been a consideration. Nevertheless, no woman had ever come close to making him feel both the mental and physical attachment he felt with Brenna. He still had every luscious curve of her body embedded in his mind. He had never forgotten the distinctive sound of her voice with the southern Delaware inflection, the graceful way she tilted her head whenever she looked up at him, and most of all he remembered her declaration that she would love him forever.

Jabarie gave a bitter laugh then brought the mug to his lips, emptied it and dropped it down hard onto his desk. Even now he spent considerable time wondering if anything they had shared was true. After she had left him, he wondered if all they'd shared had been a lie.

"I thought you were going to stop working on Saturdays?"

Startled, he glanced up to find his mother standing in the doorway. Jessica Beaumont was one woman who always managed to look amazing so early in the morning. Her slender frame looked elegant in a peach Chanel suit. Her long salt-and-pepper hair was pulled up in a neat chignon that emphasized her round face and slanted dark brown eyes. A small Coach purse was tucked under her arm as she sashayed across the hunter green carpet toward his desk.

"Didn't get much sleep last night," he confessed with a slight shrug of his shoulders beneath a black tailor-made suit.

"I can tell." He watched as his mother's concern appeared in her eyes. "I can have my doctor prescribe you something."

Jabarie groaned inward. Pills were his mother's answer to everything. "No, I'm fine." He reached for his mug and took another sip and remembered it was already empty. "What brings you here this early?"

"Your father and I are taking a tour of the new wing of the hotel and then having brunch with the Johnstons."

He nodded. His mother spent most of her day having lunch with her society friends and planning charity functions while his father traveled around to each of their two dozen hotels, insisting on seeing if they were being run properly. As if he didn't trust his son to do his job. Roger Beaumont rarely held a conversation that included a topic other than work.

"How's everything with the Las Vegas deal going?" His mother asked, breaking into his thoughts.

"Fabulous. We should be breaking ground some time next month."

She crossed her legs and looked pleased. "Your father and I are so proud of you."

"Thank you." His father had groomed his children to take over the family business since the moment they first started school. Roger Beaumont had taught his children they could have or do anything they wanted as long as it involved the Beaumont Corporation. Another career field was never an option. Luckily he never dreamed of doing anything else. Unlike his brother who was a disgrace according to his parents. Jabarie admired his brother Jaden because he had his own mind and was doing what he wanted to do, unlike Jace, who was in charge of hiring and recruitment for all of the hotels, but who'd rather have been an engineer.

He stared down into his mug and thought again about managing the Las Vegas office. Maybe change was what he needed.

"You want to talk about it?" His mother asked, breaking into his thoughts again. Jabarie glanced across the desk at her impatient face. "Well, I'm waiting. I knew something was on your mind last night at dinner."

He stared down at the polished mahogany desktop before answering. "Brenna's back in town."

He looked up in time to see his mother's eyes grow large and round and a disapproving frown bunched her forehead. "And what does that have to do with you?"

Every fiber in his body warned him not to even have this conversation. His mother had never made her feelings about Brenna a secret, but he'd always thought it was clearly unfair. She believed fruit didn't fall far from the tree and that she was a gold-digger just like her mother had been. There were times when he had considered the possibility, but he just couldn't allow himself to believe that of her.

"It doesn't mean anything except that I realize that after all these years I still haven't gotten over her."

"Are you serious?" she asked with the tightening of her lips. "The gold-digger left you the night before your wedding. I had to stand up in front of that church and tell everyone the wedding was off. Do you know how humiliating that was for me?"

And what about me? It was always about his mother.

"What could there possibly still be there?" she asked tentatively.

He wasn't sure yet, but it was definitely something that wasn't just going away.

"I think starting anything with her would be a big mistake. Claudia's said her daughter Brooke has been asking about you."

Brooke Washington was perfectly painted and groomed, and expensive and spoiled just like her mother. Past the sexual gratification there was no satisfying her. He leaned back in the chair and gave his mother a long, hard look. All his mother ever cared about was securing a daughter-in-law of the same financial class. It didn't matter if she had no brain. The last thing he needed in his life. He scowled inwardly. His mother had been setting him up with women for years even while he was engaged to Brenna. Anika Arnold. She was definitely a piece of work. She had been stalking him for months and then the night before his wedding day, she had appeared at his apartment in nothing but a long trench coat that she had graciously dropped in a heap at the door. The bubbleheaded girl had nothing but dollar signs in her eyes. No way. He wanted a woman who loved him for the man he was, not for all the diamonds he could afford to buy. One thing about Brenna, she never wanted anything from him. She loved him for him not what he could give her. At least that was what he had thought before she had taken the money and vanished.

"I hate to see you get caught in her web again. Don't forget about the money she took."

How could he forget when his mother made it a habit to remind him. "I'm a big boy, Mother. I think I can handle myself around Brenna."

"Why is she here?"

"Ms. Nellie sprained her ankle."

"Oh." He noticed the moment of concern before she hid it behind a look of discontent. While teenagers his mother and Ms. Nellie had been good friends before his mother met his father and deemed herself too good. Sometimes his mother's behavior really bothered him.

"She's not staying, is she?"

"No."

"Good." Noticing the look on his face she quickly tried to explain. "I know you think I never liked that girl and I don't have anything personally against her except that I don't think she is good enough for you. Jabarie, honey, you could do so much better."

Suddenly in need of another cup of coffee, he rose with his mug in his hand. "Well, I don't think we have to worry about that. She doesn't want to have anything to do with me."

Brenna arrived at the store and had another long day and was glad she had convinced her aunt to hire more help. The students dropped in that morning and she hired them both to work during the busiest time of the day. By the close of business she was tired. It had been so busy she didn't realize until she was closing out the register and dropping the money into a floor safe that she hadn't heard from Jabarie all day.

Thinking about last night, the loneliness of the last five years welled up inside of her, and at that moment she knew that she had made a mistake coming back. The emotional wounds had reopened. She wasn't angry with him, she was mad at herself. Now it was bleeding again and that was the last thing she wanted to happen. She needed to get rid of the scar and heal so she could finally move on with her life.

Just as well he hadn't come around, she thought while she turned the deadbolt and headed towards home. No point in starting something again that had ended badly a long time ago.

It was a lovely evening. The breeze was warm for an eighty degree evening. Brenna decided to take her time heading home and stopped to browse in several stores along the way. She spotted a shop with Delaware memorabilia and dropped in looking for angels. She had been collecting African-American angels for as long as she could remember. While staring into a glass case, she felt a light tap at her shoulder. She swung around. After a stunned moment of silence, Brenna recognized the woman standing behind her, squealed and pulled Sheyna Simmons into a bouncing hug. When she leaned back to look at her, her eyes sparkled with excitement. "Hey, girl!" She curved her arms around her shoulders and hugged her good friend again.

"I heard you were in town," Sheyna said as she pulled back. "I said uh-uh, there is no way my best friend is back in town and didn't tell me." She pressed her lips dramatically while waiting for an explanation. Brenna knew she definitely owed her one.

"My coming was so sudden I barely had time to pack." Her eyes swept her tall, slender frame. "How are you?"

"Better now. Come on. We've got a lot of catching up to do." Sheyna draped an arm around her shoulders and led her out the store and down the street to a small coffee shop on the corner. They found an empty booth near the window and took a seat. They each ordered a cup of coffee.

"So tell me. How long are you here for?"

"Just until Aunt Nellie is better."

Her mouth drooped. "I was hoping you were here for good. This place isn't the same without you."

Brenna smiled at her childhood friend. The dark mahogany beauty with her wide eyes and generous mouth. She loved what she had done with her dark chestnut colored hair. The ponytail was gone, and in its place was a sophisticated style that fell into layers and framed a rounded face.

"I've got to get back to Dallas. I opened a bookstore last year."

"You finally did it. That's wonderful!"

She nodded proudly. Her life hadn't turned out quite the way she had planned but at least some of her dreams had come true.

The moment their waitress brought them both a glass of water and moved to the next table, Brenna should have known that Sheyna was going to cut to the chase.

"Why didn't you keep in touch? I haven't heard from you in almost fifteen months. I thought we were friends?"

She could hear the hurt in her voice and regretted her decision. After she had found Jabarie in the arms of another woman, Brenna had called Sheyna to tell her the wedding was off with only a few brief details. Since then she sent her Christmas cards and an occasional phone call, but as soon as Sheyna mentioned Jabarie or Sheraton Beach, she quickly ended the conversation. After awhile, the contact became less and less. "After I left I wanted to cut all ties to this place."

Her generous mouth turned downward. "But I'm supposed to be your best friend or at least I thought I was."

"I know, and I'm sorry." Reaching across the table Brenna squeezed her hand. "I guess I've got a lot of making up to do."

"I forgive you as long as you promise not to do that again," she replied with a smile that brightened her face. "I really miss having someone to talk to about Jace."

Their waitress arrived with their coffee. Brenna waited until she left to help another customer before she replied. "You still working with him?"

Sheyna rolled her eyes heavenly. "Yes, and that man is still impossible. Nothing is ever good enough." Jace was the president of human resources for the Beaumont Corporation. Sheyna managed employee relations, and she and Jace bumped heads on a regular basis.

"We still don't see eye to eye on anything," she began with a scowl. "I am interested in building employee moral and starting referral and incentive programs, and he's more interested in cutting manpower."

Brenna brought the piping hot liquid to her lips. "It sounds like he still has a major crush on you."

A soft blush spread across Sheyna's cheeks. "Oh, puhlease! No matter how handsome he is, Jace's the last person I'd ever date," she ended with a rude snort. Sheyna then took a sip from her mug. She studied her friend over the brim and something in her eyes told Brenna she was lying. She knew Sheyna well enough to know when something was bothering her. Sheyna wasn't telling the truth about her feelings but as stubborn as her friend had a tendency to be, she decided to let it slide for now.

Leaning forward her eyes sparkled with curiosity. "Have you seen Jabarie yet?"

Brenna tried to nod as if it was no big deal.

Sheyna arched a delicate eyebrow. "And?"

She met her piercing gaze. "And what? We spoke and he and I both understand what happened between us was a long time ago."

"You don't mean that?"

It took everything Brenna had to keep a straight face. "Yes, I do."

Shaking her head, she gave her a long look of disbelief. "The two of you were so in love. I just can't see how you can just casually say hello, how're you doing and then it's business as usual. I would be in his face demanding to know why he had been with that skank Anika."

She reached for her mug. "Well, I'm not asking because it no longer matters."

"Uh-huh."

Brenna saw the question in Sheyna's eyes, but she

hoped she wouldn't ask it because she didn't want to talk about him.

"She married an NBA player last year. It was in *Jet* magazine and everything."

So much for wishful thinking. Although she felt a wave of relief knowing that Anika and Jabarie's relationship had ended. That's what he gets, she thought. He had a peach and settled for a lemon.

"Good for her." She took a sip then leaned back on the bench. "Aunt Nellie told me you're buying a new house," she said, smoothly changing the subject.

Excitement lit Sheyna's eyes as she eased gracefully back into her chair. "I close next week."

She was relieved when the subject shifted. While they finished their coffee, Sheyna spoke in detail about the three-bedroom home she had bought in a new development within walking distance of the beach. After several failed relationships, she had given up on finding a husband and decided to buy her own house. By herself.

"Well, we'll have to give you a housewarming party."

Sheyna frowned. "Please, no parties. Although I could use some help moving."

"I'd be happy to help."

They talked about what they had been up to the last several months while they finished their coffee then made a promise to call in a day or two and said their goodbyes.

Heading home, Brenna cut across the beach and came through the back door. She stepped into the house and was met by the smell of Chinese food. Her favorite. She dropped her purse on the kitchen counter and moved into the dining room and spotted Jabarie sitting at the table across from Aunt Nellie.

Her breath caught in her throat. Heat traveled down low and she took several deep breaths and willed her body to behave. What happened between them had ended five years ago. *So why am I feeling horny?* She hadn't thought about being with a man in years. Yet as soon as she took one look at him her body seemed to come alive and hummed with needs she hadn't felt in so long.

Aunt Nellie's eyes lit up when she spotted her standing in the door. "There you are. I was wondering if you had gotten lost and needed me to send the dogs after you."

"No. I ran into Sheyna and we went and had a coffee," she somehow found her voice to say.

"Hello, Brenna."

It was as if the man had put a spell on her. The very instant their eyes met her mind went blank. All she was aware of was a strong sensation that radiated through her body. "Jabarie."

Her aunt patted the place setting beside her. "Come sit and eat with us. Jabarie was nice enough to come by and check on me. We were both hungry so he ordered Chinese."

"I remembered it was your favorite."

He gave her that familiar smile that always made her want to rush back to his apartment with him and slip beneath the covers. Brenna's heart wasn't cooperating. He rose and moved to pull the chair out for her. He was dressed in a red cotton T-shirt that strained against his muscles and a pair of jeans.

"I'll be right there." She spun on her heels and moved into her room where she took several deep breaths. What in the world was he doing here? She thought she had made it clear that it was best if they kept their distance. Why was she even surprised? Jabarie always did have his own mind. Now she just had to find a way to make it through dinner without falling for his charm.

Aunt Nellie chatted nonstop while she tried to concentrate on her food and not Jabarie who was staring across the table at her. But that wasn't easy to do. She was aware of his broad shoulders and muscled body. As he ate she glanced at his long fingers holding the fork as he brought it to his thick delicious lips. A tremor passed through her every time she noticed his hands or pictured them in her mind, she thought about what they felt like against her skin.

An hour later, Aunt Nellie insisted that she was tired. Jabarie helped her back to her room while Brenna put the food away. She had just wiped down the dining room table and had moved into the kitchen when she felt his presence in the room.

She glanced over her shoulder to find him leaning inside the door. She remembered how they used to spend countless evenings together, washing and drying dishes and stealing kisses when Aunt Nellie wasn't looking.

She gave a nervous smile. "Thanks for dinner and helping with Aunt Nellie. You know she adores you."

"I adore her as well."

They stood there for a long silent moment, looking at each other but not saying anything before she finally cleared her throat. "Well, I don't need to walk you to the door but I do need to clean the kitchen."

Instead of leaving, Jabarie entered the room. Swallowing, she took a step back and fought to maintain her composure.

He cornered her against the counter. "We need to talk. I can't stop thinking about you."

Her heart fluttered wildly against her chest. "That would be a mistake."

He leaned in close, close enough for his breath to caress her cheek. "My only mistake was ever letting you go."

Her skin flushed hot and she couldn't seem to catch her breath. She looked up at him and the look in his eyes was so intense she forgot what she was about to say.

The heat exploded the second his lips touched hers. It was as if no time at all had passed since their last kiss. His mouth was hot and hungry and every hard line angle was pressed tightly against her. She kissed him back, meeting his mouth with matching passion. He tunneled his hand into her hair, holding her head with a strong grip as his tongue slipped between her lips. All she knew was that she wanted to dive in, to hell with the consequences. She closed the distance that was left and placed her hands on his shoulders and lifted onto her tiptoes.

"I want to finish what we started yesterday," he whispered against her mouth.

Every cell in her body screamed, "yes!" She wanted this. She wanted him and responded by resuming the kiss and arching toward him.

Moments later, when he ended the kiss and raised his head, she nearly cried out in protest.

"Have dinner with me tomorrow?" he breathed against her lips.

Drawing a deep breath, she forced herself to speak. "I can't."

His eyes were looking directly into hers, making it impossible to look away. "You can't or you won't?"

It had only been twenty-four hours and already she felt the seductive pull of his spell. Scraping up what strength she had left, Brenna pushed herself away from him. "Both."

"Brenna, I'm not going away. I plan to spend every second, every moment with you until whatever is supposed to happen between us, happens."

She stepped back and stared at Jabarie, fighting the hard throb of her body and the knowledge that men like him knew how to break a woman's heart. "And I'm supposed to be excited about that?"

"I would hope that you'd want to spend time with me."

Anger ripped at her. "Well, I don't."

"Your kiss says otherwise."

She rolled her eyes heavenward. "Listen, I'm really not in the mood to have this conversation right now."

"Okay," he said but something in his eyes told her he wouldn't stop until she agreed. "I'll be by tomorrow."

Her heart jackhammered. "Please, don't bother."

"I told you I planned to spend as much time with you as I can." His voice had the ability to lull away all the defenses she put up.

Brenna stepped away from him, yet his body heat clung to her even after there was several feet between them. "Why?"

"It's the only way I'll ever get you out of my system."

He ran a hand against her cheek. "See you tomorrow." With that, he turned and walked toward the door.

Brenna moved over to the sink and immediately filled it with soapy water. While stacking the dishes, she took a deep breath and tried to calm her nerves. Jabarie still had the ability to turn her world upside down; unfortunately she didn't want her world rocked. Nor did she want the kisses he was intent on showering her with. The power of the kiss still had her lips tingling.

Reaching for the faucet, she shut the water off and reached for the first plate and tried to ignore the arousal humming through her body. Her desire was alive and her body was yearning. She hadn't been with a man in five years because the only man she had ever wanted was Jabarie. He had been her first and only lover and no man made her feel the way Jabarie did. But being around him made her realize that no matter how much she tried to deny it she still wanted him in her bed. And that would be a big mistake.

Chapter 6

The next morning Brenna woke up slowly. She rolled onto her back then tossed her arms happily into the air. It was Sunday. Her day off and she planned to do something she hadn't done in a long time. Relax.

Since she had opened her bookstore last year, she had been spending every waking hour making it the success that it was today. Unfortunately, as a result, she'd had little to no life at all. Other than an occasional happy hour with her partner, Rhonda, the only place she visited often was her queen-size bed. Brenna frowned. It was sad to admit, but outside of work, she had no life at all. She had been too busy with her store to think about her non-existent sex life, but not anymore. Jabarie had awakened desires she hadn't felt for years. Now her body was demanding things she refused to give it.

Stretching her arms over her head, a smile curled her lips. She was looking forward to a day of strolling along the boardwalk, checking out all of the new shops that emerged in the last several years. But what she wanted most of all was to spend the afternoon sitting out on the beach with her book in hand.

Brenna sat up in the bed then reached up and removed the scarf from her head and combed her fingers through her hair. Glancing over at the window, she watched the yellow curtains sway due to a gentle ocean breeze filtering through the room. She sighed. It was going to be another lovely day. Staring out the window, she thought about how different the two cities were.

The only complaint she had about Dallas was the humid summer heat. It was so hot that she had started taking a change of clothes with her to work. The greatest advantage was there wasn't any snow. When she had first run off to stay with her cousin Latoya in Denton, a suburb of Dallas, she vowed to never return to Sheraton Beach. That winter, every time she left the house dressed in a light jacket she'd smile. However, last year she had found herself missing ice-skating on Sheraton Pond, the sleigh rides, and sliding down the hill on the back of Jabarie's toboggan while holding on tightly to his waist.

Brenna closed her eyes as thoughts of him filled her mind. Sundays they used to spend together. Traveling along the coast. Going to New York for the weekend for dinner and a Broadway play. Or even staying home out on the beach, jet skiing or engaging in some other water sport. But what she enjoyed most was the two of them spending afternoons swinging in a hammock that hung from a large tree in Aunt Nellie's backyard. Opening her eyes, she stared out the window again and couldn't help but wonder what he had planned for the day. He was probably planning to spend the day with some special woman in his life. The thought caused a wave of jealousy that she didn't want to feel. She yawned and tried to push the feelings and thoughts aside, but it was too late. It had already been embedded in her mind. The thought of Jabarie being with another woman bothered her. Why, she wondered. After all, their relationship ended five years ago. And she would be a fool to think that like her, he had been celibate all these years. But as she dragged her legs up to her chest and leaned back against the headboard, she realized that a part of her would always love Jabarie. After all, he had been her first for so many things.

Brenna rested her chin on her knee as she remembered their first kiss. She was thirteen at the time and even though it was awkward, and her braces had gotten in the way, it was an experience she had never forgotten. When she was fifteen, Jabarie had taken her on her first date to the movies. The whole time they held hands. At eighteen she had given him her virginity. She released a heavy sigh. There was no way she could think about her past and not think about Jabarie.

With a scowl, she pushed back the sheets and swung her legs over the side of the bed then she rose slowly and put her feet inside her slippers. There was no way she was going to spend her day lying in bed thinking about Jabarie. She moved to the shower and quickly climbed beneath the water. But as she closed her eyes and relaxed her shoulders while the hot invigorating water massaged her shoulders, memories of her past, flooded her mind again.

When she thought of Jabarie, she had no choice but to think of the way her body had responded to him. Jabarie knew she wanted him because she was certain he'd felt the tremors and her panic when he kissed her. All it had taken was a kiss and the sound of his deep baritone voice to bring her so close to giving herself to him.

Why am I thinking about him? She needed to get dressed and enjoy her day off, yet she was wondering if Jabarie was thinking about her as well. Angrily, she reached for the soap and lathered her washcloth then started to sing, determined to rid him from her mind. As she washed her body, she sung one song after another, occupying her mind with everything but them. But it didn't last. Before long she was singing what had once been considered "their song" and screamed inwardly. Damn that man for insisting on being a part of her life again.

Within minutes she turned off the water and returned to her room. She slipped on a pair of pink cotton shorts and a white spaghetti-strap shirt. As she oiled her legs she thought about what Jabarie had said and wondered if they really could work on their friendship. It was worth a try. Otherwise, he was never going to give up and if she wasn't careful she might find herself letting her guard down only to face heartache a second time.

Rising from the bed, she padded into the kitchen and was pleased to see that Aunt Nellie had already made coffee. She moved over to the cabinet, removed a funny red mug she had given her aunt for her birthday six years ago, and filled it with coffee.

Sitting at the table, she brought the hot liquid to her

lips and stared off in a daze as she remembered last
night and their explosive kiss. She took several deep
breaths and tried to calm the throbbing down low that
only he could soothe.

For the last five years she had done just fine without
Jabarie, now all she could think about was him and her
and what could have been. Bringing the brim of the cup
to her lips again, she took a gulp of her coffee, annoyed
at her feelings about him. So many questions about her
past tormented her. Maybe Jabarie was right. They still
needed to let whatever was supposed to happen, happen,
so they could each get the other out of their systems once
and for all.

Brenna closed her eyes and asked for strength where
Jabarie was concerned. If he continually insisted in being around her, getting over him was not going to happen. Instead, she would run a risk of losing her heart
again. Although the new Jabarie had matured and was
more confident and determined than ever, whatever
they once had was over, and she refused to start it again.

Opening her eyes, she tilted her chin defiantly. When
she decided to return to help her aunt, it was not to become love struck over Jabarie again or for her feelings
to resurface. *Get a grip.* This was only a short-lived
thing. Once her aunt was back on her feet and she returned to Dallas that would be the end of her thoughts
about Jabarie Beaumont.

A surprising wave of regret met that thought and
caused Brenna to shiver. Briefly, as she stared out at the
ocean, she allowed herself a few moments to fantasize
about a life beyond her temporary visits. A life with
Jabarie Beaumont. She traced the brim of the mug as

memories of them making love filled her mind. She sighed. It would be wonderful to make love again. A tingle started in her belly and began to travel outward. Abruptly, she shook her head, scattering the intimate thoughts before they could claim her mind completely. *It's sex, nothing else.* She had to believe that and after all this time it was only natural. Her fantasy was based on a physical need. Yep, that's it. She released a sigh of relief. Sexual attraction was easier to deal with than any possible emotional attachment.

"What are you thinking about?"

Startled, Brenna glanced up to find Aunt Nellie standing in the doorway dressed comfortably in seer-sucker walking shorts and a T-shirt, leaning her weight on her wooden cane.

"Nothing," she replied with a smile. "Just thinking about spending the afternoon sitting out on the beach." Setting down her coffee cup, she folded her trembling hands in her lap.

"How did the evening go with Jabarie?"

Brenna groaned inward. Leave it to her aunt to get right to the point. "What do you mean?"

"Have the two of you talked yet?" Brenna noticed that worry darkened her eyes and a line formed between her brows.

"No." Every time she was around him, talking was the last thing on either of their minds. Memories of their kiss came flooding back to her and she quickly pushed them aside.

Her aunt limped over to the table and took the seat across from her.

"How's your ankle this morning?" she asked.

"Still sore," Nellie said with a smile. "I'm afraid I've been overdoing it lately. I guess I need to spend the afternoon resting. Now enough about me, I want to know what you and Jabarie are going to do."

Brenna faced her aunt across the kitchen table. "Nothing."

"You know he still loves you."

The knot in her throat thickened. "Did he tell you that?"

"No, but he doesn't have to. It's written all over his face every time he mentions your name."

Frustrated, she raised her mug to her lips and peered at her over the rim. "If he loved me so much why did he deceive me the way he did? Why didn't he come after me?"

The dismay her aunt tried to hide brought a sad grin to her lips.

"That is something the two of you need to discuss. But before you leave and return to Dallas, I think you need to find the time to talk."

Her eyes traveled around the small kitchen that was filled with knickknacks. Counter space was occupied by ceramic jars. She looked everywhere but at her aunt because she didn't want her to see the fear in her eyes.

She reached across the table and squeezed her hand. "Bren, don't you want to be happy?"

She gave a laugh that she noticed lacked humor. "Who says I'm not happy?"

Aunt Nellie gave her a who-are-you-trying-to-fool look. "You forget. I used to change your diapers. I'm the one who raised you, which means I know you better than anyone else ever could."

Brenna could only swallow because what she said was true.

"All your life you dreamed of having two things. Do you remember that?"

Pressing her lips together, she nodded. "To have a family with Jabarie and open my own bookstore."

She nodded. "And there is nothing worse than losing sight of your dreams."

"One out of two ain't bad," Brenna replied teasingly.

"Yeah, but two is even better. Why don't you just talk to the man and then follow your heart."

"My heart is what got me in trouble the first time."

"Yeah, but now the two of you are older and wiser. The two of you were so in love."

Yes, we were.

"I just hate to see you give all that up."

Brenna hated to see the look of disappointment on her aunt's face. "Aunt Nellie, a part of me will always love Jabarie, but I just can't risk losing my heart to him again. I don't think I could survive the pain a second time." Rising from her chair, she moved over to the pot and refilled her coffee mug then reached up into the cabinet and fixed her aunt a cup as well. Aunt Nellie waited until she had returned to her seat before she responded.

"I remember when your mother was a teenager. Hell on wheels. It didn't matter how much leather my daddy put on her butt, Shaunda was going to do what Shaunda wanted. She was determined to find her a rich man. I remember when she found out she was pregnant. She came home excited. She was dating this rich developer

who was in the area at the time. She just knew he was
going to marry her. Instead he claimed that you weren't
none of his and even had his lawyer show legal proof
that he'd had a vasectomy several years before. It wasn't
until after you were born that she admitted that Aaron
was your father." Smiling, she paused long enough to
take a sip before continuing. "He was so happy because
he'd been in love with your mother for as far back as
we could remember. But Shaunda only saw him as her
rebound man. He wanted to marry her but she refused;
however, she had no problem taking his money. He
didn't care. He adored you so much there wasn't anything he wouldn't have done for his little girl." She
brought the mug to her lips again and her face saddened.
"I remember when he was killed. You were about three
at the time and after a lot of hard work and determination on Aaron's part, your mother had finally admitted
that she loved him and agreed to marry him. He had
rushed off to get a ring to make it official and I guess in
his haste to get back to the two women in his life, he
didn't see that truck as he came around that curve. I was
at the house when Shaunda got the news."

Brenna had heard the story many times before and
each time a sob lodged her throat at the thought of the
daddy she had lost. The father she never had a chance
to know.

"After that your mother was more determined than
ever to marry for money. And when she met Clyde
Powell, and he offered her to be in his life, I knew
nothing I or anyone said was going to make a difference," she added with a scowl.

While sipping her coffee, Brenna thought about her

mother. To her a man was more important than her own daughter. As much as she hated to think about it that knowledge still hurt.

"What I'm trying to say is life is too short. You've already spent the last five years running from Jabarie and your feelings. I just think it's time the two of you talk and try to work things out."

An hour later, she was sitting out on the beach with a book. Instead of reading, she was thinking about what her aunt said. *Talk.* What in the world did they have to talk about? Five years ago Jabarie deceived her. Not the other way around. Memories of his betrayal were still fresh in her mind and her heart. She thought he loved her and wanted to spend the rest of his life with her yet she walked in to find him lying on the couch with another woman. Anger bubbled up inside her that she quickly pushed aside. Was she ever going to be able to get past the pain and get on with her life? At this point, she still wasn't sure. With a weary breath, Brenna decided that maybe Aunt Nellie was right. Before she left, they did need to talk. She would rather avoid the discussion; however, before she left they were going to have to dredge up the past. If she was ever going to get on with her life she needed to understand if everything he had told her was a lie and why. Finding him in the arms of another woman had hurt her far worse than the lawyer standing on her porch holding a prenuptial agreement.

Brenna had just opened her book when she glanced across the sand and noticed Jabarie coming from the direction of Aunt Nellie's. She groaned inwardly, knowing good and well her aunt had been more than happy to tell him where to find her. Not that she was hiding.

She watched him as he approached her not at all surprised that he'd shown up. The man had a head like a brick wall. Of course, that was one of the things she found most attractive about him—his stubborn determination to have things his way. Brenna knew last night when she refused to have dinner with him that he would be back again today. Jabarie had never been a man to give up easily, not when he wanted something badly enough. She just wished he had been that determined about their relationship.

Brushing the past aside, Brenna focused on the here and now.

As Jabarie moved toward her, she shook her head, hating the sudden ache in her belly that indicated that even after all these years he could still get to her. But, as her eyes traveled to the leather sandals on his feet back up to his dark bedroom eyes, she admitted that forgetting someone wasn't easy when they were that fine. Jabarie had a body that made a woman's panties fall off voluntarily. Today he was wearing blue jean shorts that emphasized his muscular thighs and calves. Her gaze swept up to his massive chest in a white cotton T-shirt that strained across the chest. She wasn't ready yet to admit it, but a small part of her had actually been looking forward to seeing him.

"Hello, Bren," he said in a silky smooth voice that still aroused her.

She nodded. "Jabarie."

He lowered onto the red beach blanket beside her and the familiar scent of cologne ruffled her nose and for a second she allowed herself to get lost in the memories of their life together. God, she missed him. The arguments, the laughter and great makeup sex. She once loved this handsome man sitting beside her. It had taken months for her to get to the point where she didn't miss him every waking hour and again in her dreams. Now here he was, back in her life, trying to put her through all that pain again. Well, she wasn't having it. She still cared deeply about him. That was a given. But she was not about to give her heart to him a second time no matter how much she missed him. Somehow she had to find closure while staying strong.

"You like Walter Mosley?" he asked as he reached for her book and read the blurb on the back.

"Oh, yeah," she replied, glad that they had found a safe subject to break the tension floating around them. "I got hooked on him about two years ago."

Nodding, he glanced up from the book jacket and met her eyes. "My secretary gave me a copy of his newest release for Christmas last year. I read it in a week."

Smiling, Brenna stretched out her legs in front of her. "So you're reading now?"

Jabarie chuckled amusingly then set the book down on the blanket beside him. "Yes, I've been reading for pleasure for several years now. Remember how I used to tease you all the time about having your head buried in a book?"

Brenna nodded. "I remember, and you didn't believe me when I said you didn't know what you were missing."

With a smile, Jabarie crossed his ankles, then leaned back and rested the weight of his body on his forearms.

"I know now. Reading has been a wonderful escape for me. Ask your aunt. I've become a regular customer at her store."

"Really?"

His grin deepened. "I've been reading at least two books a month. With work it isn't always easy but whenever I get the opportunity to hide out on the yacht for the weekend, I always take a book with me."

Brenna swung her head around with surprise. "You have a yacht?"

He nodded. "My dad bought one about a year ago to impress his clients. She is a beauty, too. She belongs to all of us, but I think I use her more than anyone else."

"Does that mean you've learned how to sail a boat?" She remembered it being a dream of his.

"No, not quite yet, but I'm learning. We have a captain and a full staff available whenever we take her out on the water." He gave her a long dreamy look. "There is nothing like being out there. I've made a rule that when I go out I leave all my worries at the dock, then I enjoy two nights of catching up on reading and relaxation."

As kids they used to call him water boy because every chance he had Jabarie was outside playing in the water. "Sounds like fun."

"It is." Reaching over, his hand caressed the length of her arms and their eyes met. "How about going out on the yacht with me next weekend?"

It took her a few minutes to find her voice. "No, that wouldn't be a good idea. That long, all by ourselves, we might end up killing each other."

He fingered his neatly barbered mustache. "Or we'll find other ways to utilize our time."

His sexual reference angered her. He was determined to get her back in his bed. Although, right now, that idea didn't sound too bad, she wasn't even about to go there with him. "I don't think so."

Leaning forward, he asked, "Are you afraid to be alone with me?"

"Absolutely not!" Brenna cried louder than intended. The side of the beach where they were sitting was relatively empty, but a woman in a lounge chair a few yards away turned and peered over the top of her sunglasses at them before returning her attention to her book.

"I think you're lying," he finally said.

"I'm not afraid of you, Jabarie."

"Then prove it," he challenged with a wide smirk.

Jabarie had been leaning toward her and when he realized that their mouths were only a few inches away, he pulled back. Physical desire was one thing, but he couldn't confuse it with the emotions she stirred within him. Lust surged through him as he breathed deeply. Brenna's scent was lightly floral and uniquely feminine and cried to everything that was masculine about him. His loins screamed at him not to take no for an answer. Damn, he needed to relieve his sexual frustration more than he'd thought, but they were lying on the beach, not in a bed. He leaned back onto his elbows and crossed his ankles.

"Okay, then if you're not afraid of me, why don't you want to go out?" he asked again. Talking was the only way to distract his attention away from her mouth, or so he thought before he watched her nibble nervously on the succulent bottom lip. He groaned to himself. They reminded him of a ripe red strawberry. Sweet and juicy.

"You know why. So I don't know why you keep asking me the same question over and over."

"Because I'm not going to be happy until I get my way."

"Too bad," she replied with a stubborn tilt of her chin. "Now leave, you're bothering me." Brenna then reached over for her book and flipped to the folded page and started reading as if he was no longer there. He didn't bother to leave. Instead, he took the opportunity to study her.

Her hair was pulled up and held in place by a rubber band. A tendril of hair had escaped and hung loosely along the side of her face. The contrast of honey brown hair and smooth caramel skin wasn't lost on him. He reached out and brushed the strand back into place then trailed a path along her cheek down to her neck. Brenna flinched.

"What were you out here thinking about?"

"Nothing," she replied without looking up from the book.

"What do you mean nothing?" Sitting up, he snatched the book from her lap and held it behind his back so she couldn't reach it, despite her protest. "If you're sitting out here alone then you're thinking."

Her eyes sparkled angrily. "And why do you think that?"

"Because I come out to the beach all the time when I want to be alone with my thoughts."

"Really, and what do you think about?"

"You…and what happened between us five years ago."

She looked away but her hand trembled slightly. "Sometimes it's better to leave well enough alone."

He sat up abruptly. "But I don't want to. I need to understand why things went so wrong between us."

Her shoulders slumped and she gave a resigned sigh. "I don't want to talk about it."

"Yes, Brenna, I do. We need to clear the air and talk about what happened."

"Why? That was five years ago. I've moved on."

"Well, I haven't."

She licked her dry lips and took a deep breath. "That's not my problem."

"You're wrong. It is your problem. Every time I think about marriage and kids all I can see is you. I've tried having relationships with other women and they never last because all I can think about is you."

She went completely still. She would never have expected him to say those words.

"I still love you. Nothing about that has changed."

Her chest constricted and it hurt to breath. Everything started closing in and becoming too close for comfort the second he told her he still loved her. Liar! *If you loved me why were you with Anika?* She wanted to scream but could not find the air to do so. "Well, I don't love you."

He took in a lungful of air then nodded. "I didn't expect you to."

Her eyes darkened dangerously. "What is that supposed to mean?"

"Nothing. Nothing at all."

She shrank back from him, carefully, and replaced the shield she'd worn when he had arrived. All traces of sadness left her face even though an aura of vulnerability lingered around her. If they hadn't grown up together, he may not have recognized it.

"Are you going to tell me what you were out here thinking about before I bothered you?"

She hesitated. "I told you. Nothing."

"Tell me," he said softly, knowing from his sister that women liked to talk about the things that were heavy on their minds. "Were you thinking about me?"

"No," she said and let out a deep sigh as her eyes traveled out onto the water. "I was thinking about this place. I can't believe how much has changed. I really miss being here."

Without really thinking Jabarie curved his arm around her waist and pulled her closer. She laid her head against his shoulder. For several moments he offered strength and comfort. Closing her eyes, it was like they had slipped back in time when they could talk about anything. A time when they were young and eager to share all their secrets. When they had been hopelessly in love.

With her nestled so trustingly in his arms he knew he shouldn't betray that, but holding her petite frame had a distinct effect on him. When she tilted her head back and stared innocently up at him, he lowered his and brushed his lips over her mouth. The kiss only lasted a few seconds but it was long enough to send his hormones into a tailspin.

"If you miss it here that much then move back."

Brenna frowned and eased out of his embrace. "I have a life in Dallas."

"You also have a life here that you can come back to."

She shook her head. "It's not that simple."

He gazed over at her trying to read her thoughts the way he used to be able to, but he couldn't. There was no way she could have had changed that much. Somewhere deep down inside had to be that girl he had once been hopelessly in love with. When she noticed him staring, she dropped her eyes. "Is there someone in Dallas waiting on you?" he asked.

Brenna thought about the few meaningless dates she had. There was not one man she could consider a strong possibility. "Yes…" she began and when she saw the muscles at his jaw flex, she continued. "My store."

His expression softened. "You can always open another store."

"And compete with my aunt, no way."

"You can always take over her store. You know she's seriously thinking about selling."

"She is?" That was the first she heard of that.

He nodded. "We talked about it last night."

Brenna wasn't about to explain how much it hurt her that her aunt shared her feelings with Jabarie instead of her. "As much as I missed being on the coast, I love living in Dallas," she stated in an even tone.

Shifting slightly on the blanket, Jabarie studied her profile while she gazed out onto the ocean. Intense heat flowed to his groins as he remembered making love to her on that very blanket. He shook the thought off and quickly reminded himself that the beautiful woman sitting beside him was the same person who had walked out on him. She had made a mockery out of him then went on to start a new life that she loved. New friends. Her own bookstore. What she was trying to say was that in her perfect new world she had no room for him, or them. She had gotten on with her life while he was still here, in Sheraton Beach, trying to figure out how to get his life back. He couldn't forget her or maybe he didn't want to. One thing for sure, Brenna was imprinted on his brain. And, to his dismay, for some reason what she had done didn't seem to matter anymore. It didn't matter that after all these years Brenna continued to haunt him, and he thought about her more often than not while he was awake and again while he slept. The problem was he couldn't go on because there was still unfinished business between them. Somehow she had cursed him and if it was truly over, he had to find a way to free his mind once and for all.

Brenna glanced over at him and it was as if she had read his mind. The lonely look in her eyes screamed she wanted the same things. Before he realized what he was doing he had lowered her back onto the blanket and covered her mouth with his.

Trouble, Brenna knew, came often when you least expected it. She'd known being around Jabarie was a bad idea from the exact moment he spotted her in the bookstore window. Though he'd broken her heart, her body couldn't seem to remember what the heart knew all too well, and even it wasn't listening at the moment. He was just too damn tempting. And she'd always been able to resist temptation. Except when Jabarie was involved.

The pressure of his lips against her own tempted her

and she willingly gave in to the impulse. What harm was in kissing, anyway? However, as he rolled over and lined their bodies together, she realized her lips were saying one thing and her body was screaming something altogether different. Her nipples hardened. Her bud throbbed down low. She was woman enough to know what her body was trying to say.

As Jabarie deepened the kiss, she couldn't help parting her lips and inviting him deeper. He took the invitation and her body yearned for more than she intended to give him. As soon as his tongue slipped inside her mouth, she forgot about the protective barrier and how badly he had once hurt her.

His heat surrounded her. She felt feminine, sexy and alive in a way that no other man had ever made her feel. Her stomach muscles churned and knotted while the walls she'd built carefully around her heart began to crumble.

No other man had ever held her so tenderly. She'd forgotten how intimate it was to lie out on the beach with a man. She'd forgotten how the brain shut down and hormones took over. She'd forgotten how it felt to be wanted.

Finally, Jabarie pulled back and gazed down at her.

She didn't want it to stop because she knew she would make sure it never happened again. She closed her eyes so he could not see how vulnerable she was. So that Jabarie wouldn't be able to read her thoughts she'd tried to shut away, Brenna reached up and cupped the back of his head, urging his face toward hers.

He deepened the kiss and it felt like it had gone on forever. Everything inside her body sprung to life and became conscious of everything she was feeling and yearning. When she was seconds away from turning to putty, Jabarie rained light kisses on her mouth, cheek and neck then pulled back slightly to stare down at her again. This time Brenna kept her eyes wide open, wanting to make sure everything that was happening was real and not just another one of her dreams. Staring across, his eyes watched her carefully.

The sound of children playing, startled her into releasing him and sitting up on the blanket. She felt unkempt and tried to smooth her hair back into place. *Goodness, what in the world was I thinking?*

"Well…" he said.

Obviously, Jabarie wasn't sure how to approach the situation. Talk about the store, or revisit his love for books, she thought. But she couldn't. Her mind was in shambles. Her heart still raced and her nipples were still hard and erect.

"Yes, well, I better go. I'm meeting Sheyna for dinner," she said, as she grabbed the book and rose. "When you get done hanging out, would you please leave the blanket on Aunt Nellie's porch?"

"Sure." Quickly, before she could get away, Jabarie reached up and grasped her hand. "Why are you running off?"

"I'm not running. I just don't want to talk about what just happened." She was surprised by her outward display of calmness although her stomach churned with uneasiness.

"That's the problem. You don't want to talk and until we do neither of us are going to be able to get on with our lives."

She snatched her hand from his grasp. "Jabarie, that's where you're wrong. I've gotten on with my life a long time ago."

He ran a hand across his head. "Then prove it by having dinner with me on my father's yacht next weekend?"

Brenna pursed her lips. Jabarie was starting to sound like a broken record. "I already told you, no."

"And I'm not going to stop asking until you say yes."

Brenna frowned. "You are so stubborn."

"Good."

"Why is that good?" she asked and couldn't keep the shiver from her body.

"Because eventually you'll have to say yes, just so I'll leave you alone."

She couldn't help smiling. "Goodbye, Jabarie."

"Brenna, I—"

"I've got to go," she said, cutting him off; then she walked away and didn't look back. She'd always prided herself on her self-control and now she knew that confidence was false. She'd been in control before because she hadn't been tempted.

"This isn't finished," Jabarie called after her as she moved across the sand.

Jabarie sat there for the longest time, watching her leave. After everything that had happened between them, he wished to God it wasn't so, but his mind and body had already decided he had to be with Brenna. Seeing her and kissing her was never going to be enough. Being around her stirred emotions he had hid away a long time ago, and nothing in his life was ever going to be normal again until he reached inside her soul and found out what had happened all those years ago. He also wouldn't be satisfied until he had her honey brown hair spread out on his pillow and he was buried deep inside her sweet body with those shapely legs wrapped around his waist.

Lying back on the blanket, he folded his arms beneath his head then closed his eyes. Yep. He wasn't going to be happy until he got exactly what he wanted. He just hoped that once he had her squirming beneath the weight of his body, he could finally find closure and get on with his life. However, something stirred inside his chest and he had a sinking feeling that it wouldn't possibly be that easy.

Chapter 7

On Wednesday, Sheyna came storming out of Jace's office just as Jabarie came around the corner.

"You okay?" he asked.

She stopped long enough to glare up at him. Her chest was heavy. She was fuming. "You need to send your brother on a long vacation because he's impossible." With that she turned on the heels of her red stilettos and he watched as she stormed down the hall to her office at the end. Shaking his head, he thought the red suit was an appropriate replica of her mood.

"What's wrong with her?" Jabarie asked as he stepped inside his brother's spacious corner office. Jace was sitting behind his large mahogany desk with his head buried in a report.

He shrugged a shoulder beneath his navy blue suit jacket. "Your guess is as good as mine."

The fact that he didn't look up indicated there was more going on than he cared to admit. While moving farther into the room across plush royal blue carpet, he observed Jace rubbing his hand vigorously across his neatly trimmed goatee. A clear indication that something was bothering him.

At thirty-three Jace had managed to recruit some of the most talented hotel managers in the world. He was a salesperson and damn good at staffing. However, the day-to-day work environment was an area he had no business dealing with. Sheyna's job was employee relations manager; she worked on incentive programs and building the morale of their employees. When an employee had a problem she was the go-to girl. And because of her, employee retention was up considerably. Although the two rarely ever saw eye-to-eye, she was too damn good at what she did for Jace to step on her toes too often.

"You're quiet. I know you didn't come here to watch me review benefit packages," Jace commented, breaking into his thoughts.

Jabarie moved over and took a seat across from his desk and grinned. "Maybe I just came down the hall to watch my big brother in action."

"I doubt it."

He chuckled then glanced up at the mahogany paneling covering the wall of his office before saying, "Guess who's back?"

"Who?"

"Brenna."

Jace looked up from his desk. "Your Brenna?"

Jabarie met his brother's surprised look then replied with a frown. "She's not my Brenna."

"You know what I mean," Jace replied impatiently. He leaned back into the plush chair. "Yeah, that Brenna."

Jace's sable-colored eyes, studied him. "Does that mean the two of you finally talked?"

Jabarie ran a finger under his collar and loosened the tie that had tried to choke him for the better part of the afternoon before answering, "No."

"Why not?"

His brother had made no secret of his disappointment that Jabarie hadn't gone after Brenna demanding an explanation.

Jabarie leaned back in his chair and met his brother's gaze. "Because she doesn't want to talk to me."

"And when has that ever stopped you before?"

"In case you've forgotten, she left me," he said angrily.

Jace snorted rudely. "And with good reason."

"What?" he asked, startled by his brother's confession.

"You dated her and for years she had to deal with mom and dad snubbing their nose down at her. She never felt comfortable around them and you never did anything to make sure that she did," Jace added, glaring at his brother. "Hell, I would have taken the money and run myself."

"What are you talking about? I loved her. I was ready to spend the rest of my life with her regardless of how against it Mom and Dad were."

Jace gave him a look filled with contempt. "Then if that was the case, you wouldn't have let her walk out of your life. You would have gone after her and brought her back kicking and screaming. Instead you let her go then spent the last five years blaming her instead of yourself."

Jabarie rose, refusing to sit and listen to this, and stormed out the door, but not before hearing his brother call after him and say, "If anyone owes her an apology, it's you."

"I have one word to describe Jabarie. Stubborn," Brenna replied with a groan.

She and Sheyna were sharing a booth at a small bar and grill, sipping apple martinis and eating wings.

A smile tipped Sheyna's lips as she glanced across the table at her best friend. "What else is new? He's always been stubborn. So is Jace. It must run in the family."

"But this is worse than stubborn," she began between chews. "He's been calling and popping up at either the store or Aunt Nellie's all week. He's determined to get me back in his bed."

"And what's so wrong with that?"

"I don't want to start something I have no intentions of finishing. I have a new life in Dallas."

Sheyna took a sip of her drink. "You can't blame the man. The two of you were engaged."

"But we're not," Brenna interjected as she brought the wing to her lips and took another bite.

"That didn't stop you from kissing him."

Color filled her cheeks and she regretted ever saying anything. "I never said I wasn't attracted to him."

"So date him," she said and licked her fingers.

Brenna waited until their waiter had exchanged their empty water glasses for full before responding. "Why start something that I have no intention of finishing?"

Sheyna shot a straight no-nonsense look. "You're only here until Ms. Nellie gets better, so why not enjoy yourself and Jabarie while you're here?"

Brenna shook her head. "I don't know."

She met her gaze. "Oh my goodness! You're still in love with him!"

"I am not," she quickly denied.

She chuckled and her eyes crinkled attractively. "Oh, yes you are."

She didn't waste her time denying it. No doubt the truth was written all over her face. Brenna breathed in a deep sigh. "A part of me will always love him."

Sheyna gave her a sympathetic smile. "Look, I love you, and other than Anika, I don't know what really went wrong between the two of you, but I know that a love like the two of you had only comes once in a lifetime." She reached for a napkin and wiped sauce from her fingers. "I'd rather have loved and lost than never loved at all."

Brenna's brow lifted. "Is that your way of telling me you're in love with Jace?"

She managed to look truly insulted. "Hell no. I can't stand that man."

Brenna chuckled. "Whatever. Instead of being all in my business, I need to be trying to hook you up."

"Don't even think about it." She reached for her martini glass and scowled. "I tried to get him to start a new employee referral program and he rejected it. Sometimes I just don't understand that man."

"Sounds like love to me."

"Me and Jace?" she shuddered. "Never. Now you and Jabarie, that's another sad love song. Girl, enjoy your time here and that man. It ain't like you haven't slept with him before. He was your first and he can be your—"

"He's my only," she confessed between chews.

Sheyna almost tipped over her glass. "What? You're kidding, right?" When Brenna shook her head, she leaned forward and dropped her voice down almost to a whisper. "You're telling me you haven't had one sexual relationship since you left this town?"

"Nope. Not one."

"Well hell, you should be ready to have someone knock the cobwebs off."

"Sheyna," she warned then looked around embarrassingly.

"What are you ashamed of? A lot of women aren't getting any. Didn't you hear, black women are out numbered," she added as she reached for another wing and took a bite. "Which is why I can't believe you're turning down the opportunity to get you some from a brother who is not only fine but was your first and only lover." She shook her head. "I don't get it. Unless of course the brotha wasn't satisfying you…" she purposely allowed her words to fade off as she looked across the table.

"Goodness, no. I had no complaint." Just thinking about having him buried deep inside her caused her to shift uncomfortably on the bench.

"Well, then. Enjoy."

"I just don't want any misunderstandings." She

knew sleeping with him would stir up old emotions that were best left alone.

Sheyna reached for a napkin. "Then just do like I do. Lay down some ground rules. Let Jabarie know that this is a summer fling and nothing more. As soon as Aunt Nellie is better things are going back to the way things were. That way everyone is happy."

She didn't know if she could pull it off, but at least it would satisfy the sexual yearning she felt every time they were in the same room.

"I'm going to give it some serious thought."

"You do that."

Quickly changing the subject, Brenna raised her glass. "Here's to your new house."

Sheyna grinned and reached for her glass. "Thank you. This has probably been the most exciting day of my life before Jace spoiled it for me. But you know what, I'm not letting him get to me today." She shook her head then tapped her glass lightly against Brenna's and took a sip. "Nope. This is my day. I have finally gotten what I always wanted. Me, Sheyna Marie Simmons, just closed on my first house."

"And I'm so happy for you for getting everything you've always wanted." Brenna brought her glass to her lips and wished she could say the same. All she'd ever wanted was one thing. Jabarie Beaumont.

After leaving Jace's office, the rest of the afternoon was a big waste. All Jabarie could do was think about what his brother had said and wonder if maybe there was some truth to it. He had allowed his parents to dictate his life for so long that maybe he hadn't defended

Brenna the way he should have. He squeezed the pen in his hand until his fingers hurt. *Was I that blind and stupid back then?*

At six, he decided to call it a day and instead of going straight to his empty condo, he dropped by a new bar and grill he'd been hearing about to have a drink. Luckily, he found parking in the small lot behind the building. He parked his Navigator then walked around to the front of the building. Even from outside he could hear the heavy thump of R&B music. He stepped inside and was quickly swallowed up by a lively crowd dancing. All of the tables lined the walls, allowing plenty of room for dancing. He moved over to the bar to order a drink when something told him to look over his shoulder. He turned around and spotted Brenna and Sheyna in a booth with two guys sitting across from them. His jaw dropped. She looked sexy as hell. He sucked in a deep breath as his mouth went dry.

Her hair was spiraled on top of her head. Stray curls caressed her neck and framed her shoulders. Where were her clothes, he wondered. She was practically naked in a mini dress. The front of her dress gaped open and his eyes were drawn to her tantalizing cleavage. He knew enough about dresses to know that beneath that thin material she wasn't wearing a bra.

The smile on her face said she was enjoying whatever it was the man sitting across from her was saying. She fluttered her lashes and perfected a pout that made his pulse race. He couldn't believe she was flirting shamelessly with that man. Just watching her look that way at someone else caused jealousy to bubble up inside him. He forced himself to take a deep breath then reluctantly listened to the voice inside his head who reminded him Brenna no longer belonged to him.

He moved over to the bar and took a seat where he could have a clear view of the table across from them. After ordering a cognac and a glass of water, he allowed his eyes to stray over to Brenna. His eyes traveled down to her slender legs that were sticking out from underneath the table, showing off the sexy strappy sandals on her feet.

He sat there for the next half hour sipping his drink, trying to think of a way to approach Brenna without pissing her off when he spotted Tyrone Cole, escorting Brenna onto the dance floor. He didn't like the way he placed his hand only inches above her butt. He moved closer to where they were dancing and glanced at Brenna who was staring over at Sheyna with a panicked look in her eyes. Focusing his attention on Tyrone, it didn't take him long to realize the man was drunk. What else was new? Since he'd lost his job at the plant he'd found another way to passed the time. Obviously, Brenna was eager to get away from him.

Quickly he moved over to the booth where Sheyna was sitting across from some guy with a receding hairline. As soon as he approached, the two glanced up at him looking equally surprised. "Will you excuse us a moment?" Without waiting for a reply, Jabarie took her hand and pulled her gently to her feet and they joined the other couples on the dance floor. It was a slow number so he draped his arms loosely around her waist.

"What are you doing here?" she asked with a knowing grin.

"You know why I'm here." He forced a smile then glanced over his shoulder at the couple dancing on the other side of the floor. "Sheyna, you know Tyrone, right?"

She glanced in the direction of his eyes. "Sure, who doesn't," she murmured then snorted rudely.

"Here's what I want to do. I'm going to cut in and rescue Brenna."

"Oh, great, and I get to dance with the town drunk. Thanks a lot. I thought we were better than that."

"We are, and I know you know how to handle yourself with someone like Tyrone."

Looking over at her friend, Sheyna noticed the uneasiness in Brenna's eyes. "Okay, you're right. Brenna doesn't know when it's best just to kick a man in his nuts."

"Ow!" Jabarie winced jokingly although in this case, it might not be a bad idea. Laughing, he spun them neatly into their path and tapped Tyrone on the shoulder. "I'm cutting in."

Tyrone looked confused for a moment before Jabarie tugged Brenna from his arms and Sheyna led him away.

"Thanks, I owe you one," Brenna said with a smile and she wrapped her arms around his neck.

"No, you owe me two and I'm ready to collect."

Shaking her head, her smile deepened. "Okay, you win. What do you want?"

Jabarie groaned inwardly. Didn't she know she should never ask a man that? "Dinner with me on my father's yacht this Sunday."

Their eyes locked. He knew she was about to say no, but before she could, he kissed her, covering her mouth with his. The moment their lips touched he was tempted to swing her into his arms and carry her back to his condo. When he finally released her, Brenna gave a weary sigh.

"Okay, I'll have dinner, but only if we go angel shopping first."

"Oh, boy." He chuckled. Brenna would have him in every antique store on the coast. "You're still collecting cherubs?"

"Oh, yes. You should see my collection. I had to buy a second curio cabinet."

His brow rose. "Then shouldn't that be a sign that it is time to stop?"

It was her turn to laugh. "Sorry, that's one habit I can't let go of."

He wished he was a habit she had held on to. Jabarie pulled her tighter in his arms as they swayed to a new love ballad. There was a softness about Brenna that was so feminine that it screamed at ever vein in his body. It made his chest swell and excitement buzz through his blood. He knew better than to dance with a woman he wanted so badly, but he didn't want to be anywhere else. Jabarie lowered his head and his nose nuzzled the side of her neck. Her perfume was hypnotic and filled his every breath.

"I always loved dancing with you," he breathed against her ear.

"So did I," he heard her say.

He tightened his grip on her waist and pulled her closer. With his eyes closed, he listened to the words of the song. *My one and only love*. It couldn't have been more appropriate if he had written the lyrics himself. A part of him would always love the woman he was holding in his arms. Even though they could never go back to the way things were, he hoped that by the end of her trip the two of them could find closure and continue their mutual respect for each other. But even as he finished that thought, Jabarie didn't want to think about her leaving him and Sheraton Beach, not yet. Instead, he held her in his arms and looked forward to an evening on his yacht that was full of possibilities.

After another slow ballad, the music changed to a fast number and Brenna released him and tried to leave the dance floor, but Jabarie held on to her hand, refusing to let go.

"Dance this song with me."

Nodding, she started to gyrate her hips.

Jabarie hadn't done this kind of bump and grind in years, but he wanted to see Brenna in action. As soon as he tried to imitate some of the new moves he'd seen the teenagers doing, Brenna threw her head back with laughter then relaxed and cut loose.

He wanted to stop dancing and watch her move. He missed her laughter and her dancing which she had always been good at. Her breasts jiggled with each step and he loved the way she wiggled her hips. Her body moved with the rhythm of the music. She was amazing. Watching her, all he could think about was touching her and taking her to fill the sharp need within him.

It's only a need, he reminded himself with an inward groan. Yet, his reaction to her wasn't helping any. But she was a challenge and he had never been one to back down. Now that she had agreed to dinner, it was only a matter of time before she was back his bed and by the time she left for Dallas he would have her out of his system. Finally the song ended. Smiling, he reached down for her hand. "Come on. Let me buy you a drink."

Brenna followed Jabarie over to the bar where he ordered her another apple martini and a shot of cognac for himself.

Half of her yearned to agree to anything he wanted while the other half of her screamed a warning for her to stay away from him. When he'd asked her again to have dinner with him, Brenna started to say no, but she realized she didn't want to, and there was no point in denying herself a few hours of fun. His satisfaction was evident in his expression when he gave her a faint smile.

While they waited for the bartender to return with their drinks, Jabarie moved up behind her and wrapped his arms around her waist. She found herself snuggling closer and leaning her waist against his body.

"Who's that guy Sheyna's dancing with?" he asked.

Her eyes darted across the dance floor until she spotted Sheyna grinding against the man with the receding hairline.

She lifted her shoulder. "Somebody in town on vacation. Believe me, she isn't the least bit interested."

"Hmm. What's the deal with her and my brother?"

Brenna swung around in his arms and met his penetrating stare. "I was going to ask you that same question."

He shrugged then leaned closer and stole a kiss that momentarily took her breath away. "I don't know, but whatever it is, I wish the two of them would hurry up and figure it out. Their constant bickering and disagreements are starting to wear on my nerves."

She nodded. "I think they're fighting their attraction."

"That's too bad. They might never find out what they're both missing."

He gave her a long hard look and she noted the meaning behind his statement. Her eyes widened, the only indication that her heart had begun to pound wildly.

He pulled her even closer, burying his lips against her hair. "I don't want to waste another moment fighting what I feel for you."

"I thought we were working on being friends," she shot back.

Pulling back slightly, he stared at her, his gaze narrowing. "Didn't you tell me that too much has happened between us to be just friends?"

Briefly closing her eyes, Brenna smiled. Damn, she had said that. "I think it's a start." Her gaze swung back meeting his and she didn't miss the gleam of determination in his dark eyes.

"I think we need to start by talking about what happened between us."

Brenna shook her head. "How about we just enjoy our time together with no pressures or expectations, and I promise before I leave, we'll talk."

He winked at her, smiling. "Ms. Gathers, I think you've got yourself a deal."

Chapter 8

"Where do you want this box?"

Sheyna swung around and looked at the box labeled dishes that Brenna was carrying in her arms and pointed at the counter.

"Just set it there. When I get a chance I'll toss them in the dishwasher."

"Okay." Brenna slid the box onto the counter then retrieved two bottles of water from the refrigerator and handed one to her friend.

"Thanks," she said then gave her a tired smile as she removed the cap and brought the bottle to her dry lips. "Remind me to never move again." Sheyna groaned as she slumped back against the oak cabinet "This is hard work."

"Well you don't have to worry about moving for a very long time. Your house is adorable!" Her eyes traveled around the spacious kitchen cabinets and counter space to die for. The three bedroom, two-story house was a first-time home buyer's dream.

"It is nice, isn't it?" she said, beaming with pride.

Brenna took another swallow then wiped her damp hand across her shorts. "Come on. We better not leave them alone for too long. They might decide to take another break."

"When aren't they on a break."

She gave her best friend a sympathetic look then turned on her heels and followed her back outside. Sheyna had hired a small local moving company to move her out of her apartment and into her new home. Thank goodness she packed her own stuff because as slow as they were, they would still be at the apartment. They were late getting there and every time she looked around one of them was taking a break. Paid by the hour, the movers were trying to milk Sheyna for everything they could get.

Stepping through the door, her eyes traveled over the white truck and her brow furrowed. Sure enough, they stepped outside and found all three leaning against the truck taking a cigarette break.

"Enough!" Sheyna exclaimed and stormed over to the truck. Within seconds, her tongue was wagging loud across the yard.

"Oh, brother." Brenna groaned and started across the yard when she heard a vehicle. She turned around.

Jabarie!

Her heart did a backflip when he climbed out the passenger side of his brother's gray Escalade. She gave him a smile then shifted her gaze to the driver.

She had known Jace for as long as Jabarie and he had always treated her like a sister. Like his brother, he was also over six-feet tall with the same piercing sable eyes. His nose was straight and he had an attractive cleft in his nutty brown chin that was surrounded by a neatly barbered goatee. As soon as Jace noticed her, a smile softened his mouth, and she moved over to greet him with a big hug.

"Hey, Bren." He wrapped his arms around her and gave her a hug then pulled back and planted a kiss to her cheek. "How have you been?"

"Good. How about you?"

"Can't complain. Although your friend is driving me crazy," he added with a wink. His eyes then traveled over to Sheyna yelling at the man talking on his cell phone. He raised his curving eyebrows. "What's going on over there?"

Brenna gave a frustrated breath and glared across the grass. "Those are a bunch of lazy morons. We've been trying to get them to actually work all morning."

Jace's body stiffened and his grip loosened. "Excuse me a minute." He glanced over at his brother and signaled for him to follow.

Jabarie gave her a quick look then strolled across the lawn with determined strides to the trio that was doing nothing. Brenna followed and noticed that the one with the bald head, when he spotted them heading in their direction, startled then quickly jumped back onto the truck and got back to work. The other two continued to lean against the truck smirking as Sheyna pointed her finger in their faces.

"Excuse me," Jace said as he drew near. "Do we have a problem?"

Sheyna swung around with her lips twisted. "What are you doing here?" she demanded to know.

"Came to rescue you," he replied with a wink.

Defiantly, she planted her fist at her waist. "I don't need your he—"

Brenna yanked her over beside her, cutting off her words and gave her the eye to be quiet.

As soon as she was out of the way, Jace walked over to the owner of the truck and stared down at him. "Is there some reason why you're not working?"

"We're taking a break," he mumbled without even bothering to look at him.

"They've been taking breaks all morning!" Sheyna screamed before Brenna clamped a hand over her mouth.

The tall lanky man, in his mid-thirties, scratched his head and came over and said apologetically, "Sorry Massah Beaumont. We's gonna get right back to work," he said mocking his ancestors.

Jabarie's face was a mask of stone as he moved up into his face. "You're going to get back to work now, and when you're done you're going to give this lady a twenty-five percent discount, otherwise I will report you to the better business bureau."

Red faced, the man stuttered and Brenna could tell he wanted to challenge him but thought better of it.

Jace walked over to the other, who looked barely out of high school, and bunched his brow when he noticed the smirk on his face. "Aren't you Charlotte's son?"

His eyes narrowed suspiciously, and he shrugged his shoulders as if to say, so what. "Yeah? What about it?"

"Your mother came to my office just yesterday asking me about a job for you." He paused dramatically and stroked his mustache. "I guess this is an example of the kind of work you do."

Shaking his head, he sputtered. "Oh, no, I'm a hard worker. Just watch and see." He then jumped onto the back of the truck and started carrying furniture into the house. The others followed.

Beneath her fingers, she could feel Sheyna's body relax and she glanced over and saw a silly smirk on Jace's face as she stared over at him. Brenna shook her head. She had it bad and didn't even know it.

Glancing over at his brother, she could understand why. The brothers were fine. While Jabarie watched the crew work, she took in his stance with his legs slightly parted and his arms folded across his massive chest. He was wearing a short sleeved T-shirt and blue jeans that hung low on his waist and looked sexy as hell. It wasn't the hot summer heat that traveled down between her legs.

Brenna jumped when she felt someone touch her arm.

"Girl, what are you thinking about?" Sheyna asked jokingly.

"I should be asking you the same thing." Their laughter drew Jabarie's attention and as soon as he turned to her and their eyes locked, she stilled and could do nothing but stare.

A wave of longing rushed through her body. She had been celibate for far too long. That's all it was, she told herself. Lust. Plain and simple.

Sheyna gave her an encouraging shove. "Go over there and talk to him. You know you want to."

Yes, she did and that was the problem. She needed to keep her distance from him but there it was, that magnetic pull again drawing her to him. On wobbly legs, Brenna moved over to him and was greeted by another warm smile.

"Hey," she said unable to resist a grin of her own.

"Hey, yourself."

Recovering quickly, she swallowed, hoping to relieve the dryness in her constricted throat. "Thanks for getting them back to work." They were now unloading the truck the way movers should. "It's a shame that a person has to scream and holler and act like a damn fool just to get work done."

"No problem."

Her lips twitched with amusement. "I guess that means I owe you again."

"It appears so." Jabarie crooned softly, his handsome mouth curved into a wide grin.

Her lashes came down, concealing her inner-most feelings for him before she nodded and said, "Okay. I'll spend the night with you on your yacht," she said then turned on her heels and moved into the house.

Jabarie waited until the storm door closed before he let out a deep breath. He almost didn't believe his ears. Brenna had agreed to spend the night with him.

Woohoo!

Finally, he was getting somewhere because he wasn't sure how much more he could have taken watching her standing in the center of the yard in khaki shorts that hugged her sweet round behind and showed off her long legs that sent his loins screaming. Did she just agree to sleep with him? He didn't want to get ahead of himself but that was what it had sounded like. Yes!

Anxious to join his brother in the house, Jabarie moved over to the truck and grabbed a large box and carried it into the house. He stepped into the Berber carpeted foyer directly into the living room and carried the box over to the corner where the movers were stacking all the others and lowered it to the floor. He rose and swung around to find Brenna staring up at him holding a plastic bottle of water in her hand.

"I thought maybe you'd like a bottle of water."

He could use a whole lot more water than that. A cold shower would be good and not because he was sweating, either.

"You look hot," she commented in a sensual tone that sent his libido racing.

"So do you," he said. And as he unscrewed the top, his eyes traveled down to her breasts that strained against the tight midriff T-shirt. He brought the bottle to his lips and almost choked when he realized she wasn't wearing a bra. Two succulent nipples were visible through the thin material. He took a long drink, welcoming the chill before warmth spread through his body. He finished half the bottle while he tried to think of his next move.

"How's your aunt today?" he asked while being careful not to let his gaze rest where he wanted to and looked in her eyes instead.

"She's fine. Ms. Lucy is going to come over and hang out with her today," she said and licked her lips.

Jabarie leaned closer and stared down at the moisture left on her smiling lips.

"What am I going to do with you?" he asked, and didn't even wait to see if she had any suggestions because he already had some of his own. Most of them he would save until they were alone on his yacht but there was one thing he wanted now and there was no way of resisting the urge. Angling his head, he touched his mouth to hers, increasing the pressure until she responded. The kiss was glorious and full of heat and hunger.

The sound of the door swinging open startled both of them. They jumped back like the time they'd been caught with their hands in her aunt's pie filling.

"Oops," Sheyna said, skidding to stop. "My bad."

Jabarie looked from her to Brenna's startled face and replied, "I think that will do for now."

After Sheyna paid the movers and sent them away without a tip and at the twenty-five percent discounted rate that Jabarie had instructed, the four of them worked together to put her house into order. Jace paused long enough to pull out his cell phone and order a couple of pizzas. As soon as the food arrived, he tipped the delivery boy and called for the others to join him in the kitchen.

Brenna loaded the last glass into the dishwasher then turned the unit to a light wash. The dishes were already clean; she was just trying to remove the dust that had accumulated during the move. She then removed four plates from the drainer, dried them off with a paper towel and carried them over to the table. She moved over to the table just as the others came in and washed their hands at the sink one after the other and took a seat.

"I ordered one pepperoni and one sausage," Jace informed as he reached for the first box.

Brenna's stomach growled. "Sounds good to me."

Jabarie's eyes grew round and amusing. "I hear. Please, bro, feed this girl."

She slugged Jabarie playfully in the arm then held out her plate so Jace could serve her up a slice.

"Thanks." Quickly she brought the pizza to her mouth and took a bite. A moan escaped her lips. She didn't think pizza had ever tasted so good. While chewing, she gazed over and found Jabarie watching her. She enjoyed the warmth of his eye contact.

"I take it you like the pizza."

Giggling, she nodded.

Sheyna reached for her glass. "Garamond's has been here for about a year now. They have some of the best pizzas on the coast."

"It's really good." She reached for one of the colas on the table and popped the can open. "What made the two of you decide to come and help out?" she asked between sips.

Jace finished chewing his food before answering. "Who didn't know miss motor mouth here was moving. She'd been complaining about this day for weeks."

"I have not," Sheyna objected with a frown.

"Oh, yes you have," he replied in a challenging tone. "Woe is me? I have to move. I hate moving," he said in a false soprano voice, trying to mock Sheyna's sultry tone.

"Now he's really lying," she barked and tossed a sausage at his head.

The table erupted with laughter.

Brenna dabbed her mouth with the corner of her napkin. "He is right, Sheyna. You have been complaining."

Her friend's eyes snapped to hers. "You're supposed to be on my side."

Shrugging her shoulders, she gave her a sheepish, "sorry."

"Speaking of sides," Jabarie began then paused and took a sip. "As soon as we're done setting up your bedroom, how about a friendly game of Spades?"

Brenna glanced over at him and saw the challenge gleaming in his eyes. In high school, playing cards was how the four of them had spent many Friday nights.

"Y'all don't want to mess with us," she heard Sheyna say.

Jace gave a dismissive wave. "We're about to spank that behind."

"Yeah, whatever. Then let's make this game a little more exciting."

Leaning back in the chair with a look of confidence, he replied, "You're on."

Waving her hand in the air, Brenna jumped in. "Ooh! Ooh! How does this sound? For every hand you lose, you've got to strip one article of clothing."

Her best friend nodded then folded her arm against her breasts. "That sounds like a plan." She made the comment a dare.

Jabarie and Jace looked at each other then turned to the women. Brenna immediately noticed the desire lurking in the depths of Jabarie's eyes and wished she could take back what she'd said when she heard him say those two little words.

"You're on."

They had been playing for almost an hour and as Brenna stared down at the last three cards in her hands, she nibbled nervously, wondering if they had bitten off more than they could chew. So far they had five books. Two more and they'd win the hand. She glanced over at the chair to her left where Jabarie sat with his shirt off and his feet bare. As she waited for him to throw out a card, she nibbled on her bottom lip to stifle a moan. He looked delectable. Staring at his chocolate nipples, she had the strongest urge to lean across the table and lavish one with her tongue.

"Come on, you don't have all night," Sheyna said impatiently as she sat in the chair fully dressed minus her shoes.

Jabarie gave her a hard look before he tossed an ace of spades onto the table. Her pulse raced. Glancing down at her hand, she looked at the big joker. She was all out of spades. If Sheyna didn't have the other joker then she would use it. She glanced across the table and met the look in her partner's eyes. Silently, she was trying to find out what she had in her hand. Brenna raised a brow then watched as the corner of Sheyna's lips turned upward before she slammed a ten of spades on the table.

Brenna glanced over at Jace's naked torso as he slid a jack of diamonds on the table, meaning he was all out of spades. Soaring inside, in one swift move she slapped her joker onto the table.

"Ha!" she cried then leaned across the table and gave Sheyna a high five.

"Yeah, yeah. It's your turn," Jabarie said in a playful voice.

Reaching to her hand, she dropped an jack of hearts onto the table. Jabarie dropped a two, Sheyna a nine, then Jace's eyes lit up as he dropped king.

"That's what I'm talking about!" Jabarie cried.

Brenna rolled her eyes heavenward and tried to keep a straight face. "Whatever." The men continued to yell across the table.

Impatiently, Sheyna snapped her fingers. "Excuse me, but can we get on with this?"

"Hold your horses, little mama," Jace said, sobering.

Brenna's eyes traveled nervously down to her king of clubs then around the table. Both of them needed one book to win. If they lost, she and Sheyna would have to take off their shirts. For the men, it was time to remove their pants. One of them was still holding the other joker. Glancing at Sheyna, she tried to read the expression on her face, but she seemed to be distracted by Jace's chest. Finally, he lowered an ace of clubs onto the table. Groaning inwardly, Brenna flung her king onto the stack. Jabarie followed with a ten of spades and Sheyna slapped the joker on top. They had won!

Excitedly, Brenna sprung from her chair over to her friend and they joined hands and jumped up and down while screaming, "Take it off. Take it off!"

Jabarie growled and rose from the chair. Jace followed.

Sheyna shook her head. "Uh-uh. We're gonna take

this into the living room so we can get a better look." She hooked her arm through Brenna's and the two moved into the other room and flopped down on the couch. Shortly after, the men followed.

"Ooh! Wait one more second." Sheyna quickly rushed over to her entertainment center and put on "Shake Yo Money Maker" by Ludacris then returned to her seat. "Now we're ready."

Brenna was in stitches as she saw the looks of discomfort on the brothers' faces. "Don't be scared," she taunted.

"Scared!" Jabarie repeated then turned to his brother. "I ain't scared of nothing. Come on Jace, let's show these women what we're working with."

They started moving to the beat of the music in some old Temptations' moves before turning around and shaking their butts at them. Brenna was laughing so hard, her side hurt. However, the second Jabarie started rocking his hips and reached for his belt buckle, she quickly sobered and tuned out everything else that was going on in the room. All she saw was Jabarie. She swallowed deeply then forced her eyes up to his face. Big mistake. Jabarie was staring intensely as his tongue slipped out between his teeth and slowly slid across his bottom lip. Her nipples hardened. Oh boy. Her eyes slid back down across his chest and down to where he was lowering his zipper. Her lips parted and her body quivered. With his eyes on her, he lowered his pants down to his feet before he kicked them away. There he stood in a pair of red cotton boxers. The fine hair sprinkled sparingly across his chest traveled downward, disappearing inside the waistband. Her breath caught in her throat. He continued to gyrate his hips to the music. His moves were sensual and taunting, and she had to admit he was better looking than any of those Chippendales.

"Smile for the camera."

Brenna was shocked back into reality at Sheyna's laughter and the sound of her camera phone as she snapped a picture of the two of them.

"Give me that!" Jace demanded then lunged at Sheyna who dashed off the couch and down the hall.

Brenna's eyes followed her, laughing, before she turned to face Jabarie again. He was still standing in the same spot watching her. Her laughter faded abruptly.

"Come here," he said in a soft commanding voice. She rose from the couch and moved over to stand before him. As soon as she was within arm's length, he snaked an arm around her waist and grabbed her like he was afraid she would slip away. Overwhelmed with desire, Brenna couldn't have said no even if she had wanted to and she didn't. She threw her arms around him.

"Jabarie?"

"Brenna?"

She wasn't sure what she wanted to ask him, but he seemed to know the answer when he pressed his lips against hers. On contact, she felt an explosion stronger than any Fourth of July celebration. He explored her with his hands and his mouth. She groaned when he reached beneath her shirt and rubbed her breasts. Moaning, she leaned into his touch. It wasn't long before she felt the evidence of his arousal throbbing against her stomach.

Hearing arguing in the other room finally brought an end to the kiss.

Brenna shook her head. "I don't think those two are going to ever get along."

Shaking his head, Jabarie leaned in and whispered against her lips. "I disagree. I think it is just a matter of time before they realize what has always been standing right in front of them."

Their eyes locked for another long intense moment before Jabarie groaned, reached down for his pants and they moved into the family room to referee.

When Brenna got home she immediately moved to the shower, anxious to relieve her body of an entire days' worth of sweat. She turned on the spray of water and while the water reached the right temperature, she shed her clothes then stepped in. Closing her eyes, she moved directly beneath the showerhead, soaking her hair and face. Taking a deep breath, she allowed the hot steam to relax her as thoughts of Jabarie invaded her mind again.

This afternoon they had reached a turning point in their relationship. It was almost as if no time had passed and the four musketeers were back hanging out and laughing. That was the way it had been between them starting in the fifth grade. But they weren't kids any-more. They were grown-ups. She was a woman, and Jabarie was a man. All six-foot-two, one hundred and ninety pounds of chocolate flesh.

Brenna lathered her body and her skin tingled with thoughts of what tomorrow would bring. One thing for sure, it was nothing more than two people satisfying their sexual hunger. Nothing more. Absolutely nothing would change. As soon as the trip was over she would return and help her aunt, and as soon as she was better, she'd head back to Dallas to life as she knew it.

She was in the shower for the longest time contemplating what she had agreed to do. One thing for sure, after Sunday, her life would never be the same again.

Chapter 9

Brenna wished she hadn't agreed to spend the night with Jabarie.

Last night, she couldn't sleep. She spent most of the night tossing and turning and then she finally settled down, only to find herself waking up at the crack of dawn. To pass the time she took a long, hot bubble bath, hoping a book and the steam would calm her nerves, but instead she spent the entire time thinking of Jabarie. Finally she climbed out and after getting dressed made breakfast for her and her aunt. When they sat down to eat, she barely remembered what the two of them talked about. As soon as the dishes were washed and put away, she disappeared into her room and retrieved a tote bag from her closet. It took her almost an hour to decide what to pack before she finally fell back onto the mattress with a heavy sigh. *I don't have time for this.*

Her pulse hammered, palms sweat, and any thoughts about how the evening might end, made everything feminine in her come to life. She touched her queasy stomach and prayed her decision to go out with Jabarie didn't come back to haunt her. But after yesterday at Sheyna's, Brenna knew that anything was likely to happen now that she had agreed to spend the night with him aboard his yacht.

The uneasiness at the back of her mind refused to be still. Dammit! This was why she had rather leave well enough alone. The way she was acting reminded her too much of when they had first started dating. The excitement, the anticipation of seeing Jabarie each day, she just couldn't put herself through all that again. Besides, too many years had passed and it wasn't a good idea to start something she had no intentions of finishing.

When she finally had her bag packed, Brenna took a seat on the couch in the living room and took several deep calming breaths. She could do this. All she had to do was stay focused and remember they were ex-lovers, spending the night with no promises for anything more.

The doorbell rang and Brenna practically jumped off the couch. Frantically, her eyes darted around the room. She knew there was no way she was going to survive the two-hour drive down the coast unless she had a distraction. Spotting her book on the coffee table, she grabbed it, tucked it under her arm and headed toward the door. Jabarie was standing on the porch, with his hands buried inside his pockets, smiling.

"Hey," she greeted breathlessly.

"Hey, yourself," he said with a smile. "Ready to go?"

She nodded. "Let me grab my bag and I'll be right out." Brenna spun on her heels; heart pounding, she moved to her room to retrieve her bag. Before leaving the room she took several deep breaths. *You can do this!* All they were going to do was have a nice quiet day together like two friends, nothing more. But even as the thought filled her mind she knew that wasn't true. Today was going to be a turning point in their relationship, and once they stepped over it, there was no turning back. If she was having any last-minute doubts then this was her final chance to back out. But as she pressed a palm to her stomach, she knew that there was no way she could cancel their night together, even if she had really wanted to, and she didn't. As she swung her purse over her shoulder, Brenna remembered what Sheyna had told her. She was in control, which meant it was up to her to lay down all the rules. Nothing more could happen than what she allowed to take place. The most important thing was for her to keep her heart out of it. The last several days, Jabarie had managed to slip between her defenses and that was something she refused to let happen again. Sliding her sunglasses onto her eyes, she moved out onto the porch and locked the door behind her.

Jabarie took her bag and carried it out to his Porsche. "Where's Aunt Nellie?"

She followed him to the sidewalk. "She said she felt good enough to go to church this morning."

"That's a good sign."

Brenna nodded. Although her aunt still couldn't apply a lot of pressure on her ankle, Brenna knew it was just a matter of time before she would be heading home again. Pressing her lips firmly together, she decided it would probably be a good idea if she kept that thought close to the front of her mind. A constant reminder that her visit here was only temporary would help make the next twenty-four hours that much easier to manage.

"Beach traffic is going to be heavy."

She gave Jabarie a knowing look. "What else is new this time of year?" People from all the surrounding states migrated to the beaches on Friday and headed back on Sunday.

As she waited by the curb, her eyes gazed admiring at the sleek vehicle with a beautiful metallic gray finish. "You have a beautiful car."

Jabarie's lips curled upward. "Thank you. I bought her last month for my thirtieth birthday." His eyes shifted to her hand. "Why are you bringing a book?" Jabarie asked as he opened the trunk and put her bag inside.

"Because I'm at the middle of this mystery and dying to know what happens," she lied. As much as she was enjoying the book, she hadn't been able to concentrate on it since she had arrived at Sheraton Beach.

"I'm dying to find out what happens, as well."

At the tone of his voice, she gazed up into his eyes to find him moving around to the passenger's side while staring down intensely at her. She swallowed as she realized that he wasn't referring to the book in her hand but their relationship. Even before he reached her, she knew he was planning to kiss her.

"Hopefully this weekend, we can figure out the mystery together."

As his gaze zeroed in on her mouth, desire streamed through her, fast and hot, and she found herself tilting her head with anticipation. To hell with reason and logic. She never could think straight where Jabarie was concerned. The next twenty-four hours was going to be all about them and she was going to try to live for the moment and get everything she wanted. And what she wanted was Jabarie.

When he stopped in front of her, her pulse raced. And when he lowered his head, she automatically parted her lips and met him halfway. As soon as their lips touched, she released a soft sigh as if she had been waiting all morning for this moment.

While his hands ran along the contours of her back, his kiss was as thorough and skillful as it always had been. One thing Jabarie knew was her mouth. He took his time mating their tongues before sweeping every corner of her mouth. The strong sensation sent heat traveling down to her inner thighs.

Reluctantly, he ended the kiss, struggling for control.

"Before this weekend is over, we're going to sit down and talk about everything that happened between us." He gave her a long look that let her know that he would no longer accept any excuses.

Nodding, Brenna slid inside the car and lowered her purse onto the floor in front of her. As she got comfortable on the seat, she felt the heat of his gaze on her legs in a raspberry skort.

"What's wrong?" she asked, finally finding the words to speak.

Shaking his head, he made a long wolf whistle that made her giggle before shutting the door.

Jabarie walked around the front of the car and she took a moment to take in his appearance. He wore khaki shorts and a polo shirt that looked fabulous on his body. Her heart was still pounding from the kiss and as she stared at him, she knew that when she returned home tomorrow things were going to be different. They would each finally have the answers they needed to move on with their lives.

Brenna pushed her sunglasses back onto her nose, and smoothed her hair along her head for any strands that might have escaped the ponytail she'd pulled it into this morning.

Within seconds, Jabarie had his seat belt fastened and pulled away from the curb. Brenna leaned back against the butter-soft leather seat and pushed her nervousness aside and enjoyed the drive. It was her first time in a Porsche, and she was amazed at how roomy it was. There was plenty of room for Jabarie's long legs. Watching him, she was impressed at the way the car handled, especially since Jabarie was a speed demon. But she wasn't worried. He had always been an excellent driver. Besides, she had never been any good at driving a stick.

Just as he warned, the traffic was heavy, but he wove through it effortlessly. After a few minutes of silence, Brenna opened her book. Staring down at the pages, she pretended to be reading, but all she could think about was Jabarie.

Out the corner of her eyes, she watched the muscles in his arm and leg flex each and every time he shifted the car. She found herself extremely conscious of this virile man. With each breath, Brenna could almost smell the testosterone as he drove, and wondered if she was going to be able to stay strong tonight. So far things weren't looking too good.

By the time he pulled onto Route 1, heading south, Jabarie couldn't stand the silence anymore. It just left his mind free to wander with thoughts about where the afternoon might lead. Usually, he played the radio on an R&B station but today there was something, or in this case, someone, much more interesting sitting right beside him.

Briefly, he again glanced out the corner of his eyes and beamed approval. Brenna's outfit was encasing a body that he was dying to hold. The little skirt with the shorts attached was dangerously short, and the barely there shirt was transparent enough that her nipples showed through. The outfit was definitely a turn-on. Her long slim legs and generous curves caused his blood to race fast and furiously through every region of his body. It took everything he had not to reach over and slide his hands up her legs, certain that it would feel as smooth as silk. Blood flowed to his groin area. Jabarie shifted uncomfortably on the seat. Dammit, he needed a diversion.

Brenna was deeply engrossed in the book. Jabarie knew it shouldn't bother him, but it did. The old Brenna would have been laughing and joking with her hand resting lovingly on his thigh. And that's what he wanted. Even if she didn't feel comfortable touching him, he wanted Brenna to direct her attention toward him. Reaching over, he fiddled with the CD player until Prince's latest CD came blaring through the speakers.

The soulful lyrics didn't help the situation; instead suggestive words made things worse.

Jabarie's fingers tightened around the steering wheel as he frowned. She hadn't even glanced over at him when the music came blaring out the speaker. He shifted his attention to the road and hummed along with the music, trying to ignore her sweet scent that engulfed the car and his need to reach over and bring her closer to him.

After several seconds, he turned the music down and concentrated on his driving, annoyed at her for ignoring him. Unable to help himself, he reached over and removed the hair tie holding her hair in place.

"Hey, what you do that for?" she asked with a gasp.

"I like your hair down."

"Well, I don't. It gets all in my face."

But even saying that she buried her head back in the book and didn't bother to tie it back up. He felt the long strands of hair brush his arm every few seconds and decided with an inward groan that maybe letting her hair down had been a bad idea. As he drove he thought about her lying on her back with her hair spread around the pillow and her arms spread open, inviting him to bury himself inside her—

He quickly shifted the thoughts from his mind. This weekend he was supposed to be trying to get her out of his system. So far it wasn't working.

Since the yacht was in Ocean City, Maryland, they decided to spend the afternoon there looking for black cherubs. They drove to the boardwalk. Holding hands they traveled into one store after the other. Eating funnel cake and hotdogs they passed the time talking about nothing in particular, simply enjoying each other's company. They had walked clear down to the other end when Brenna found a beautiful angel that was way more than she'd ever spend, but Jabarie insisted on getting it for her. At first, she thought that maybe he was trying to buy her affection, but after he reassured her that wasn't the case, she agreed after reminding herself it probably hadn't made the slightest dent in his pocket.

Afterwards, they walked over to the amusement park and Jabarie dragged her kicking and screaming onto a roller coaster. It was almost dinnertime when they finally left and drove to the dock. As soon as they pulled up to the marina, the first thing she noticed was that the air scented of water even more so than at the boardwalk. Even now after years of living near the ocean, she was still impressed by the marina and the gorgeous boats bobbing in the water. Each spelled a level of wealth that she knew nothing about. It also was a reminder of how different their worlds were. She'd never been within fifty feet of a yacht, while Jabarie owned one. He'd never had to hustle a day in his life, while she had every day. That's why they weren't right for each other. A feeling of sadness rushed over, that she quickly pushed away. None of that mattered. All they were doing was sharing an evening together, nothing more.

Jabarie parked his Porsche then escorted her over to the boats. He then took her hand and led her over to the *Beaumont Beauty* whose name was written in fine gold lettering along its side.

He wasn't exaggerating when he said they owned a yacht. It was over seventy feet long. She was actually relieved to see that it was more than a big boat because she had been worried about motion sickness. It was more like an apartment on the water. The yacht was big and quite impressive just from the exterior.

"Very nice," she said as they stepped onto the deck.

"Thanks."

Her eyes darted up to his profile to find his lips pressed firmly together. Jabarie said thanks in a tone that said he was embarrassed by his wealth. One of the things she had always admired about Jabarie was that he didn't take money for granted. He had worked hard to make his own mark in the world.

"Let me show you around before we leave port." He began and pressed a palm at the small of her back. "The *Beaumont Beauty* is a powerful yacht. Our cruising speed is fifteen knots, and we normally have a crew of four aboard. This cruise we're down to two, but we'll do our best to make sure you have a pleasant and safe cruise."

"I'm just sure you will," she mumbled under her breath. He led her inside the yacht and she couldn't believe the interior. The room reminded her of the suites at the Beaumont Hotel. "Wow! It's decorated just like—"

"The hotel," he interrupted, knowingly. "I know. It was my mother's idea to give people a taste of the real thing."

"Good idea," she replied as she continued to glance around the posh interior design of the sitting room. Thick beige carpet beneath her feet covered the entire room. A sofa upholstered in a vibrant tropical print was at one end. Overstuffed matching chairs were at another. There was a fully stocked bar with three bar stools. There was also a large television hooked up to a DVD player. But out here, who in the world would want to watch television? she thought with a dreamily smile and she took it all in. The room was definitely bigger than her living room at home.

Taking her hand, Jabarie led her down a narrow stairway to the lower level where there was a small hall that opened to three staterooms.

He opened the first hardwood door. "Brace yourself for what you're about to see," he said with a teasing smile.

Brenna walked around each of the rooms that were quite impressive. However, it was the master suite that caused her to gasp.

She stood in the middle of the luxurious room taking it all in. She stared at the dark woodwork and opulent ivory furnishing to the huge bed, dominating the elegant room. Wow! She ran her fingers over the cream and green plump comforter, tempted to snuggle into the numerous plump pillows, in various shapes and sizes, clustered against the headboard. Behind the bed was a large window overlooking the clear water. Along one wall were built-in drawers. Stepping into the adjoining bathroom, she found a spacious room with a Jacuzzi, complementing the suite.

"Wow!" she commented as she moved back into the room where Jabarie was awaiting her approval. "This is definitely a home away from home."

He nodded, and appeared relieved by her answer. "It is for me." He stared at her for a long intense moment as if he was about to say something before he blinked rapidly and said, "A life jacket is located on the back of your room. There are also more on the deck."

"Okay. This is great." Once more Brenna allowed her eyes to travel around the room. "Jabarie, she is truly gorgeous."

"Yes, she is."

Brenna swallowed. By the way he was staring at her, she knew only one of them was talking about the yacht.

"I'll leave you to freshen up. Dinner will be ready in about an hour. Is there anything else I can get you?" he said in a tone that could have been considered suggestive.

She was ready for a kiss and it took everything she had not to drag her mouth to his. Jabarie had been a gentleman all afternoon. Other than holding her hand and brushing against her, he had kept his distance and as much as she didn't want to start anything her body still yearned for his touch. "No, I might take a quick nap."

Jabarie stared at her for a long time before nodding. "Okay, I'll be right next door if you need me."

Brenna closed the door behind her and took a seat on the bed. It was a bed for lovers. Closing her eyes she couldn't help imagining that things had been different. That Jabarie was still her lover and they had sailed out into the Atlantic, enjoying each other while they made love under the stars.

Jabarie went down to the kitchen to check on dinner. After the chef assured him that everything was going according to plan, he moved out onto the deck and stared off at the water as the captain prepared to sail on their romantic dinner cruise. Everything had to go according to plan. Brenna had made it clear that it was only one date, and when her aunt was better, she was leaving his life again. So tonight was the only chance he had. They had to get past this lustful need for one another, then they needed to talk. If they didn't, the weekend would be a bust and the split this time would be far worse than the first. Somehow he had to come to terms with their past and with that came answers that would aid him into removing her from his heart. Staring off into the ocean he tilted his head confidently. He was certain that a night of making love to her would be enough time to get her out of his system once and for all.

Chapter 10

Standing in front of the mirror, Brenna examined her reflection from all angles. The sundress she had purchased while at a book exposition in Chicago last spring was perfect. The peach dress had thin spaghetti straps and molded her shape in all the right places. The stretchy material wrapped around her narrow waist then gently flared to a flirty hem that stopped a couple of inches above her knees.

Her eyes traveled down to the high-heeled gold sandals she'd bought, complementing the look. When she found them on a clearance rack last season, one would have thought it was Christmas at her excitement at finding a pair of Steve Madden's marked down over eighty percent.

Reaching up, she brushed a strand of hair into place.

She decided to leave it loose, using only a polished gold clip to pull the hair back away from her face.

Brenna reached over into her tote bag on the bed. A little makeup was in order. Leaning toward the mirror, she brushed her lashes with mascara then added a little shadow to her lids. Turning her head from side to side, she was pleased at the results. She was now ready for her evening with Jabarie to begin. Her heart jolted in response.

"If you go through with this, there is no turning back," she murmured to the woman staring back at her. But even as she said that, she noticed the corners of her mouth turn upward as she replied, "I know." She wanted this night as badly as she needed her next breath.

Brenna heard a light tap at the door. Glancing into the mirror, she gave herself one final appraising look, then took a deep steadying breath and opened the door. For the longest time he said nothing, but the hungry look in his eyes and the low whistle he blew between his teeth exactly the reward she had hoped for.

"Damn, you look good," he complimented as she stepped outside the room.

"You clean up well yourself." She returned the admiring stare, nodding her approval at his black pleated slacks and gray short-sleeve shirt.

"You look like you're ready to get this evening started," he said then moved closer and cupped her chin, tilting her head so she'd have no other choice but to look at him. "Are you sure you're ready?"

Brenna knew what he was asking. This was her last chance to say no. "More sure about anything in a long time." The moment she'd stepped out of the stateroom she had known there was no turning back.

He looked relieved. "Good."

She smiled and started to walk past him but Jabarie stretched a restraining arm in front of her, barring her passage. At her questioning look, his face split into a wickedly sexy grin. "I believe we need to start our evening off with a kiss."

Jabarie lowered his arm and pulled her close. He bent his head until his lips barely brushed her ear. "I hope you're prepared for a long night," he whispered, his breath a gentle caress.

She felt a shiver of anticipation course through her veins as he slowly moved in to claim her mouth. Her lips parted and her eyes slid closed. She rose onto her tiptoes as he pressed his lips to hers. With a moan, Brenna opened her mouth to him and he accepted, tracing her lips with his tongue then entering. Jabarie tasted and explored, leisurely at first with slow thrusts of his tongue then more quickly, claiming her while giving her a preview of what was to come. She leaned into him meeting each stroke while letting him know that she was looking forward to everything the evening had to offer, until he finally pulled back.

Disappointed, she opened her eyes and looked up at him with her brow raised. "Is that all you got?"

Jabarie gave a rich robust laugh that filled the lower deck. "That was only the beginning," he promised.

"It better be." Smiling, Brenna eased her way up the narrow stairs to the deck. Moving over to the rail, she took a long moment to stare off into the water. The captain had piloted them out towards the middle of the ocean. The shore was already quite a distance away. Brenna took a deep breath. The evening was nice and a warm gentle breeze ruffled her hair around her face. Feeling Jabarie move up behind her, she glanced over her shoulder and smiled up at him. "I think I need to go and tie my hair up."

"No," he insisted, twining a strand around his finger. "Leave it that way."

She hadn't forgotten that he loved it when she wore her hair down. Swallowing, she simply nodded.

Jabarie wrapped his arms around her waist and she closed her eyes and gave in to the moment. Right now, she was the happiest she had felt in such a long time.

"Dinner's ready," he replied while planting a kiss along the side of her neck.

"All right."

He dropped his arms then laced her fingers with his and led her down the stairs. Stepping into the dining room, Brenna gasped at the romantic setting. Violin music. Flickering candles. Two delicate glass flutes filled with white wine. A vase of deep red, long-stemmed roses at the center of a table covered with a white linen tablecloth. The atmosphere screamed love and passion.

"I take it, you like what you see."

"Oh, I love it!" she exclaimed. Jabarie pulled the seat out for her and she lowered. "Thanks."

As soon as he settled onto the chair across the table from her, their server came out to pour their wine.

"Brenna, this is Toliver. He is the person who prepared all the wonderful dishes we're about to eat."

She glanced up at the slender man with berry black

skin, large round eyes and full lips. "It's so nice to meet you. I can't wait to see what you've prepared."

"I hope everything is to your liking," he said with a distinctive Caribbean accent.

"I'm sure it is."

It wasn't long before he came out carrying two hot bowls of lobster bisque. Reaching for her spoon, Brenna brought the creamy liquid with chunks of meat to her lips and moaned. "Oh, my, that's good."

Jabarie's eyes danced knowingly. "I thought you would like it."

"Like it? I love it." While they were dating the two had made it a habit to order the lobster bisque, constantly in search of the better bowl. So far a small upscale restaurant in Northern Philadelphia had held the number one spot on their list but after sampling Toliver's recipe, it by far topped the charts.

After their empty bowls were removed, a starter salad was served with a homemade raspberry vinaigrette dressing. Music filled the silence of the room while she ate every crispy vegetable in her bowl.

Dinner was her favorite: lamb chops, sweet potatoes and asparagus.

"Tell me about your bookstore."

She didn't want to mention that if it hadn't been for him betraying her, she'd never would have been able to afford it. "I opened a large bookstore right near campus. We have a spoken word night. A small coffee and sandwich shop and play light jazz music. We occasionally even have a live jazz band."

"Sounds nice."

She smiled, pleased at what she had accomplished.

"Yes, I wanted something different than your traditional bookstore. A place where people could relax and gather."

"Sounds like you have a winner."

"Yes, business has definitely been good," she replied between chews. "So tell me, how's life been at the Beaumont Corporation?"

"Never a dull moment." She listened as he told her about the six new hotels they had built in the last four years with the goal to open three more in the next two years. Their latest was among the glitz and glamour of Las Vegas.

After dinner, she moved out onto the deck and scanned the area. No other sailors, just miles and miles of water. The sun was preparing to set and looked like a bright red ball sitting on top of the water. Taking a seat, she kicked off her shoes and allowed her feet to hang over the water.

"How long again have your parents owned this yacht?"

"About a year now. I love it."

"I can tell." A love for water was one thing they had shared.

Jabarie took a sip while he stared off ahead for a long thoughtful moment. "I enjoy being out here where it's quiet and I'm all alone. So I can think without interruptions."

"What do you think about?"

He shrugged. "Life. My career. Sometimes, you."

"What about me?" She dared to ask.

He turned so that he could look directly at her as he spoke. "What you're doing and how I wish that things had been different between us."

So do I. There was a long pause before she sighed

and reached for her drink. "I think about you and the same things sometimes. Then I tell myself that things happened for a reason."

"You don't really believe that."

She forced herself to nod. "Yes, I'm afraid that I do."

"Come here," he said, taking her hand and pulling her to her feet. Nervously, she licked her lips.

He leaned forward and retraced her moistened lips with his tongue. Desire coiled low in her belly. Her breasts tingled and her nipples hardened and all she could do was hold on.

Pulling back slightly, he stared down at her, eyes burning with desire. "I want to know if leaving Sheraton Beach was it worth it. Are you happy?"

Right now the only thing that made her happy was being here on this yacht, alone with him. With his body pressed against hers, she felt the heat radiating against her skin. She stared up at his beautiful brown eyes that she had been dreaming about for the last five years. Was she happy without him in her life? No. But she couldn't tell him that. She couldn't tell him that since she left her life had been empty and lonely. The only thing holding her together had been seeing her dream of opening her own bookstore turned into a reality, but even that was no longer enough. She looked down at his chest as she spoke. "I'm living my dream."

"That's not what I asked you. I want to know if you're happy?" He tilted her head up to look into his eyes and when she did, the deep dark pupils were impossible to withstand.

"I am quite content."

"But are you happy?" he demanded. His eyes burned with the need to know the truth.

"Yes." She lied. She looked right up at him and lied because the truth would have caused her to crumble. It was too late to go back and revisit that exact moment his lawyer had come to her house, or when she rushed over to his apartment and found him in the arms of another woman. Maybe they could have talked and worked things out, if she had stuck around long enough. But she hadn't, and there was no point in resurrecting those emotions and feelings that obviously had never gone away. They were both hurting for different reasons. She because she had felt betrayed. Him…she wasn't sure why. Never understood that one. All that she knew now was that after five years, neither of them had moved on with their lives. And a small part of her was glad to know that he had never gotten over her walking out on him. As much as she missed him it was good to know that he had felt the same way.

"I don't believe you," Jabarie said then pulled her even closer in his arms. Her torso brushed against his chest. "You forget. I know you well and can always tell when you're lying."

"You're wrong," she said barely above a whisper.

"No, I'm not," he began while brushing light kisses on her temple. "You missed me. Didn't you?"

Her pulse pounded. "No, I didn't."

"Yes, you did, because I missed you."

Her heart did a backflip and down between her thighs she felt herself dampen with need. Her breathing became shallow as she watched him watching her. "Jabarie, I think we need to…"

Jabarie placed a finger to her lips, silencing her. "I can't Brenna. I can't keep pretending I don't still care about you because I do," he said, clearly not listening to a word she had said. "You're the last thing on my mind every night, and the first thing when I wake up. I still get hard just thinking about you."

Excitement spiraled throughout her body. She slid her arms around his neck wanting him with everything she had. She arched her body against him and felt the thick, hard strength of him. He was solid, but then she knew that. Had never forgotten. Her heart knew what her mind had been hiding from all these years. Jabarie was the only man who could bring her body to life. And she wanted him with all she had.

He slid his fingers gently up her arm, along her shoulder until he cupped the back of her neck and pulled her closer to him. Brenna offered no resistance, instead she leaned into the solid wall of his chest and closed her eyes while his hot breath caressed her nose, sending delicious shivers raging through her body. Then he planted kisses from the corner of her mouth, along her cheek, down to her throat. Oh, did his lips feel good! How had she gone five years without experiencing this? Cool air brushed against her skin, but she didn't seem to notice, not with the heat Jabarie stirred. Somewhere in the back of her mind, Brenna knew she should stop him, knew that she would soon be completely lost to the passion he fired within her. She knew all that, and yet she decided not to say a word.

His lips retraced their path along her cheek, inches closer to her mouth. Gazing down at her, he cupped her face in his hands. "I want you, Brenna," he whispered in a voice husky with passion. "But I won't do anything until you let me know that this is what you want, as well." His questioning eyes searched her face.

Brenna looked deep into the dark depths of his eyes. She knew then that she'd worry about the consequences later because she needed him now.

To answer his question, she raised on her tiptoes and pressed her body against his. Jabarie pulled her even closer and ground his hips against her. She felt his erection, hot and hard, against her belly and she smiled, loving the fact that she could still invoke such a passionate response from his body.

Jabarie needed no further encouragement. He took her hand and led her down to the lower deck. She allowed him to lead her into the room, knowing this was her last time to say no. But why say no when it wasn't at all what she wanted. She wanted him. She wanted him in her, over her, beside her. This was her choice, her decision and she had made it. And whatever the consequences were, she would deal with them later.

As soon as the door was shut, Jabarie bent to capture her mouth with a passion that could no longer be denied. His tongue sought hers and they entwined.

His mouth incited a firestorm in Brenna. He nibbled on her bottom lip, sucking gently on her flesh and sent shivers of awareness pulsing through her.

His kiss consumed her. His arms held her against him, and the warm pressure of his chest against her aching nipples was enough to make her knees weaken.

Pulling back slightly, Jabarie caught her hand in his, brought it to his lips and stilled her trembling.

She forced a smile. "Is this where you seduce all your women?"

His grip tightened on her hand. A muscle at his jaw ticked before his mouth softened into a slow smile. "You're the only one I've ever brought aboard the *Beaumont Beauty*. The only one I've ever wanted to do everything for, give everything to."

Brenna tried to shrug off his sweet words, believing he was saying what he thought she wanted to hear. But as she stared into his face, reading his expression, she saw the truth as clear as his desire. His words had a clear meaning. Part of her brain was flickering a red warning light, while the other challenged her to be as honest with him as he was with her. He had arranged this cruise so that he could spend time with her alone. How could she find fault in that? Brenna swallowed hard and no longer feared the feelings and emotions the night would resurrect; instead she was ready to take everything he had to offer. She felt only an overwhelming heat that surged through her and burned out everything but her deepest needs.

She took a step forward. He slipped a hand between the folds of her dress and caressed the underside of her breast.

She shuddered at his touch. "I can't think."

He came back and nuzzled her throat, then her ear. "Don't think, just feel. I've missed you, missed this." He cupped her breast then kissed his way down from her ear past the hollow in her throat to the moist valley between her breasts. "You smell good."

"Oh," she sighed. With his hands and mouth on her

body, it was hard to remember why she had been angry with him, or how rejected and alone she'd felt after she'd left. All she could think about was what was happening now.

While staring intensely at her, Jabarie reached out and cupped her bare breast, teasing her nipple in lazy circles with his thumb. "Do you like that?" he asked. "Tell me you like that."

"You know I like that," she gasped. "I always have." Jabarie had always known what she liked.

Her nipple hardened into hot pebbles. He lowered his head and drew her nipple into his mouth and suckled the sensitive bud. She arched beneath him with a little cry that exploded from her lips. After another sharp intake of breath which was quickly followed by a low moan, he painted a path with his tongue, moving from one nipple to the other. Her pulse raced and her nipples were tight knots of desire, while her breasts ached in his hands. When she didn't think she could stand a second more, he released her and stepped back.

With his eyes holding hers, Jabarie removed his shoes and socks. His hands went to the buttons of his shirt.

"Let me," she whispered then stepped forward. She undid the buttons slowly, then put her lips to his chest as she parted his shirt and licked his nipples.

He groaned then yanked his shirt off and threw it on the floor, revealing a torso that had haunted her dreams for years. It was hard and defined and covered with a fine coat of dark black hair. Encouraged, she kissed and licked his chest, the ridges of his ribcage and the flat torso, causing him to shudder.

Laughing, Brenna blew warm air on his belly and

unzipped his trousers. They fell to his ankles followed by his boxers. She took his stiff rod in her hand and lowered to her knees in front of him and caressed him. He was slick and hot, pulsing in her hand.

She enjoyed the feel of him, anticipating what would come, then took her hand away and allowed her tongue to travel the long, hard length of him until he groaned.

Breath coming fast, he reached down and lifted her to her feet. "No more."

He put his hands at her waist, and she put her hands on his shoulders as he walked her back towards the bed, easing her down onto her back, her legs open.

He stood between her legs, looking down at her with possessive intent. Reaching out, he slipped her silk thong off, and brought it to his nose. "Hmm. I've never forgotten your fragrance." He held her eyes as he breathed deeply, absorbing her scent. "This smell has always belonged to me."

Brenna shuddered under his gaze, uneasy with his claim to her, thrilled that he still found her attractive. He dropped her panties to the floor and took her ankles, lifting and spreading them wide, and studied her intimate secrets.

"Put your legs on my shoulders."

She did as he asked, and he studied her while he ran his hands down her calves, then her thighs, stopping short of touching her where she wanted his hand most. She couldn't hold back the whimper of disappointment and arched her hips in invitation. But he ignored her and had every intention of doing this his way. She groaned inwardly. It was apparent as he retraced his path, that rushing was not on the agenda this evening.

Just as she was prepared to scream, he turned his head and used his tongue to outline her ankle. She quivered on contact. It was a combination of a tickle and erotic delight that she couldn't begin to describe.

"My shoes." She wiggled the foot still wearing high-heeled gold sandals.

"Leave them on."

Impatiently, she waited for what he would do next. He let her legs slide down his body until her feet rested on the bed.

"Would you like me to taste you?" he asked.

When she nodded, he pushed her thighs apart and sank between her legs. Brenna wrapped her legs around his shoulders. "Yes."

Jabarie lowered his head and Brenna felt his hot breath on her tender folds. She quivered, waiting for his tongue, and when his finally touched her there, no more than a gentle caress, she clutched the sheets and caught her lower lip between her teeth.

"Oh, yeah," she moaned. "More, please."

He looked up at her and replied, "No worries, sweetheart. I've been waiting five years to taste you again."

After his declaration, Jabarie slid his large hands under her bottom to lift her to his mouth. His fingers kneaded her buttocks; his thumbs held her firmly in place. He buried his face in her essence, inhaling deeply, rubbing his mouth across her damp channel. She closed her eyes, all her senses concentrated on the hooded area. When his mouth closed over it and pulled it gently into her mouth, she gave a strange, tortured cry and her fingers moved to the back of his head to hold him in place.

In the distance, the soft crash of the waves rolled in

a rhythm as mesmerizing as his mouth on her. He pleasured her with long strokes, lazy licks, even tiny nibbles on her flesh, pushing her ever closer to the edge. She cried out in pleasure and bucked her hips to his face. She wanted every morsel of what he had to offer. It wasn't long before heat flared through her body and her breath caught, her body arching as she cried out his name and climaxed.

Jabarie lowered her cheeks back onto the bed then his fingers traveled around to her entrance and he slipped two fingers inside. Her hips rocked against his mouth while she begged and pleaded for him to take her. Instead, he spread her legs wider. He dipped one finger into her warm juices, then eased the tip into her as he teased her bud with his tongue. His tongue and his fingers worked together, alternately driving in and withdrawing. He was driving her wild. Every move he made sent a whirlwind of awareness through her. Panting heavily, she arched her hips into his face again.

"Oh, yes, don't stop!" she pleaded.

He kept up the dual thrusts for a few more moments then drew back and positioned her at the center of the bed. When he lowered on top of her, it felt right. A sob clogged her throat. She felt protected in his arms.

He lifted himself up on his elbows and looked down at her. "Everything okay?"

Right now everything in her world was right. "No."

"Is there something you want me to do?"

Her mind was a jumble of sensations, of arousal. "Yes. I want to feel you inside of me."

After reaching over to the side table, he pulled on a condom and her hand followed his, moving quickly to the base. He groaned then kissed her slow and deep as he positioned himself at her entrance. He teased her by rubbing against her clit, easing inside, then withdrawing, pushing into her an inch, letting out a low groan and pulling back.

Brenna writhered beneath him. Her nipples were so hard they grazed against his bare skin. Each touch threatening what little self-control she had left. She wanted him and she wanted him right now. "Stop teasing." She grabbed his hips and tugged him into her, demanding more than he'd given her.

He plunged, satisfying her demand, thrusting deeply. His breath escaped him in a long hiss as he sank deeply inside her. She cried out at his penetration. It had been too long. She felt filled, her muscles working with his, tightening and releasing as he plunged and pulled back.

"Please," she pleaded. "Make love to me."

"I wouldn't have it any other way." He smiled down at her and started moving again. This time slow, deep thrusts. Her thighs opened wider and she locked her ankles behind his back.

It lasted forever. It was over in a moment. She held him as he rode her. The tension built. Each thrust brought intense pleasure and speed as he rode hard inside her body. It was wild. It was madness. She came an instant before he did. Her orgasm went on and on, as she tightened her inner muscles around him.

He came long and hard, his body arched. Every muscle in his arms corded with tension. His breathing came in furious, hot gushes, scorching her face and temples as his face contorted with passion.

At last, he collapsed and dropped his head onto the

pillow beside hers. His breath now was labored, deep pants that matched hers.

He stilled. As her breath evened out, she became aware of the length of his legs wrapped around hers, his smooth torso resting on hers. She lifted her arms and drew him closer, nuzzling at his neck. The pulse in his throat beat hard and fast. He had his eyes closed and his mouth partly opened as he recovered.

"I didn't expect things to get that out of control. I had planned to make it last a lot longer," he muttered.

She panted still. "Any longer and I'd have passed out."

He smiled. She watched an expression of supreme satisfaction cross his face. "Next time."

Brenna clung to him. She'd never experienced anything like that before. Not even when they were together. Oh, the sex had always been the bomb, but today it was in a category all of its own.

Chapter 11

The next morning, sunlight beamed through the small window. Brenna woke slowly, not ready yet to let go of the tranquility that surrounded her. She rolled over, aware of a slight ache between her legs, and smiled. Last night, Jabarie made love to her! Part of her had expected to wake up to find that it had all been a dream. Reaching out for Jabarie, she found him gone and his side of the bed was cold. But she knew he had been there. She could see the indentation on his pillow. Grabbing his pillow, she brought it to her chest and could smell the faint, masculine scent of him. *Unbelievable.* She was astonished by the sense of fulfillment she felt because for the first time in five years, she felt complete.

Closing her eyes, her smile deepened as the events of

the night before came flooding back. Jabarie had made her feel like a woman, but then, he had always been an excellent lover. He'd touched, kissed and stroked then held her tenderly as she came apart in his arms. Afterwards, when their hearts had slowed, he'd whispered passionate words near her ear. He'd made her feel truly special and most importantly, missed. And she could no longer deny that what was happening between them was a lot more than just sex.

Brenna tightened her hold on the pillow as feelings she had thought were long since dead, swelled her heart. Her own driven need to have him buried inside her body last night, again and again, shocked her and had conjured up the possibility that maybe they had a chance of getting back together and getting it right this time.

Impossible. She squeezed her eyelids together afraid to even think that thought completely through. What if they could? Would she be willing to risk her heart a second time? But then came the scariest question of all—what if she was wrong and just caught up in the moment?

She groaned and rolled onto her back as her mind continued its tortured train of thought. It was ridiculous. There was nothing going on between them but lust. What she thought was happening wasn't really happening and just an unconscious yearning to go back to the way things used to be. Regardless of what she was feeling, she just wasn't willing to risk her heart again. Opening her eyes, she released a heavy sigh, expecting at any moment now to feel a hint of regret. But despite everything, she had no second thoughts about what had occurred last night. Even if she had wanted to there was no way to change what had happened between them. Last night had been special, a brief rekindling of what they once had and she would hold the moment forever close to her heart. The worse thing she could do at this point was to make it more than it really was.

Laughter and raised voices caused her to sit up and peer out her window. She blinked as a powerboat passed, creating waves and zipping through the ocean. Growing up on the ocean, one thing she loved was water sports.

The phone on the wall rang and it took a moment for her to realize the call was probably intended for her. She moved across the bed and grabbed it on the fourth ring.

"Get up, sleepyhead. I'm sending Carmen down with some coffee. Meet me on the deck for breakfast in twenty minutes." Jabarie didn't give her time to agree or to protest. With a smile, she rose from the bed and moved into the shower.

When Brenna came out of the bathroom, a pot of coffee waited for her on the dresser. She filled a mug and sipped while she dressed in red shorts, a white tube top and flip-flops. Coffee in hand, she moved up onto the deck and found Jabarie sitting at a small table chewing on a croissant. He smiled when he spotted her coming and slowly rose from the chair to greet her. "Good morning."

He was wearing swim trunks and nothing else. Her throat went dry, while she stared at his broad chest. He was fabulous with large biceps, washboard abs, defined pectorals and lean legs. Jabarie came around the table and circled her in his arms, pressing his lips to hers. With him staring down at her, Brenna knew he was thinking about last night. She too remembered and it brought a flush to her cheeks.

"You hungry?" he asked, and the look in his eyes told her he was talking about something other than food. The thought of his hands on her body made her skin sensitive all over again. Her knees wobbled. She felt moisture gathering between her thighs, even her breasts felt heavier, more tender. She leaned closer to him, absorbing his heat and scent.

"Yes, I could eat a little something." She wasn't sure where she found the strength to step back and lower in the chair.

Jabarie returned to his chair as well and slid over a tray of croissants, fresh fruit and bacon.

Brenna reached for a slice of bacon. "What time are we heading back today?" she asked between chews.

"We're not," he replied as he reached for his coffee mug.

Her smile faded. "What do you mean, we're not?"

"I mean we're going to stay out here until tomorrow morning."

"But I have to get back to open the store," she protested.

Shaking his head, he speared a slice of honeydew melon. "No, you don't."

"Jabarie, I'd appreciate it if you'd stop speaking in riddles," she snapped.

The corner of his mouth twitched then inched upward as he tried and failed to bite back a grin. "I mean that Ms. Nellie and I had a long talk and we both agreed that you needed to take some time off and relax. So she decided to close the store for two days," he added when a frown appeared between her eyes.

Crossing her arms against her breasts, Brenna glared across the table at him. "How dare you trick me into coming out here with you!"

"I didn't trick you into coming out here, you agreed. But now that we're here we can use this time to ourselves. Whether you want to or not, we need to talk about us. Besides," he said quietly, "I needed a break and I'm sure you needed the same."

She bit down on her bottom lip until it pulsed between her teeth. He was right. She hadn't had a vacation in years. Some weeks, Brenna worked seven days straight, barely stopping long enough to rest. What he said was true, but that didn't make it right.

Reaching across the table, he lightly stroked her arm. "Consider this a mini vacation."

She couldn't resist staring off into the peaceful blue water. Even though she was angry, he was right. She did need a vacation.

Brenna finished her food in silence and Jabarie who had sensed her anger, left to check with the captain while she finished her food in private. As soon as she was done, Brenna moved onto the bow of the yacht and lowered onto one of the chaise lounge chairs. It was a gorgeous morning. A cool gentle breeze caressed her skin while she lowered her sunglasses onto her eyes and enjoyed the Maryland sun. She wouldn't admit it but she was glad to be spending another day aboard the *Beaumont Beauty*.

"What are you thinking about?"

"Nothing, just enjoying the moment," she replied, eyes still closed. "I'm on a beautiful yacht. The weather is gorgeous." Brenna sighed. "It don't get no better than that!"

He laughed along with her. "I guess that means you're no longer mad at me."

She pursed her lips. "I'm not mad. Just don't appreciate you and my aunt scheming."

"You can't blame a brotha for trying." He bent down over her chair and captured her lips in a hot, searing kiss. "There is no place I'd rather be. I'm hoping to spend the day together, relaxing and being adventurous."

Brenna sat up some on the chair. "What do you have in mind?"

Jabarie wagged his brow suggestively. "You'll have to wait and see."

She snorted rudely. "I think I'd rather read my book instead."

He threw his head back and laughed. "Too late. I tossed it over the side of the boat while you were still sleeping."

She snatched her glasses from her eyes. "You didn't?"

"Okay, maybe I didn't," he teased. "But it's hidden where you won't find it until we return to shore tomorrow." He scooped her up into his arms and she squealed. "We are out in the middle of nowhere. And I'm holding you captive."

"Does that mean I'm your prisoner?" she asked around a giggle.

"Yep."

His words swept over her. He was teasing her, yet it didn't stop the tingling she felt at the pit of her stomach. Smiling, Brenna hadn't felt this comfortable in years. While in Dallas she was serious, professional and lived by a schedule. But back on the East coast, she was rediscovering herself and seeing a side she hadn't realized was missing until now. She was laughing, feeling relaxed and living for the moment.

"How about a swim?" he asked as he lowered her back to her feet.

She frowned as she lowered back onto the lounge chair. "I didn't bring a suit. If I had known you planned to kidnap me I would have come prepared."

"You don't need one," he said with mischief gleaming in his eyes.

Her brow rose. "Are you serious?"

"Sure. There's nothing wrong with skinny dipping." With her brow raised, he continued. "There's nothing out here for miles but me and you."

Brenna remembered the motor boat disturbing the water this morning and the couple behind the wheel, then she looked at him for a long, thoughtful moment before she giggled and rose from the chair. "Last one in is a rotten egg," she said then kicked off her flip-flops and reached for her shirt.

Jabarie was a competitor who liked to win, but as he watched Brenna slip the white tube top over her head he froze. All he could do was stare at her heavy, firm breasts. When she found him watching her, she tilted her head to the side. "Are you letting me win?" she asked as her fingers toyed with her waistband.

Her voice was a purr that tickled his senses and left him speechless. Jabarie struggled to get his thoughts under control. "No, not at all," he answered, his voice thick with desire. Watching her, he realized that he wanted more from this day than just a pleasant outing.

Their relationship was more complex than a man simply wanting a woman. No longer was he trying to get her out of his system. It wasn't going to happen. Deep in his heart, he knew he wanted her back in his life permanently and was willing to do whatever he needed to do for the next twenty-four hours to show Brenna that she, too, in fact, wanted the same.

Giggling softly, she reached for her shorts and pushed them over her hips and down her legs. A pair of pink low-riding panties hugged her hips. He balled his fists at his sides as she straightened.

Frowning, Brenna glanced over her shoulder at him. "I'm going to win," she said, taunting him as she pivoted on her heel and lowered her panties.

His throat turned dry and lust throbbed at his groin. The sight of her naked body had his pulse racing.

Brenna looked over the side of the rail at the ocean below. "I'm curious. Once we jump how are we going to get back up?"

Jabarie swallowed hard. "There's a ladder at the back we can use to reboard."

"Cool. I guess I'll see you in the water." Then she took a leap off the edge of the boat.

Jabarie's trunks caught on his feet and he kicked them off just before he tumbled over the side. As the water closed over his head, he heard the sound of her laughter filling the air. He pushed to the surface and enjoyed the feel of the water flowing around him. It was surprisingly warm. He swam over to Brenna and came up behind her. Reaching for her, he skimmed his hand down her spine. He felt her tremble beneath his touch.

"I won," she said while doggy paddling.

He glanced over at her. "I let you win."

"Oh really?" she said, as he pulled her closer and treaded water to keep them both above the surface.

"Yes. We both know I'm a better swimmer than you," he said.

She pulled away from him. "Since when?"

"Since always."

"That's what you think," she said, and took off. He followed her easily, making out the shape of her caramel legs under the water. Jabarie caught her ankle and pulled her to him, using a powerful scissor kick to bring them both to the surface.

He loved the way she moved against him. Already, he had a hard-on and felt as if he was going to explode if he didn't get inside her soon. He wrapped an arm around her waist and pulled her closer before cupping her breast in his hand.

"I'm good at everything I do," he murmured close to her ear.

"Sounds like someone has a big head," she replied with a wry grin.

"I'll prove it," he said. Already he wanted, needed her again. Five hours had been too long. Still, he knew he had to take this slow, because despite her teasing Brenna still wasn't ready to talk about their past, and he didn't want to cloud their relationship with sex.

Brenna pushed away from his hold and dived under the water. She still hadn't surfaced when he felt her hand on his knee, skimming up the inside of his thigh. She cupped his length in her hand.

"Oh!" he gasped, then forgot to tread water and started to go under.

She surfaced a few inches from him. "I don't know if you noticed, but I'm also good at what I do."

He laughed. "I've definitely noticed."

This was what had been lacking from his life. Teasing, fun and relaxation had been missing in all of his relationships, until now. He paddled over to her, capturing her around the waist again.

Brenna turned in his arms and pressed her lips to his, tasting and exploring with her tongue. Jabarie held on tight with one arm while he stayed afloat with the other. What he wanted to do was climb back on the yacht and bury himself inside her. He wanted to bind her to him, so that they'd never be separated again.

She lifted her head, light twinkling in the depth of her eyes. "Why are you staring at me?"

"Because you're beautiful when you're being silly."

Her wet hair draped over her shoulders, tickling his. He liked that feeling, and pulled her closer. "Is that the only time you think I'm beautiful?"

"Hell, no," he said then nibbled playfully at the side of her neck, while she giggled and reminded him how ticklish she was. With a smile, Jabarie closed his eyes, allowing the feel of her in his arms to consume him. He needed her in his life as badly as his next breath.

"All right. Time to swim." She pushed away from him and dove under the water. With a groan, Jabarie followed. Swimming was the last thing he wanted. His body pulsed with something he hadn't felt in a long time—urgency. As soon as he could manage it, they were going back to bed. He wanted them so deeply intertwined she'd forget everything except being with him.

* * *

Brenna swam until she was too tired to take another stroke. Her ears were just below the water so the only thing she heard was the throbbing of her own heart. Closing her eyes, she floated limply on her back. It wasn't long before she felt the gentle swish of water as Jabarie swam around her. Finally, he came up beneath her, raising her out of the water before dropping her with a splash.

Brenna screamed as she hit the water then quickly came up for air. "I'm going to get you for that." She wiped the water from her eyes just in time to see Jabarie move up beside her. He took her hand and gently pulled her to him, pressing his warm salty lips against hers. She couldn't get close enough as she pressed her body against his firmness then wrapped her legs around his waist and deepened the kiss. It was a priceless moment. She held on to the strong insistent presence of him, and it wasn't long before she felt her body respond. She was engulfed with a desire so thick she was having difficulty breathing. Warmth spread to every nerve in her body before settling between her legs.

Grasping her waist, Jabarie lifted her slightly and lowered his mouth to her bare breast. He needed more and he needed it now. He wanted to be so deeply embedded in her that one wouldn't know where one ended and the other began. And though he knew that was impossible, that there were too many issues that needed resolving first, his body refused to listen. He continued to suckle hungrily until her nails dug into his shoulders and she cried out his name. As they both sank beneath the water, he realized they needed to get out of the water right now.

Holding her carefully with one arm, he swam them both back to the yacht and lifted her up onto the ladder. Jabarie followed closely behind. The second he was on the deck, he scooped her up. The remains of their breakfast and clothing were as they'd left them.

Brenna was a little embarrassed, but there was a sense of rightness about being in his arms that made her understand this weekend was God's will. A kind of confirmation that she'd made the right decision to join him on the yacht to resolve the past and cement the future. She and Jabarie weren't finished.

She wrapped her arms around his neck as he took heavy strides across the deck of his yacht and down to the lower deck. With each step, she felt the power of his upper arms as he held her to his chest, and despite the damp skin, heat emanated from him. Holding tight, she took a deep breath, inhaling his clean masculine scent. His heart beat strongly against her cheek and she closed her eyes as anticipation flowed between them.

As soon as they were in the stateroom, Jabarie set Brenna on her feet next to the king-size bed. She was dripping on the carpet, but he didn't seem to notice. His eyes were still glued to hers. "Stay right there."

You're not the boss of me, she thought with a defiant tilt of her chin. She followed him into the adjoining bathroom and as he reached for two thick bath towels, she swatted him playfully on the butt.

Startled, Jabarie glanced over his shoulder then turned around. "I thought I told you to wait."

"I wanted to see what you were doing," she giggled as he playfully backed her into the room. Just before she fell onto the comforter, Brenna stepped aside and snatched one of the towels from his hands. "Let me dry you off."

"I like the sound of that." Jabarie moved and stood before her with a lustful look in his eyes.

Brenna gave him a long wicked look then dropped the towel onto the floor. "I think I'm going to use my tongue instead."

He noticeably swallowed and she chuckled inwardly. Their relationship had always been aggressive. Role reversal, one of them always played the dominant lover, sometimes her, and more times him. His dominant behavior was one of the things that had always appealed to her. But she learned a long time ago two can play that game and she gave as good as she got. Glancing over at his dampened body, her lips curled in a smile. Right now, she was running things.

"Close your eyes," she said, and as soon as he complied, she pressed her lips against his chest. He flinched but that didn't stop her from licking the drops of water. His breath caught as she dipped her head to catch one pebble-hard nipple between her teeth. Her tongue caressed a moist path from one nipple to the other, stopping long enough to pay a little extra attention, and suckled each before traveling downward following the trail of hair. Lowering to her knees, she nibbled and licked and moved closer to his erection but barely brushed it. She heard his groan of frustration as she moved back to kiss the water from his powerful thighs instead.

Her body burned with arousal. Today she wanted to be more daring than ever before, and push their lovemaking to the limits. Jabarie was the only man who'd ever made her feel this way. She kept tasting him, mesmerized by every inch of his strong body. The upper body she loved and his legs were lean and hard. The hardest part was his erection that thrust toward her.

She lowered her head, letting her breath ruffle over his erection. He smelled wonderful and she took a deep breath while running her cheek along his thigh. She released a sigh and slipped out her tongue and licked up the underside then tilted her head back and gazed up at him. Not only was he hard as steel but his gaze was so hot that she heard the room crackle with anticipation. Slowly, she took him into her mouth. His hands came to her head, rubbing her hair but not holding her or pulling her closer.

"Yeah," he hissed out loud.

"You like that?" she purred.

"You know I do."

So do I. Her hand closed around him and he felt like velvet under her fingers. She lowered her head and ran her tongue up and down his length. He groaned and she took her time, tasting and rediscovering, then retraced her path. She reveled in the taste of his body and the effect it had on her. Sparks shot through her entire body. She looked up at him and his eyes were glazed and his lips parted as he looked down at her. She sucked him deeper in her mouth, felt his body tighten as she worked up and down his length. Under her tongue and hands, she could feel his tension building. She began to work faster while his hands moved through her hair. He seemed to grow large, and groaned before he pulled her away and lifted her to her feet.

Jabarie carried her to the bed then lowered her to the

sheets, pulling the comforter onto the floor. She loved the feel of his solid frame against her. He wrapped his arms around her, anchoring her to him with his hands on her back.

He lowered his mouth to hers and she was consumed by the fire that only he could ignite inside her. She loved the way he kissed her, savoring the moment with no intentions of stopping until he'd explored every corner of her mouth. Reaching up, she stroked his jaw and whispered affectionate words.

He groaned and his erection pulsed between them. She felt him growing even harder and reached between them to enfold him in her grasp. Jabarie shuddered.

Not about to be outdone, he placed her at the center of the bed. Leaning over, he squeezed and molded the flesh of her full breasts. Each touch caused her to moan aloud. He teased her nipples with the tips of his fingers. Her heart was thudding and her mind running feverishly. Arching her chest, she needed to feel his mouth against her skin.

"Jabarie, kiss me there," she whimpered.

"Yes, baby." He lowered his head and sucked. She arched off the bed with a little cry that was lost in the sounds of sexual frenzy going on in the room. Reaching up, she cupped the back of his neck and held him there.

Jabarie waited until her breathing slowed before he pushed himself up onto his elbows. Brenna smiled at him with swollen lips still wet from his kisses.

Watching her he knew that once would never be enough for him. She ran through his body and soul. This is where they were connected. Sex had never been a problem between them. When he was lying between her legs, buried deep inside her body, it was the one time when he'd always felt that he was truly seeing the real Brenna Gathers. Sexually aroused, there was no way she could put up barriers.

He brought his lips to her damp skin and kissed a path between her breasts then down across her abdomen. Gradually, he felt the heat building within as her breathing became labored. While he continued his exploratory journey, Brenna's fingertips caressed his back and buttocks, feeling the muscles and contours. He licked her belly, then slipped a finger between her folds. He knew he'd find her hot and slipper; thank goodness her arousal was something she couldn't hide. It made him tremble that she wanted him so much. With his thumb on her clit, and a finger inside her, teasing her, he stroked and aroused her further. "That's it, baby. Say it. Tell me you like it," he said in a deep, husky voice.

Brenna moaned, and wiggled and spread her legs wider as she lifted her hips off the bed to meet his hand. "Please, now. No more foreplay. Just make love to me," she managed to get out between moans.

Jabarie kissed his way back up her body, lingering at her breasts. He sucked against the hardened flesh and nibbled softly until she was calling out his name.

Unable to wait a moment longer, he climbed out of the bed long enough to retrieve a condom where he had left them the night before, then slid one on before returning to his place on top of her.

He positioned himself between her legs, wrapped them around his waist and drove into her. He set the rhythm, thrusting and withdrawing as her legs locked around him. Her hips rose, sucking him deeper, deeper still, until he felt he'd explode. He lowered his head and kissed her lips, cheek and neck. Sweat popped out on his brow, dripped down his chest and made their bodies slick. His breathing became labored as he tried to hold on until she found her pleasure. Finally, she cried out and he groaned. Her inner muscles clamped down, refusing to let him go as an orgasm ripped through her body. He came an instant later; his entire body spasmed. A few moments later, he pulled out and rolled onto his side. With his eyes closed, he fought for breath. "Damn, Brenna. That was even better than the last time."

"I have to agree." Chest heaving, she rested her face close to his chest and drifted off to sleep.

Much later, Jabarie sat on the side of the bed beside Brenna and watched her sleep.

He had been determined to sleep with Brenna and get her out of his system once and for all so that he could get on with his life. Only it didn't happen that way. Once again he couldn't get enough of her taste, her smell, being buried inside her body. Was it love? He tried to tell himself no and ignore the emotions stirring inside. There was no way he could possibly be fooled twice by the same woman. No way. No how. He wouldn't do that to himself again. However, there was a knot in his chest that he couldn't ignore. A knot of hard, raw emotion that just wasn't going away. Something had to give. Something had to change.

Jabarie pulled her closer to him and lowered his lids as a sharpness tore at his heart. He didn't know what it was about Brenna that still made him want to hold her in his arms and never let her go. But he couldn't go on like this. Either she wanted to be a part of his life, or not. And he planned to find out. Tomorrow, before he returned Brenna to her aunt's house, the two of them were going to have a long talk.

Chapter 12

As soon as Jabarie pulled off the highway toward Sheraton Beach, Brenna released a heavy sigh of despair and said, "Time to get back to reality."

Jabarie took his eyes away from the road long enough to give her a look that made her instantly regret her words. The sparkle in his eyes was gone and his mouth set in a firm line.

"Back to reality?" he repeated as he pulled onto the shoulder of the road. "What was this, some kind of fantasy vacation?"

Puzzled by his abrupt change of mood, she didn't answer.

Jabarie put the car in park then turned on the seat so that he was facing her. "Is that all I am to you, a big joke?"

Brenna shook her head. The last two days had been so perfect. Yesterday after making love they spent the afternoon on the yacht teasing, playing and simply just spending time together. The captain even let her take a turn piloting the yacht. Dinner had been more scrumptious than the first and that evening was spent dancing on the deck before Jabarie had carried her to bed where they stayed until it was time to leave this morning. On the way back from Ocean City, they had held hands and talked about nothing in particular, she enjoying the sound of his voice. Why did he want to ruin that? She met his direct stare. "This isn't the time."

"You're wrong. This is the perfect time."

"I rather not," she said, although one thing she knew about Jabarie was that you couldn't persuade him to do anything he didn't want to do.

"Too bad. I've waited five years for this discussion. I've tried to get you to talk all morning and each time I tried to bring it up you quickly changed the subject. Well, enough is enough. We are going to talk about us *now*."

Brenna briefly lowered her eyelids. The weekend had been so magical. The last thing she wanted to do was ruin it by talking about what could have been. "I think we should just leave the past in the past."

Jabarie shook his head in silent amazement. "I can't believe you."

She shifted an eyebrow. "What are you talking about?"

Reaching over, he grabbed her hand. "Brenna. We made love. It wasn't just sex. What we have is an emotional bond that no matter how much you try to deny it, it's not going away."

"I...disagree."

"You're lying," he said then pulled her across the seat so fast that she startled before taking a deep breath. Jabarie would never lay a finger on her. However, his jaw tightened as he clenched his teeth. "It was more and you know it." His mouth was so close, she felt his warm breath across her nose and cheeks.

She freed her hand of his grasp and slid back over to her side, putting a little distance between them. He was right. There was more going on between them. A lot more, but there was no way she was going to put her feelings out there just to be crushed again, no matter how wonderful the last two days had been. "What difference does it make? What happened between us ended a long time ago."

"You don't mean that." Rage burned from his eyes and she could tell he was hurting because the muscle at his jaw twitched.

Well, too bad. What about all the pain and heartache she'd had to endure?

Yes, the past two days had been magical and meant everything to her. Making love again was everything she remembered and thought of constantly of the last five years. Her body had never forgotten and neither had her mind. Her body was still experiencing aftershocks and was still damp with yearning. If he asked her to get in the backseat she wouldn't think of saying no, or refusing him. But as she stared up at his face of stone, she pushed the thought away. He wanted to talk about it. Fine. He asked for it.

"What were you expecting me to say?" she asked, then brought a hand to his chest and pushed him away.

"That you were the bomb? That it doesn't get any better than you and I. Okay, I'll admit it. Having you make love to me is something I can't even begin to explain." She paused with a sigh. "The past two days mean more to me than anything has in years, but it doesn't change anything."

His nearly black eyes narrowed dangerously. "You know, I can see you haven't changed one bit in five years."

Her gaze widened. "What's that supposed to mean?"

"It means you are the same scared, little girl who is afraid of taking a chance."

The long deep look they exchanged infuriated her. "I'm not scared."

"Prove it, and stay in Sheraton Beach."

She stared at him for a long painful moment before dropping her eyes to her lap. "There is nothing here for me to stay."

"What about me? Stay because I want you to." Reaching out, he cupped her chin and tilted her head so that she was forced to look at him.

He was asking things she was unable to give. "Why Jabarie?" she asked and held her breath as she waited to hear, what, she wasn't sure.

"I'm surprised you have to even ask that question."

"Obviously, if I knew the answer I wouldn't be asking. I need to know why?" she asked softly.

She watched him watching her and suddenly she wanted to be anywhere but in his car with him. There was something in his eyes that made her think he could see exactly what she was feeling.

He lowered his head until their mouths were only inches away. "Because I love you. I've always loved you."

Brenna reared back as if she'd been struck. "Well then that settles it," she said sarcastically. "Because you love me, I guess I better sell my half of the bookstore and move back to Sheraton Beach."

"Where is all this anger coming from? I always loved you. Never stopped loving you. Five years ago I wanted to marry you before you decided to walk out of my life."

She sobered quickly, staring at him as her heart pounded erratically, stunned by his response and expression. Moments later, rage distorted her face. "How dare you!"

"What?"

"I'm not in the mood for playing games. Been there. Done that. You already made me the laughing stock of this town once, and I refuse to go there with you again."

He stiffened as though she had struck him. "What are you talking about? You're the one who ran out on our wedding day, not me."

She glared at him. "Of course I did. After your lawyer arrived I was so hurt I fled."

"Yeah, with a check. I'm sure that made leaving quite easy. Why did you take the money?"

She blinked; there was no way she heard him correctly. Did he just ask her why she took money from his mother? She took a deep breath and reminded herself that she had already spent the last five years waiting for him to come for her, to say he loved her, yet, he never came and now he wanted to blame her.

"I hope you don't expect an answer," she retorted.

His temper flared. "That's why I brought it up. It's time for us to talk about the past so we can have a future…together."

She stared at him, stunned by his statement. "If you were so concerned about the past you should have tried to talk to me then."

"Well, I'm asking you now. Why did you leave with the money?"

She couldn't believe this line of questioning. "If you had asked me that five years ago I would have given you an answer."

Jabarie shifted on the seat and she noticed his knuckles whiten as he tightly gripped the steering wheel. Without saying another word he started the car and she sat there with her arms crossed and pouting. She'd always thought the behavior childish, but believed at this moment it was indeed warranted. She didn't look at him again until he pulled up in front of her aunt's house and killed the motor.

"Why can't you just answer the question?"

Brenna raked a frustrated hand through her hair. "Look," she began. "Too much time has passed."

"No," he disagreed. "Too much time has been lost."

"Lost?" She was so furious she could hardly speak. "How dare you!" Her right fist pounded his hard chest. When that lawyer appeared at her door she had called him every name in the book. Now she wasn't going to give him the satisfaction of making her go there. "It was you that sent the lawyer to my house telling me to either sign the prenuptial agreement, or walk away with the check."

He wore a puzzled look on his face. "Lawyer? Prenup? What are you talking about?"

She rolled her eyes. She wasn't the least bit interested in playing this game. "The night before our wedding your father's lawyer came to my house on your behalf."

When Jabarie spoke again his voice was quiet, yet held an undertone of cold contempt. "I never sent Victor to have you sign anything."

Why was he lying? Her bitterness resurfaced. "Then why else would he have showed up at my door?"

"I have no idea, but I didn't send him. Now let me get this straight…because my lawyer paid you a visit and stuck a piece of paper in your face, you just walked out of my life without even speaking to me first?"

She seethed with anger and humiliation. "I did come looking for you! I came to the condo and found you with Anika."

He stilled as he remembered the evening Anika popped up at his apartment, wearing nothing beneath a trench coat but a thong. "That was a big misunderstanding."

Brenna held up an open palm. "Save it. It really doesn't matter anymore. It's too late to go back."

Jabarie dragged a frustrated hand across his face. "It does matter. Believe me when I tell you this. I didn't ask you to sign a prenuptial."

"Then who did?" she asked, eyes darting around the car in frustration.

The expression on his face hardened. "Probably my parents."

A sudden, thin chill hung on the edge of his words. She couldn't believe her ears. Were his parents actually responsible for ruining her life?

"So now what?" he finally said following a long uncomfortable silence.

"It doesn't change anything."

"It changes everything. My mother told me that you came to her for money. Obviously that was a lie."

"Me?" Her own anger and hurt could no longer be controlled. But there was no way she was going to break down in front of him.

Reaching down she grabbed her purse and swung it over her shoulder. This discussion was getting them nowhere. "The only reason why I took the money was because you offered it to me. I needed to get away because there was no way I could stay in Sheraton Beach and have everyone talking about me again. I just couldn't bear it."

He remembered first hand what she had gone through with her mother. "I would never have offered you money to leave town when all I've ever wanted was to marry you. I loved you too much."

The dam broke and tears flooded her eyes. She had lost the man she loved. "It's too late. We can never go back to that time."

"The hell it is. I love you and refuse to lose you a second time around." She opened the door and Jabarie reached for her, but Brenna wrestled her hand away.

"Goodbye." She climbed out the car and moved into her aunt's house. Distraught and with tears blinding her eyes, it took her several seconds to realize her aunt was bouncing around the living room, doing jazzercise. Brenna gasped, then stood there for several seconds hoping her eyes were playing tricks on her before Aunt Nellie swung around and noticed her standing there and released a quick intake of breath.

"Oh! Brenna. I didn't know you were here."

"Obviously." She dropped a hand to her waist and gave her a look of disbelief. "How long have you been faking?"

Aunt Nellie hesitated for a moment before offering her a sheepish grin. "For almost a week now."

"Why?"

Aunt Nellie reached for a towel and mopped her forehead while she tried to catch her breath. "Because I wanted you to come home and give Jabarie a second chance. The two of you are meant to be together."

"And that makes it right?" Brenna tossed her hands into the air and stormed to her room where she started laughing and crying at the same time. It was just too much for her to have to deal with at one time.

Jabarie found his father in his study. As usual, Roger Beaumont was deep in thought. Standing in the doorway he took a moment to observe the man who had ruined his life. He was a tall man who over the last several years had gained a great deal around the middle. He had just celebrated his sixty-third birthday. As soon as Jabarie cleared his throat, Roger opened his eyes and stared over at him.

"Oh, good. You're back."

Acknowledging him with a quick nod of the head, Jabarie strolled straight for the bar in the corner and poured himself a glass of cognac. Taking a sip, he allowed a second for the liquor to warm his stomach before moving over to the chair across from his father, who sat with a puzzled face, and lowered onto the seat.

"Tell me…" he began "…what the hell happened

five years ago that caused Brenna to walk out of my life?"

The pen dropped from his father's hand and slowly he raised his head and looked across the desk at him. "I made a big mistake."

"Father, what did you do?" he asked, struggling for control.

His father looked up at him, his eyes practically begging him to forgive him. "Jabarie, I was just trying to look out for you."

Anger blazed from his eyes while fear of what his father was about to say tightened his chest. "I'm going to ask you again. What did you do?"

His father slumped back in the chair, which he found so out of character for the overly confident man. "I paid her to disappear."

"Why would you do that?" Jabarie already knew the answer, but he had to ask anyway.

He father looked up at him, eyes clear, unblinking. "Because I didn't think she was right for you."

Fury almost choked him. "Who are you to say who is, or isn't right for me. It's my life. Not yours."

"You're right. I was wrong for interfering." His gaze lowered as did his voice. "I had Victor draw up a prenuptial agreement and he went to her house and told her to sign it, or the wedding was off. Instead, she ran and went looking for you."

Jabarie shook his head. It was starting to become clearer now. "And she found me with Anika."

His father cleared his throat. "I sent Anika to your apartment."

Jabarie shot to his feet. "You did *what?*"

His father nodded his head, wearily. "I knew Brenna would run over to your condo to discuss the prenuptial, so I encouraged Anika to show up at your place."

Jabarie slammed his glass down onto the desk and almost regretted his actions when he saw his father flinch. "How could you interfere in my life that way? How…how could you do that to me?"

"I was wrong. I've been regretting what I've done for the last several years, but I thought it was too late to do anything about it."

"Well, you thought wrong," he replied sharply as he paced a small path in front of him. "I never stopped loving Brenna."

"I know that. You haven't been the same since she left, and I'm so sorry."

"Brenna is the best thing to ever happen to me. She completes me."

"I understand that now. I—I was afraid she was just like her mother."

"She is nothing like her mother," he spat then sat down heavily on a leather couch close enough so that he could still see his father's face but far enough away that he wouldn't be tempted to wring his neck. "You don't have a clue as to the type of person Brenna is, because you never bothered to find out. You were too busy judging her."

Roger nodded. "You're right." Folding his hands on top of the desk, he leaned forward and after a long silence asked, "What can I do to make this right?"

Jabarie settled his head in his hands. "I can't believe this."

"Son, please understand, I just wanted to make sure

she was the right woman for you. I thought when she took the money that she was exactly who I thought her to be."

He looked up. "Well, you're wrong. Brenna has gone through so much in her life and you were responsible. After her mother ran off you made sure that everyone knew what she had done. Brenna was the laughing stock of this town. She lived through years of people pointing and judging her based on her mother's past. The reason why she took that money was because she had been humiliated a second time and wanted to get as far away from Sheraton Beach as she possibly could."

"I was wrong son, and I'm sorry," he said with a heavy sigh of despair.

He watched as his father rose and moved over to the bar and reached for a canister of his favorite brandy, then retrieved a glass from underneath. "Son, you have to understand the Beaumonts represent wealth and with wealth come people looking for a big payout."

"Brenna isn't like that."

"Please hear me out," he said as he moved over to the couch and took a seat.

Immediately, Jabarie brought the warm liquor to his lips, hoping that once it hit his stomach it would calm the anger brewing inside.

Roger took a sip as well before continuing, "I remember while I was in college, I met this beautifully amazing woman named Amber. She and I dated for almost two years and the day after graduation she found out she was pregnant." His father looked lost in the past and Jabarie's face softened as he realize that somehow what he was saying was quite painful.

"I wanted to marry her and your grandfather was livid." He gave a laugh that lacked humor then brought the glass to his lips again.

Jabarie nodded, knowingly. He remembered Roger Beaumont II as being a pistol.

"I refused to listen to anything he had to say because I was determined to marry Amber. We prepared for our wedding and our baby. I was happy and in love and nothing else mattered.

"Your grandfather pulled us both into his office and made it perfectly clear that if I married her, he would disown me and I'd lose all my rights to the Beaumont fortune.

"I told him I didn't care and sent Amber back to the apartment while I spoke to my father in private. But no matter what I said that stubborn bastard refused to change his mind. I stormed out of there and headed home to find Amber packing. She told me what good would it do her to be married to me without the money. When I told her we didn't need his money all we needed was the baby and each other, she laughed at me and told me the baby wasn't even mine."

Jabarie was stunned by his father's expression and the somber look on his face said he had taken the blow very hard. "Did you check to make sure she was telling the truth?"

Nodding, he raised the glass again. "I tracked her down living in a trailer park and demanded a blood test. She charged me five thousand dollars before she would agree. And sure enough, for once she had been telling the truth. Her little girl wasn't mine. I remember walking away feeling lost because a part of me had been holding on for almost a year, hoping it was all just one big misunderstanding and that she really did love me." The room grew quiet and he took another sip from his glass.

"What does any of this have to do with Brenna?"

"It just means that you might not always agree with me and your mother's actions, but no matter what I do or say I always have your best interest at heart."

"You thought I was going to end up getting hurt just like you did?"

"Her mother doesn't have the best reputation in town."

His father had tried to protect him, but Brenna wasn't like Amber. Brenna was never after his money. She had loved him for him, and he had been too stupid to realize that until now.

"Brenna isn't anything like that," he said defensively.

"I know that now. I just didn't know that then." He rested his elbows on his knees. "So what are you going to do?"

"Why, Dad? It didn't mean anything to you then, why should it now?"

"Because it does matter. After all these years, you still love her. You've become bitter and hardened your heart. By now you should be married, and I should have a couple of grandchildren running around." Leaning back, his father sighed. "What I'm trying to say is that if you love her, then don't let her get away a second time."

"I don't know what else to do."

He put an arm across his son's shoulders. "Since when have we Beaumonts been quitters? If you want Brenna then go get her."

"Can you forgive an old lady for trying to match-make?"

Brenna glanced over at her aunt as she stepped into the living room. She was sitting on the couch, knitting.

"Of course I can," she replied then moved over to the chair across from her and took a seat.

Aunt Nellie lowered her knitting needles to her lap. "I just wanted you to have a second chance."

Brenna frowned. She had spent the last hour lying across the bed, crying her eyes out about a life that could have been. No matter how she looked at it there was no turning back. "It's too late for that."

Her aunt was stunned by her response. "It's never too late. At least give Jabarie a chance to explain."

Closing her eyes, she settled back on the cushions of the chair. "He already has."

"And he told you he had nothing to do with the prenuptial agreement?"

Brenna's eyelids snapped open. "How do you know that?"

Before answering, her aunt moved her knitting aside and released a heavy sigh of despair. "A while back his father came to me and confessed what he'd done," she admitted, a frown turning her mouth downward. "Jabarie had never been the same after you left him, and he admitted that it was all his fault. Humph! You better believe I gave it to him for ruining your life like that."

Despite the pain she was feeling, Brenna chuckled. "I just bet you did." She had seen her feisty aunt in action on several occasions, and from experience she was not one to mess with.

"Anyway, Roger started asking all kinds of questions about you. Where you were living, if you had married, and when I told him you were still single, he wanted to know if you were happy."

Brenna was surprised to hear that he was even interested in knowing how she was doing. She had always gotten the impression he didn't like her.

"I think he truly regrets what he did because he pleaded with me to help him come up with a way to fix things."

Well, he should. Because of him the last five years had been the most miserable time of her life. They could be married with a child by now. Pressing a palm to her stomach, she realized it was all gone because of one selfish man.

"And I guess your spained ankle was part of that plan."

Aunt Nellie's eyes danced with amusement. "I really did fall and hurt myself. I just figured I'd milk it for all it was worth."

Brenna shook her head with disbelief and started laughing.

"Hey, you can't blame an old lady for trying."

There was a knock at the door, and her heart began to race because she knew before even opening the door that it was Jabarie.

"You want me to get that?" her aunt asked.

Brenna shrugged then rose from the chair. "Sure, why not? After all, you seemed to have recovered nicely," she teased then moved out onto the deck while her aunt went to the door. Just as she thought, it was Jabarie. While a gentle breeze ruffled her ponytail, she listened to the two of them talking on the other side of the door. She almost laughed when Jabarie told Aunt Nellie how glad he was to see her back on her feet. She snorted rudely as Aunt Nellie told him it was a miracle. It wasn't long before he stepped out onto the deck and slid the door close behind him.

Brenna glanced up and noticed him staring down at her. When she met his eyes her pulse jumped. She took in his snug white T-shirt defining his muscular chest and shoulders and noticed how his jeans hugged his strong legs and thighs. Tall, sexy, he made her pulse race as much as the first time they'd met. *He didn't send the lawyer.* She was still stunned by the discovery. One after another, including the fact that after all these years he still held a special place in her heart. Brenna groaned inwardly. That was her biggest problem of all. In fact, that realization made things worse instead of better. She brushed a frustrated hand to her forehead.

"Hello," he said.

"Hi."

"I see your aunt is back on her feet."

"Yes. It seems she's back to normal." So formal and stiff, nothing like a couple who was once engaged and just hours ago had been lovers. Jabarie looked as uncomfortable as she felt.

Nodding, he walked over to the rail. He stood with his legs braced apart and his hands curved around the rail while he glanced off into the ocean. "Now that Ms. Nellie's better, I guess that means you'll be leaving soon?"

"Yeah, after the big sidewalk sale on Sunday."

His head swung around and he turned to face her. "Why so soon?"

Brenna averted her gaze toward the beach. "There's no reason for me to stay."

"I think there is."

Brenna gazed over at his hopeful face. "I've got to get back to the bookstore."

"Can't you stay a little longer?"

She saw the disappointment in his eyes, but as much as she wanted to stay, she couldn't. The longer she put it off, the harder it would be to finally say goodbye. "I can't."

Jabarie moved and lowered onto the bench beside her and his warm fingers curled around her. A sense of calmness settled over her, and for the longest time they both sat there holding hands and staring off into the ocean.

"I spoke to my father," he finally said, breaking the silence that surrounded them.

Her breathing stalled while she waited for him to continue.

"He had schemed to keep us apart. The prenup and the check were all his idea."

Brenna swallowed. Hearing it from him made her feel sick all over again. "Aunt Nellie told me your father came to her a while back full of remorse for what he had done. She faked the severity of her sprained ankle to get me home so we could get back together." If it had been someone else, it might just have been funny. But laughing was the last thing she felt like doing.

Jabarie glanced over at her then back at the water. "Now what?"

She had to bite down on her lower lip to keep a sob from moving to her throat. "We can't go back. What happened between us we have to leave in the past."

"How can you say that?" Swinging on the seat, he ripped out the words impatiently. "We just spent a fabulous weekend together. Those feelings are still there. I know it, and so do you."

How could she get him to understand she couldn't go through that type of pain a second time? What he wanted was now five years too late. Leaning her head back, she looked into his eyes. "Why didn't you fight for us then?"

He appeared surprised by her question because it took him a few moments before he finally answered. "Because I thought that was what you wanted."

She fixed him with an icy glare. "So, if you loved me as much as you say you do, even after all this time, then why did you let me go? No phone calls. Letters. Nothing." She was getting angry again just thinking about it. "Do you know how that made me feel? Your lawyer throwing a prenup in my lap. Even then I didn't want to believe it because I knew the man that I loved wouldn't do something underhanded like that. So I went looking for you, so that my fiancé could tell me it was all a mistake. I arrive at your apartment and find you in the arms of another woman. My heart broke in two as I slowly crept out the door and back to my car. When I returned home feeling hurt and rejected Aunt Nellie handed me an envelope your mother had been more than willing to drop off and inside I found the check. I was so hurt I took that money and left that night. At first I wanted to rip it up, but then I decided that in some way I had earned it for all the humiliation and for having no choice but to leave and pick up the pieces somewhere else. There was no way I could stay in Sheraton Beach after that." She was actually trembling now.

"But it was a mistake. I never offered you that money. My father had even sent Anika over to distract me." Anger pulsed at his jaw.

She nodded and said calmly, "I never knew your father and Anika were that close." As soon as he prepared to speak, she held up her hand and continued. "Even knowing that doesn't make it hurt any less. It's just too late for us." A hot tear rolled down her cheek.

"It'll never be over between us." Jabarie pulled her over to his lap and held her in his arms and as soon as she lowered her cheek against his chest, the tears flowed freely. He rocked her in his arms and whispered encouraging words as deep sobs raked her insides. The last thing she'd ever wanted was for him to see her break down this way. Only she couldn't hold back any longer. She cried for every year they had lost together because of two people who never thought she was good enough.

"I'll always love you," he whispered as he pressed his lips to her forehead. When her head tipped back and her lips parted, he knew she wanted the kiss as much as he did.

Need raced through him and settled below his belt. He loved this woman and there was no way he was letting her go a second time. He slid his arms tightly around her then swooped down and pressed his lips to hers. When she moaned, he deepened the kiss, taking possession of her mouth. Brenna tasted delicious, and familiar and even with a lifetime he would never get enough.

She leaned forward, her soft curves burning where they touched, arousing him. He thought about her naked, lying beneath him. He slipped his tongue inside, taking total possession of her sweet intoxicating mouth, and felt the rapid beat of her heart keeping pace with his own.

Brenna returned each stroke with one of her own. Her tongue slipping into his mouth raised his level of desire. He slid his hand across her breast and grazed his thumb across her nipple, feeling the hardened bud. He slid his hand beneath her shirt and cupped her bare breast.

She trembled and caught his wrist with one hand and pushed him away with the other, abruptly ending the kiss. He stared down at her; heat blazed in her eyes and he tried to reach for her again. Shaking her head, she rose from his lap and moved over to the railing.

"I need some time to think," she said softly.

His gaze lingered on her until he nodded. "It's not over. I'll see you tomorrow," he said then rose in one fluid motion and walked back into the house.

Chapter 13

The following afternoon Jabarie drove down to Main Street and parked in front of Lori's Florist & Gift Shop. Now that he knew the reason behind their breakup, he was on a mission, and that was showing Brenna that he still loved her.

With a phone call he could have easily ordered her flowers from the hotel florist and had them delivered, or asked his secretary Donna to do it. But that wouldn't have the right reaction that he needed. He needed everyone in town to know that he still loved Brenna, and the best way to get the word around their little town was to shop on Main Street.

Jabarie stepped through the door and the bell over-head rung, announcing his presence. Lori, a short, round middle-aged woman with large friendly brown eyes immediately stuck her head out from behind the door behind the counter. When she realized who was standing in her office, her eyes grew wide with surprise.

"Good afternoon, Jabarie. I haven't seen you in my store in ages."

He gave her a warm smile, knowing it was just a matter of seconds before the questions started rolling off her tongue. "Hello, Lori. I haven't had a reason to buy flowers."

"That's a shame. A fine man like yourself should have women knocking at his door," she replied while the cocoa brown woman ran a hand across her short, curly afro.

He chuckled. "I'm only interested in one woman."

Lori gave him a long questioning gaze then walked across the shop toward him. "Really? Anyone I know?"

"Maybe," he said offhandedly, even though he knew good and well she knew Brenna Gathers. Instead of appeasing her curiosity, he swung his eyes to the flower arrangement on the shelf in front of the store. "I need to send some flowers."

"What would you like to send her?"

"Roses," he said confidently as he turned around to face her again.

Lori walked over to the counter and retrieved a notepad and pen. "Good choice. Did you know that roses are a girl's best friend?"

"So I've heard," he said with a saucy grin.

"What color?"

"Red."

A knowing smile curled her full mouth. "Red means love."

Jabarie buried a hand in his navy pleated slacks and rocked back on his heels. "Then that's what I want because I'm definitely in love with this woman."

Propping a hand at her ample hip, Lori studied him for a long thoughtful moment before saying, "I see…" and purposely allowed her voice to trail about before suggesting, "How about I add a little baby's breath to the bouquet?"

"Sounds perfect," he said then held up both hands, palms out. "But, I'm going to need ten dozen red roses."

"T-ten…" Lori stuttered and she swayed slightly. "Wow! That many? This mystery woman must be very special."

He tried not to chuckle. "Yes, she is. And my loving her won't be a mystery too much longer," he added under his breath before moving around to a large glass display case and gazed inside at the assortment of colors. "In each bouquet can you add one single white rose?"

"Buying that many, I'll be glad to add them at no charge." Lori offered as she scribbled quickly on the pad. "Any special note included?"

Jabarie nodded and Lori signaled for him to follow her over to a card display on the counter. He quickly selected one with a yacht on the front, thought it was quite appropriate. It took him less than a minute to write what was in his heart. *You are the air I breathe.*

He put the card in Lori's outstretched hand. Immediately she glanced inside and read the inscription. "Wow!" She gave a whistle then peered at him over the tops of her glasses. "This woman is really special," she said, obviously still fishing for information. "David used to send me poems all the time. Bless his soul. I still miss that man."

He cupped her shoulder. "We all do." David had been an honest plumber and member of the community for generations whom people had loved and respected for years. He and Lori had been married over thirty years when a massive heart attack had ended his life three years ago.

Jabarie nibbled on his lower lip. "Do you think I'm overdoing it with that many roses?"

Lori's eyes widened and got all bright and flashy before she shook her head. "Not if you're trying to get her attention and you'll definitely be doing that."

His shoulders relaxed with relief. He definitely needed to make a statement.

Lori moved behind the counter and as soon as she rang up his order, he reached into his back pocket and removed his credit card and handed it to her. "Can you deliver them this afternoon?"

"No problem. Where do you want them delivered?" she asked as if she didn't already know.

He waited until she had handed him his card back before answering, "The Cornerstone Bookstore."

She slapped a hand across her thigh. "Hot damn! About time you came to your senses. Does that mean you and Brenna are courting again?"

Jabarie chuckled. "Better late than never."

"I agree," Lori said and moved from behind the counter. "I'll make sure to have these flowers delivered by three o'clock today."

"Thanks, Lori."

"No problem."

Jabarie waved then turned on his heels.

"Oh, and Jabarie?" she called after him.

He froze in his track but didn't bother to turn around.

"Make sure this time when you decide to tie the knot you tell Lady Beaumont that a local florist is just as good as the ones in the city."

He chuckled. His mother did have a tendency to rub the local merchants the wrong way. Believing nothing was good enough unless it came for New York or any of the surrounding big cities. Glancing over his shoulder, he said, "I guarantee you, after I propose, I'll contact you right away."

"You do that!"

Jabarie bid his goodbye then whistled as he strolled out of the shop. Things were starting to look up already.

Brenna was just finishing up story time hour for the little preschool kids when she spotted the florist van in front of the bookstore. She waved goodbye to one of the parents escorting their child out the door with a brand new book tucked under his arm as the delivery guy came through the door.

"Well, what do we have here?" Aunt Nellie's eyes danced with amusement. She came from behind the desk and walked toward him and didn't stop until she was standing next to a gorgeous bouquet.

The delivery guy looked down at his clipboard. "I have flowers for Brenna Gathers," he announced then looked from one to the other.

Stunned, Brenna took the large vase from his hands. "Thank you. Let me go and get you a tip."

Shaking his head, he started backing away. "No need ma'am. It's already been taken care of. I'll be right back."

"Right back?"

He spun in his heels and headed out the door before she could ask what he meant. From the window she watched him reach inside and pull out two more bouquets of roses. She hurried over to the door and held it open for him.

"Thanks. Where would you like these?"

"Those are for me, too?" her voice cracked.

"Of course they are. I'll take them." Aunt Nellie took them from his hands.

"I'll be right back," he said and moved out to the van again.

Brenna's gaze traveled over to her aunt whose eyes were dancing with amusement.

"I think Jabarie is trying to show you how much he still loves you."

Her stomach turned somersaults. It had been a long time since a man had bought her flowers; in fact if she thought long and hard, it hadn't been since Jabarie. It was something he had been doing since they were teenagers. She appreciated it then but now holding flowers caused a sob to lodge in her throat. He was so thoughtful and kind and that's what she had always loved most about him.

For the next five minutes she watched as the delivery guy brought in a total of ten huge bouquets.

"What are we going to do with all of these roses?" she asked her aunt after the florist van pulled away from in front of the store.

Aunt Nellie shrugged. "We can take them home. Or they'll look lovely around the store."

Leaning forward, Brenna took a deep breath and inhaled the floral scent. A small smile turned her lips. "I think the store would be a good place for them." Brenna paused as she reached for the card on top of the largest bouquet. "Although, I think I'm going to take this bouquet home with us."

"I think that is a fabulous idea."

"Yeah," she said, too stunned to say more. Brenna removed the card from the envelope. *You are the air I breathe.* The words made her head spin and her heart race. Jabarie was determined to break down her barrier and make her love him again. What he didn't know was that she did love him. She had never stopped. However, what he'd never understand was that no matter how she felt there was no way she would ever allow herself to be that vulnerable again.

Hovering over her, Aunt Nellie smiled. "I think that says it all."

Brenna frowned then tucked the small card into her hip pocket and released a short sigh of despair as she moved to arrange the bouquets. It was ironic but now she had Jabarie's love and knew that everything that had happened five years ago was one big misunderstanding. Had happened because his father had butted into their business, and now, even knowing that Jabarie still loved her and wanted her back in his life and was ready to start over, she wasn't interested. The reason was obvious.

She was afraid. Afraid of loving and being hurt again. There was no way she could go through that once more. Her entire life had revolved around him. Being his wife was all she had ever wanted. After she left, her priorities changed. She had gone on to start a new life and built her own world and now that she had, there was no way she was giving all that up for a man, no matter how much she loved him.

As soon as they had the bouquets arranged around the store it was business as usual. The students came in and they helped straighten the shelves. At five the bell rang over the door, and immediately she knew it was Jabarie.

As soon as she spotted him walking into the store, she lost whatever willpower she had. Being in the same room with him, sharing the same air, stirred feelings and emotions that she was trying so hard to fight. Right now the only thing she yearned for was a kiss. As he moved toward her, she fought the panic that singed her. He was so handsome and, damn, that man had a sexy walk. Beneath the black suit jacket his broad shoulders swayed from side to side.

"Hey you," he greeted with a sensual smile on his lips.

"Hey." She took a deep steadying breath, trying to get her traitorous body under control.

Jabarie's eyes swept around the room and finally back at her. "I see you got the roses."

Nodding, she smiled at the dark eyes that stared down at her. "Thanks. They're beautiful." Stones that made up the wall around her heart started chipping away.

He reached down and cradled her face between his hands. "You're more than welcome. I love you, Brenna, and plan to do whatever it takes to show you."

Another stone fell as her heart hammered foolishly. "Oh, really?"

Nodding, Jabarie took her hand and led her to the office. "Have you had time to think?" he asked as soon as he closed the door behind them.

She gazed up at his beautiful dark eyes that searched her face, trying to reach into her thoughts. "Yes, and nothing has changed."

"The hell it hasn't," he murmured then tugged her to him and took her mouth. His kiss was slow, deep and thorough, leaving her body pounding hungrily. They were all the reasons why she had to fight him. He was everything she didn't need, while at the same time he was everything she needed.

Her lips parted for his probing tongue and she sank into the hunger, the taste, devouring him. She held him tighter, wanting to hold on to him and this moment forever. Jabarie deepened the kiss with one hand cupping the back of her head. The kiss was thorough and possessive. All he did was take and she allowed him to. As soon as a moan escaped her lips, Jabarie released her and pulled back.

"Like I said before, it's not over," he said in a husky drawl then turned on his heels and walked out of the office, leaving her unable to breathe and barely able to stand. So she stumbled back into the chair.

Brenna stepped inside to fill her glass of lemonade. She carried the glasses over to the counter then reached inside the refrigerator. Tonight felt like old times. After dinner, she and Aunt Nellie sitting out on the deck watching the sun set over the ocean. As she refilled their glasses, she took a deep shaky breath. She was really going to miss it here. In cutoff jeans and bare feet, she moved back out onto the deck, and handed Nellie her glass.

"Thank you, dear," she said with a warm smile.

"No problem." Brenna lowered back onto the chair and propped her feet on the rail as she stared out at the sky that was a breathtaking combination of red, orange and purple.

"Aunt Nellie," she said as she took a sip.

"Yes dear?"

"Jabarie had mentioned that you were thinking about selling the store."

She heaved a heavy sigh. "Yes, child, I am."

Turning slightly, Brenna's eyes came up to study her face. "Why is this the first time I've heard about it?"

"I didn't want you to worry about it."

Brenna blew out a breath, and shook her ponytail. "Aunt Nellie. You could never worry me. We're family."

"I know. I was planning to tell you as soon as I was certain."

"Why do you want to sell?"

"I'm just tired and ready to live a little before I get too old."

"Aunt Nellie, you're far from old."

Reaching over, she patted her hand affectionately. "Thanks, baby, but I'm ready to travel and see the world and I just think that maybe it's time for me to sell the store and live life to the fullest."

"You can't sell! I love that store."

"Well, what do you suggest I do, because it can't run itself?"

Brenna paused, tilted her head to the side and studied her expression. "I want to buy it."

Aunt Nellie brought the glass to her lips. "And how do you manage to run the store all the way in Dallas?"

She didn't have a clue, but right now that didn't matter. All that did was that she loved that store. "I'll find a way."

"You know this would be so much easier if you'd just come back home. Your partner can run the store in Dallas and you can run the one here."

Brenna pursed her lips. Her aunt was baiting her again and this time she was using the bookstore to do it.

"I'll figure it out. Until I do, don't sell."

"Well, you've got less than a year because on my fifty-sixth birthday I am buying myself a one-way ticket around the world."

She chuckled. "Aunt Nellie, you've never flown a day in your life."

"Humph! Who said anything about flying? I'm traveling Amtrak."

Long after her aunt called it a night, she sat out on the deck thinking about what she had said. It would be so much easier if she just moved back. Her partner was more than capable of running the store in Dallas, while she could manage the store here. But moving back wasn't even an option.

She dragged her legs up against her chest and rested her chin on her knees. She had so much to think about. But a few months would give her plenty of time to work out a plan. In the meantime all she had to do was survive the next couple of days. While at the bookstore she had gone online and booked her ticket back to

Dallas for Sunday evening. Sunday night she would be back in her own bed.

Brenna heard movement in the grass. She rose off the seat and glanced over near the bushes.

"Who's there?" she called then heard a hearty chuckle before Jabarie came around to the side of the deck.

"Very funny," she replied with a frown.

"I didn't mean to scare you," he said and moved up the stairs.

"I wasn't scared."

"Yeah, right."

Brenna leaned back in the chair and tried to ignore the masculine presence beside her. "What are you doing out here tonight?"

"I told you I was coming to see you."

A man of his word. She should have expected as much.

Jabarie moved over and took a seat on the bench beside her. "I've been thinking about you all day."

"Really."

"Yep. Thought I'd come by and convince you to take a swing with me in your aunt's hammock."

Her face flushed. He was trying to recreate the past. Quickly, she shook her head. "I don't think so."

"Don't think. Just feel."

He rose and moved down two steps before he realized she wasn't following. Swinging around, he held out his hand. "Come on, Bren."

She paused for a moment then rose from her seat and placed her hand in his. As soon as she touched him, Jabarie swung her into his arms, despite her protest, and carried her over to the other side of the yard where a hammock was hanging. As soon as he reached it, he cradled her in his arms while he slid comfortably on the ropes. "There," he said releasing his grip. "Now, isn't this nice?"

"Yes," she admitted. Brenna slid over some and turned slightly on her side so she could look him in the face. "I haven't had a chance to come out here since I've come back."

"Now you have." Jabarie closed his eyes and it gave her a chance to admire the contours of his face. The sun was low and darkness had fallen upon Sheraton Beach, but she could see enough that even if she hadn't already had his face embedded in her mind, she would have thought him handsome. Reaching up she couldn't help smoothing her finger across his thick bushy eyebrows. He stared down at her.

"I actually started having them plucked." He had such a silly smirk on his face she didn't know if he was joking or telling the truth.

"No, seriously. Can't you tell my brow is no longer connected? Bianca's been coming over once a month with the trimmers."

"Good for her," Brenna replied as the hammock swung lightly from side to side.

"She's ready to hand over the job to my woman."

Her heart stalled momentarily. "Do you have a woman?"

He drew an arm around her and pulled her close. "Yes, she's just too stubborn to admit it."

"She sounds like my kind of woman," she teased, even though deep down inside she was relieved to discover he was joking.

"She's my kind of woman, as well," he said, then lowered his lips and gave her a slow, drugging kiss. Afterwards, she rested her head on his chest. For a long time, it was silent except for the ocean raging onto the shore.

"Bren."

"Yes?"

"I love you."

She remained silent, unsure of what to say. There was no way she was going to confess she loved him as well. If she did he would never leave her alone.

"Thank you," she finally said.

"No, I should be thanking you for being the beautiful, compassionate woman that you are. I should be thanking you for giving me the privilege of being a part of your life. For allowing me to share your every breath. You are the very air I breathe. And without you in my life, I feel suffocated."

Her heart fluttered. She didn't know what to make of his confession. She just lay there with her arm draped across his chest.

Jabarie shifted his weight. "If you could have anything in the world, what would it be?"

To be your wife. Brenna was stunned by her answer and for a moment she thought she had said it out loud. That used to be what she wanted more than anything, but not anymore, or so she thought. "I'm not sure."

"Scared?"

"I'm not scared," she protested and slugged him.

He chuckled. "I think you're scared, but no problem, keep denying your feelings."

"What do you want?" she dared to ask.

"If I could have anything in the world, it would be you," he said and her eyes flew open at the feel of his hand against her cheek. His eyes were soft.

"I spent so many nights dreaming about my life with you."

"Tell me about your dreams."

He covered her hand with his then laced his fingers with hers. "In my dream I never let you go. I call you several times a day to find out how you are. I let the whole world know you're mine, then in front of the entire town I ask you to be my wife and you accept. After we're married, I make love to you so often you get pregnant right away. For nine months, I watch your body change as you carry my child. When she's born I watch her suckle your breasts and I'm amazed at how beautiful she is with your hazel eyes and caramel skin. Then I hold you both in my arms and I thank God for my family."

Jabarie lifted his head and looked down at her for the longest time, letting her see his pain and regret.

Her head was swimming and she didn't know what to say. She wanted those things so bad her stomach ached.

Jabarie kissed her fiercely. His lips crushed hers and became possessive. His arms were so tight she could hardly breathe but she didn't care, because she was holding him just as tightly.

Brenna wanted the evening to never end, to get totally lost in the moment. She wanted to stay here with him and pretend that nothing mattered beyond these stolen moments with Jabarie.

Chapter 14

Midway through the week, Brenna was in the office ordering books online with their distributor, although she was having a hard time focusing on her work. It was as if she had developed attention deficit disorder. No matter how many times she tried to focus on her orders, her brain refused to cooperate. All she could do was think about Jabarie. Since Tuesday, the roses had been rolling in so much the store was starting to look like a florist. For the last two nights Jabarie arrived at Aunt Nellie's shortly after eight to sit out on the deck together to watch the sunset. He was determined to break down her barriers but she was trying to stay strong no matter how hard it was becoming. Living in Sheraton Beach and running the bookstore was something she had always dreamed of and now she had the chance. She sighed. There was no way she could get her hopes up for something that would probably just break her heart in the end. There had to be another way.

She had finally finished the order when Sheyna came barging through the office. As soon as she saw her face, she knew it had something to do with Jace.

"I need your help," she said then flopped down in the seat across from her.

Brenna was almost afraid to ask. "What? What's wrong?"

She raised her sunglasses onto her head and Brenna couldn't miss the anger raging in Sheyna's eyes. "I have arranged a company volleyball game for this evening and we're short a player."

"And you want me to play?" she asked, toying with the edge of her desk.

"Yes."

After a long pause, Brenna shook her head. "No way."

"Why not?"

"Because I don't want to play volleyball," she responded stubbornly.

"But I've got to kick Jace's butt."

Brenna looked up sharply. Sheyna's voice had taken on a strange desperate tone. Turning on her chair, Brenna's eyes traveled to the computer screen for an e-mail that confirmed her orders. "This sounds like something personal between the two of you."

"No. It's just everything I plan, Jace tries to sabotage," Sheyna replied, clicking her tongue.

Brenna glanced over at her leggy friend. She had no

idea the way her face lit up every time she mentioned Jace's name.

"Who else is playing?" she asked suspiciously.

Sheyna looked down at her hands. "Um, Bianca, you remember Chuck from accounting, and Jabarie," she mumbled.

"Just what I thought." As much as she wanted to help her there was no way she could spend the afternoon across the net from Jabarie. He was determined to wear her down, but she wasn't falling for it. For all she knew, this was another one of his plans.

"Isn't there some other employee you could ask?"

"No," Sheyna said then leaned forward onto the desk. "Please, Brenna. You know you're the only real friend I have. Besides, can't nobody else play volleyball like you do."

She had to force back a smile. "Flattery will get you nowhere."

"Please, I'm begging you. I've got to squash Jace and I need you."

She groaned. How could she tell her no? She knew Sheyna would be disappointed if she didn't play. The idea of beating the brothers was too appealing to pass up.

"Come on, it's going to be fun."

"What time is the game?"

"Now," she said, rising from her chair. "So go get dressed and hurry."

Brenna smiled softly. "Isn't this just for fun?"

"No," Sheyna said almost too quickly. "This is pay-back time."

An hour later she found herself walking across the

beach barefoot in the sand directly behind the hotel. Jace and Jabarie were already there with several other employees ready to play the battle of the sexes.

"Hey, Brenna!"

She glanced to her right to find Bianca trotting across the sand.

"Oh, my goodness! Look at you!" She embraced Bianca in a warm hug then pulled back and assessed her from head to toe. Shaking her head, Brenna couldn't believe how much the bucktoothed teenager had changed. Bianca had transformed into a stunning woman. Her glasses were gone and no one could miss her wide walnut eyes or the dimples on either sides of her cheeks. Her ponytail had been cut into a short so-phisticated style that perfectly fit her round nutmeg-colored face. "How have you been?"

"I've seen better days. Ready to kick my brothers' butts?" she asked with a smirk.

"You better believe it." Brenna's eyes traveled over to the volleyball net. As soon as Jabarie spotted her he closed the distance between them; her mouth dropped as she watched him move toward her in shorts and no shirt. His chest glistened beneath the sun while the muscles in his thighs flexed with each step. He was an awesome athlete and looked handsome as hell. He pulled her into the circle of his arms and held her against the warmth of his skin. Lowering her eyelids, Brenna took a deep breath, drawing in the masculine scent that was so much him.

"I guess you came so I could kick your butt."

She pulled back and slugged him in the arm. "You can try."

Jabarie rubbed his arm as if trying to get rid of the pain. "What do I get if I win?" he asked with a challenge in his eyes as if he already knew the outcome. There was no way she could back down.

Brenna laughed. "How about a popsicle?"

"How about dinner tonight?" he said, his thumb caressing her cheek.

She blew out a breath and shook back her hair. "Nope. Something else."

"Why? You afraid of losing?"

"Nope."

Jabarie tilted her chin then leaned forward and kissed her cheek. "Good. Then dinner it is." He walked over and joined his team, making the wager official.

Jabarie knew the game was meant to be all in fun but with Brenna and Sheyna playing and with dinner as a high stake, the game had suddenly become quite competitive. He knew Jace, who was trying to prove something to Sheyna, had never been part of a team and not given it his total attention. He watched as Brenna hit the ball over the net and Jace sent it sailing back over to their side. The women were good, but they were better. He watched them play and found weaknesses he needed in order to win the game, which he found ironic, considering they were losing.

They could probably be winning if he was paying closer attention and not focusing on Brenna's legs. She'd always had the most gorgeous shapely legs and calves just like a dancer. You would have thought it was the first time he'd ever seen them when in fact he'd been dreaming about them wrapped around his waist for the last several nights. Watching her sent his desire into over-drive and between serves he watched her with the warm sand beneath her bare feet. And it wasn't helping that she was wearing a yellow midriff top and white shorts. As a result of playing under the hot sun, she was sweaty and her shirt clung to her like a second skin. Jabarie groaned inwardly. He wanted to run off with her, not huddle with Jace and discuss game strategy.

"Jabarie? Man, snap out of it."

He blinked and spotted Jace standing beside him, holding the ball in his hand. It was their turn to serve.

"Yeah?" he said, hoping that his older brother hadn't realized what, or in this case, who had distracted him. He even had a serious hard-on and shifted a little to hide the evidence. It was time for him to concentrate on the game.

"Are you okay?" Jace asked, his expression serious.

The girls were huddled together, but it looked like they were looking over at them and laughing instead of discussing strategy. "Yeah, I'm fine."

"Then pay attention." As far as his brother was concerned, losing wasn't even an option.

"What's the score?" he asked off-handedly.

"Three, three," he said.

"No problem. We've got this." If he wanted to win and have dinner with Brenna tonight then it was time to forget about the woman huddled with his sister and Sheyna on the other side of the net.

Jace served the ball and the game began. Brenna dived for the ball and still managed to hit it over the net. It was intense, fast, and Brenna was playing hard and her expression serious. She had no intentions of losing.

Well, we'll have to see about that. Two more serves would determine who won the game.

"Time out!" Sheyna called and walked to the center of the court and started talking too low for them to hear.

"Man, she's up to something. I just know it," he heard Jace say in a highly agitated voice.

Didn't his brother realize his mind was not at all on the game? He stood and watched as Brenna's shorts clung to her sweet curvy behind. His fingers tightened with the urge to grab on and hold one bun in each hand.

"Look at them!" Jace cried. "They're up to something."

"I'm looking." Hell, he couldn't stop looking.

"Come on, this is serious."

"I thought this was supposed to be fun and morale building for our staff?"

He glared across the net. "It was until Sheyna challenged me."

"Challenged?" His brow rose with amusement. "What kind of challenge?"

Jace took a deep breath then said, "The loser has to come to the winner's house and clean their windows wearing an apron." He looked almost too embarrassed to admit it.

Jabarie tossed his head back and laughed. "Well, then I guess we better win this," he said at last. He didn't realize how important winning was to Jace. Now they both had to win this. "Relax, we got a good shot at winning."

"Let's get this over with. Come on, girls," Jace yelled. "Are you gonna huddle all day?"

"Not on your life!" Sheyna screamed back then returned to her spot near the net.

Jace moved in near the net and watched as Brenna set up the serve. As if she knew he was watching, her eyes shifted and she stared across at him for a long intense moment before finally saying, "You ready?"

He nodded.

She served and Jace raced for the ball and knocked it back over the net and Sheyna sent it sailing back. The game had gotten personal and the tone for the next several seconds was intense. They were winning this game because losing was not an option. He had a night planned that would end with Brenna lying in his bed.

Jabarie served the ball straight to Sheyna knowing she'd send it sailing back over the net, right at Jace. He sent it back to Brenna putting the fate of the game in her hands. If they lost, she couldn't blame it on him. Brenna jumped for the ball and tapped it hard enough to send over to him. Time seemed to move in slow motion as their eyes met. In them he read a strong desire to spend the evening lying in his arms. He leaped into the air and hit the ball and sent it sailing over Sheyna's head. Brenna dove for the ball and missed it.

There was total silence before the crowd started cheering. Grinning, Jace moved over and gave him a high-five. He and Jace ducked under the net to the other side where Sheyna's arms were folded across her chest angrily.

Jace stopped right in front of her and punched her playfully in the arm. "I'll be sure to pick up some glass cleaner on my way home tonight."

"Very funny."

Jabarie gave her a sympathetic smile then moved

over to Brenna who was covered in sand and sweat. "Congratulations," she said, her voice low.

"Thank you," he replied. He tried to see if she was mad but couldn't read her. She tilted her head back to look at him. "We got lucky near the end," he said wryly.

Shaking her head, Brenna disagreed. "No, it was skill. You've always been fantastic at volleyball."

He groaned. "Don't say that too loud. I hate for my boys from college to find out I'm better at v-ball than football."

She playfully slugged him in the shoulder then chuckled. "I don't think there is anything you're not good at."

"I failed at us."

Her laughter died and she gazed up at the serious expression on his face.

"I let you go when I should have continued to fight for us. And that is one mistake I intend on fixing no matter how long it takes." His eyes were focused dead center on her mouth.

She tried to speak but he pressed a finger to her lips. He wasn't whispering, so it didn't matter who heard him. "Have dinner with me tonight."

A shiver raced through her. "That was the deal we had."

"No. I want you to have dinner with me because it's what you want, not because I won some silly bet," he said, his gaze not leaving her lips.

She stared up at him for the longest time. "I want to have dinner," she said and licked her lips. She was aware as he moved in ready to taste her, and she was more than ready to feel his hard body against hers.

He lowered his head and she tilted her head back and wrapped her arms around his waist then rose on her toes to meet him as he pressed his mouth to hers.

He surrounded her with his heat. He smelled like sweat and all man. Opening her mouth she invited him to explore. He thrust his tongue into her mouth with a skill that she appreciated. Leaning into him, she pressed her hardened nipples against his chest and felt the warmth against rock-hard flesh. Jabarie groaned deep in his throat and his hands that rested at her waist traveled down to her buttocks and held on.

A wolf whistle made her pull back. Jabarie wrapped his arms around and held her in a hug. Smiling, she turned her head then gasped. Standing at the edge of the beach was Mrs. Beaumont.

Jabarie stepped into the parlor of his parents' home to find his mother lying on a chaise lounge reading a book.

"You wanted to see me?"

A smile softened his mother's expression. "Please, come, have a seat."

His brow rose curiously as he moved over to a wing-back chair across from her and took a seat. The room was his mother's personal hiding place. It was decorated in all gold with a large picture window that looked out onto her garden.

"Nice game. I'm sure the employees really appreciated the afternoon off to have a little fun."

He nodded, although he knew that was not the reason she had asked him to come see her.

His mother reached over and poured herself a cup of tea. "Would you like some?"

Jabarie shook his head.

"Was that Nellie Gather's niece I saw playing?"

Ah, now we're getting somewhere. "Her name is Brenna and yes, that was her."

She nodded then brought the cup to her lips. "And how is she doing?"

"She's fine."

Her face softened. "I'm glad to hear that."

"Are you really?"

"Yes, I am." And for some strange reason he almost believed her.

"I've always like her independent spirit."

"You could have fooled me," he said, leaning forward, resting his elbows on top of his knees. "I remember you trying to keep us far apart."

His mother scowled. "Just because I didn't think she was right for you doesn't mean I don't admire her."

"No, you just didn't want me marrying her," he said bitterly.

She sniffed. "At the time I was just trying to protect you."

"Protect me from what?"

She smiled weakly. "A gold digger."

Jabarie pursed his lips, not at all surprised by his mother's answer. Because Brenna was Shaunda's daughter, so she expected the same of her.

Jabarie gave her a long suspicious look. "Mother, as soon as I told you she was back in town you made it clear you didn't want me seeing her again."

"I know, and your father and I had a long talk and I wanted to apologize."

"Why did you lie about the check?"

"I was trying to spare your feelings," she began between sips. "After Roger had that prenup delivered to her house and he told me about Anika being at your condo, I felt so bad I made him write her a check that I delivered to her house." Pausing she glanced across at him as if to make sure he was really listening. "Part of me expected her to take the money and leave town, yet when she did I was a little disappointed because deep down I hoped she really did love you after all."

She does love me, or at least she used to. "What I can't understand is how the two of you could set out to ruin your own child's life like that?"

She gave him a thorough once-over before saying, "We've always had your best interests at heart."

"You ruined not just my life but Brenna's, as well."

"I know and I'm sorry."

His brow raised and he shook his head. "Sorry is not going to make everything better between us."

"Do you still love her?" she asked following a long silence.

He looked her in the eyes. "With everything I am."

She took a sip and looked pleased by his answer. "Does she love you?"

Sighing heavily, he shrugged. "I don't know. She isn't as willing to give her heart to me a second time."

"Give it time."

"Mother, time is something I don't have on my side. She is leaving in a couple of days." He rose. "I better go. Brenna and I are having dinner."

She looked up at him with eyes filled with remorse. "Can you please tell her I'm sorry?"

He never had been able to stay mad at his mother for long. Leaning over, he kissed her cheek and nodded before saying, "I'll do that."

Chapter 15

Brenna made a mess of her room, pulling clothes from her closet and drawers. A lot were items that had been hanging in her closet for the last five years. Thank goodness she found something to wear because when she had agreed to come down and help her aunt with the store, bringing dress clothes was the last thing on her mind.

It was almost seven o'clock and Brenna was standing in front of a full-length mirror, turning one way and then the other before she smiled in satisfaction. She was wearing a black slip dress with the hem just above the knees, high-heeled slides and an upswept hairdo. For some reason she wanted to impress Jabarie tonight.

She heard a car pull up and stop out front. Heart racing with excitement, she glanced once more into the mirror. "You can do this," she whispered then stared at her reflection for a long intense moment.

Spending the evening with Jabarie was going to get her in a mound of trouble emotionally. What she needed to be doing was avoiding him until it was time for her to leave for Dallas. He was the last person she should be spending time with. "You shouldn't be going anywhere near him," she chastised then shook her head at her reflection. But she knew why she couldn't stay away and her racing pulse was the answer. She loved Jabarie and despite everything, she wanted to spend as much time with him as possible. She would deal with the consequences and her pain later.

The doorbell rang and she rushed to answer it and found Jabarie dressed in a beige linen suit. Her heart did a flip-flop. He looked gorgeous standing there holding another bouquet of fresh-cut roses in a cone of green tissue paper.

"Hey."

"Hey, yourself. These are for you." He handed her the bouquet.

"Wow, more roses," she said with a saucy grin. "Thank you."

His eyes twinkled amusingly. "A woman can never have too many roses."

Brenna took the flowers and brought them to her nose, inhaling the floral scent. Smiling, she looked up and found Jabarie watching her with a heated look in his eyes that sent want blazing through her body. Taking a calming breath, Brenna moved aside so that he could enter and move closer to her.

"You're beautiful," he murmured then captured her upper arm and pulled her against him.

She stared up at his heated gaze fully aware of what he was about to do, yet she didn't care. Tonight she was going to have everything she wanted, because in a couple of days the magic would be over.

Jabarie leaned down and kissed her. Temptation overtook her and she kissed him back. She might not be willing to give their relationship another chance, but she was perfectly willing to kiss him like there was no tomorrow. Leaning into the curve of his chest, she could smell his woodsy cologne, feel his body heat and she thought about how good it would feel to end the evening with him buried inside her body. Her lips parted and his tongue slid inside her mouth. She released a soft moan of delight and tasted a hunger as strong as her own, which filled her mind with all sorts of ideas. Too much more of this kiss and they weren't going to make it to dinner. With difficulty, she pulled back and looked into his eyes to see if his desire mirrored hers. Yep. His eyes were glazed and his chest heaving. With a wink, Jabarie released her.

"Let me go put these in water." She gave him a quick smile and moved inside the kitchen. Once there, she leaned against the counter and prayed for strength. Tonight she was going to need it.

Brenna reached for a crystal vase from underneath the sink and filled it with water then lowered the roses inside. It was then that she noticed her hands were shaking. "Girl, you can do it," she coaxed. All she had to do was remind herself that they were lovers spending a no-strings attached evening together. But why did that seem easier said than done?

When Brenna reentered the living room, she found Jabarie sitting on her aunt's worn couch that was covered by a multicolored afghan. He looked so out of place. *The same as you in his world*, a little voice whispered and she lowered the vase onto the coffee table. The entire time Jabarie was watching her intensely with his deep piercing eyes.

"Let me grab my purse," she said with a shaky breath then moved back to her room long enough to retrieve her purse. When she returned, Jabarie had moved over to the sliding door and was staring out back. She took a moment to take in his dominant stance and shook her head. It didn't make any sense that one man could look that good. She cleared her throat and he swung around. Jabarie grinned, but there was no mistaking the longing burning in his eyes.

"You ready to go?" she asked.

He nodded then followed her toward the door.

"Goodnight, Aunt Nellie!" she yelled loud enough for her to hear at the back of the house.

"Goodnight, sweetheart. Have a good time."

After locking the door, she moved down the stairs with Jabarie, ready for their evening to begin.

Jabarie had made reservations at Murphy's, Sheraton Beach's finest restaurant. They were escorted to a table at the far left of the room against a floor-to-ceiling window that captured a view of the ocean.

Brenna brushed up against him and whispered, "Don't look now, but people are looking our way. The gossip is about to start."

He helped Brenna into her chair then moved around

and lowered into the seat across from her. "What can they say except that I'm having dinner with the most beautiful woman in town." To prove that he could care less what others thought, he reached across the table for her hand and brought it to his lips.

Bubbling with amusement, Brenna snatched her hand back. "Quit! You're embarrassing me," she replied, and couldn't resist laughing as she glanced out the corners of her eyes. "I'm serious. I guarantee you before our dinner is over, the news of us being here together will be all over Sheraton Beach."

"In that case, let's give them something to talk about," Jabarie said then leaned over and kissed her soundly on the lips, publicly declaring before anyone who was watching, that Brenna was his, then released her.

"Would you quit it, please?"

"No, I won't," he began as he rose from his chair and moved to the one beside her. "I love you and don't care who knows it." He lowered his mouth to hers again and the instant their lips touched, she didn't have the energy to argue any further. Desire warmed her stomach and traveled to settle down low. She wanted him. It had been five days since their trip to Ocean City, but to her it suddenly felt like a lifetime.

Pulling herself together, she pushed him gently away then looked up to meet the hungry look in his eyes that sent her pulse on a tailspin. Tonight was proving to be more difficult that she had imagined.

Looking away, Brenna noticed a woman to the far right of the restaurant raising her cell phone to her ear. "Now you've done it," she said. "The gossips are already flapping their lips."

He followed the direction of her gaze across the floor to a small table and chuckled. "Now you're being paranoid. She's probably on the phone checking in with the babysitter."

Brenna giggled along with him. He was probably right. She was being ridiculous. She reached for her water and sobered quickly when she noticed Jabarie staring at her. The candle at the center of the table flickered and shone light across his face. For the longest time he didn't say anything, but neither did she. They just sat there gazing at each other.

"Did I tell you how beautiful you look tonight?" he finally said.

"No," she lied.

"You look beautiful." Jabarie reached for her hand again. "You are beautiful."

She paused, tilted her head to the side and studied his expression.

Jabarie gave her a satisfied look that was full of promise of things to come. Her heart was beating way out of control, while a hot throbbing sensation settled in her stomach. She tore her gaze from his and looked down at her hand and tried to regain her composure. There was no way she was going to let lust take over her mind. Not tonight when it was so important for her to stay in control.

To her relief, a waiter arrived. She ordered an apple martini while Jabarie ordered a glass of white wine.

Glancing to her right, Brenna noticed a familiar looking woman at a table in the back waving at her. Even though she had no idea who she was, she simply raised her hand and returned the gesture. "Who is that?" she asked behind a tight smile.

Jabarie followed the direction of her eyes and chuckled.

Her gaze returned to his. "What?"

"That's Vanessa Wayne."

"What?" she gasped, then her eyes grew large and round. "Please tell me she no longer writes the gossip column for the *Sheraton Beach News*.

"Okay," he said as he reached for his water glass. "But I would be lying."

Brenna groaned. There was no way this was happening to her.

"Look at the bright side. She'll make it clear that the two of us are still madly in love with one another."

"I don't think you left one shred of doubt about that," she remarked dryly, then they both laughed.

"I could have taken you to dinner, outside of town, but I don't have anything to hide. This way everyone knows you're the only woman I want." Leaning over he gently pressed his lips to hers again then pulled back.

Brenna wanted to correct him and make sure that he understood that what they had ended the second she boarded that plane to Dallas, but she didn't have the heart to spoil their evening.

Their drinks arrived and as soon as they were alone, Jabarie raised his glass in a salute. "May our time together be unforgettable."

She couldn't resist touching her glass to his with a faint clink.

The waiter returned with their house salads and their conversation drifted to the hotel's recent renovations and the Las Vegas construction. As the meal progressed, their conversation shifted to music and movies while they enjoyed their delicious steak and lobster dinners. By the time apple crisp and vanilla ice cream was being delivered, Brenna asked the question she'd been dying to ask all evening.

"Was your mother surprised to see me?"

Jabarie took a bite while nodding his head in amusement. "Yep, although I had already told her you were back."

"Oh," she murmured and waited for him to continue.

"She told me to tell you she was sorry," he said between chews.

Brenna practically choked on an apple. Quickly she grabbed her glass of water and took a sip then coughed.

"Are you okay?" he asked and tapped her lightly on the back.

She nodded. "I'm fine. I was just surprised by what your mother had said."

He shrugged. "I guess she's trying to change."

Brenna found that hard to believe, but decided it wasn't her place to judge.

"The evening is still early. Let's go to the Starlight Lounge so we can dance," he suggested, and she had to laugh.

"There will be no stopping the rumors about us," she said, her thumbs playing with the bowl.

"Good." He signaled for the waiter and as soon as he took care of the bill, they rose.

Happily, Brenna offered him her hand as they moved through the restaurant and out the door. They drove the short distance on Main Street to the Starlight Hotel, Sheraton Beach's oldest hotel. Jabarie placed his hand at the small of her back and escorted her across the marble lobby floor with its high ceilings and abundance of foliage complementing the area. They moved to a dimly lit lounge where a band was playing and excitement made her heart race. Jabarie led her to an empty booth in a secluded corner off the dance floor, where he ordered her another martini and a shot of cognac for himself. They then sat there for the longest time with his arm around her, listening to music and enjoying their drinks.

When he asked her to dance, she went to the dance floor and into his arms, letting go of her fears about the future and simply enjoying the moment.

Slow dancing to old school music added more fuel to the fire. Holding her close, Jabarie's hands moved gently down to the small of her back. "It's like we've been doing this forever," she said feeling herself getting caught up in the moment.

"I know," he said. "And now that I have you in my arms I have no intentions of letting you go."

"This feels really nice," she admitted, gazing up into his thickly lashed eyes.

His eyes moved to her mouth as he whispered, "It's only the beginning."

She opened her mouth to remind him that her stay was only temporary, but before she could get the words out, he seared her lips with a steamy hot kiss. She was lost and she gave as good as she got. Who was watching was the last thing on her mind. When Jabarie finally pulled back, his gaze roamed over her features. She was speechless.

His breath brushed her nose, causing her to shiver. "Brenna," he murmured, "I want you naked in my arms."

She gasped and gazed up at his intense eyes. Before

she could find the words, the music changed to a fast number. She stepped back and continued to dance, but after two more numbers, he caught her hand.

"I'm ready to go."

"Okay," Brenna replied and he took her arm and led her outside into Delaware's breezy night air.

As soon as they were in the car, they rode in silence for a few minutes. Jabarie's hand rested on her knee and her leg trembled. Her thoughts were a jumbled mess and somehow she had to get them under control. Brenna shifted on the seat and stared out the window. When he made a right at the next corner instead of a left, she glanced over to him and asked, "Where are we going?"

"To my place," he answered as he adjusted the rear-view mirror.

Brenna was certain, Jabarie's condo gave his mother nightmares. Except for the piles of paper all over the place, the three-bedroom, two-bath, beach-front property still looked the same as it did when she'd left Sheraton Beach. Clean white walls. Plush taupe colored carpet and almost no furniture.

"I see you're still bringing your work home," she said dryly as she lowered onto the couch.

"Not much has changed."

Her eyes traveled around the partially furnished room "I see. Although by now I would have thought that this place would have looked a little more, uh, …lived in."

Jabarie playfully winced as he removed a stack of papers from the glass-top coffee table and carried them over onto the dining room table. "You forget, I never intended to be in this place this long."

He was right. Two weeks before their wedding, he had surprised her by putting a deposit down on a small beachfront property not too far away that was supposed to have been their first home together.

"Whatever happened with that house?" she asked as he moved onto the brown leather couch beside her.

Jabarie reached for a remote control and pointed it toward the stereo before answering. The sounds of John Legend flowed through the room. "One of my dad's partners bought it as a tax write-off." He looked at her and shrugged. "I didn't want it if I couldn't have you. It hurt too much."

Brenna knew all about hurt. She still ached in a lot of places including her heart, but this would probably be their last night together and there was no way she could deny herself.

The thought stabbed at her heart. She was going to miss him like crazy. But it didn't make sense for her to think about what if things could be different and if maybe in time they could find a way again to be together. What they had was a closed chapter in their lives. The past two weeks had helped her find the closure she had so desperately needed.

Okay, so maybe she hadn't found closure yet, but now that she knew what had really happened, it had soothed her heart in a way that she could now quit wondering what she had done that was so wrong. The truth was she hadn't done anything except believe that her fiancé had fallen into the arms of another woman when in fact the only woman he had ever loved was her.

And he still loves you.

Oh, God, she was in trouble.

There was no way they could start over again. Love hurt too much and there was no way she was going to be able to endure that type of pain a second time. Her feelings for him were unacceptable. Being together was totally impossible.

"Did you hear what I said?" he asked, breaking into her thoughts.

"What?"

Jabarie grinned. "I said thanks for spending the evening with me. I hope you realize that even though you are still intent on leaving, I'm not giving up until I have you in my life, permanently."

She released a sigh at that thought. They needed to talk because the last thing she needed was another misunderstanding. "Jabarie, I—"

Cutting her off, Jabarie rose, scooped her into his arms and carried her into his room. Once there, he lowered her feet to the floor and she looked up at him. He smiled then took her face in his hands and pressed his lips to hers. The kiss was so different from the others, so incredibly tender, that she ached inside, knowing that this would all be over soon. Once she returned to Dallas she would be fine, she tried to convince herself. Tonight, she'd enjoy every second with Jabarie. Every kiss. Every touch.

Breaking the kiss, she reached for her dress and pulled it over her head. She stood before him in a black thong and matching bra, offering herself to him…one last time. Impossible. Once would never be enough. Her shoulders dropped as she realized it didn't matter. Somehow she would have to find a way to move on.

"You look so sad. What's on your mind?" he asked, cupping her chin so she had to look at him.

"Nothing, only you," she said then reached for his belt buckle.

His expression told her he didn't believe her, but he didn't press the issue either. Instead he drew her closer so her breasts were pressed against his chest. Jabarie ran his palms down her back and rested them at the swell of her backside. He was so familiar with her and she with him that it scared her.

It wasn't going to be easy parting tomorrow. The next couple of weeks would probably be ten times lonelier than the last time she had left him. Nevertheless, it was the way it had to be.

Pushing tomorrow aside, she reached up and unfastened the buttons of his shirt and slid it open, grazing his nipples with her fingertips. He hissed on contact at the same time she felt him jerk behind the zipper of his pants.

She smiled. "I think someone is waking up."

Chuckling, Jabarie pulled the pins from her bun and tangled his fingers in her hair. "Sweetheart, he's always awake where you're concerned."

"Man, I like the sound of that," she purred as her hand slid down his chest and smoothed over the hard ridges of his abdomen. With her index finger, she skimmed over the narrow trail of hair leading inside his pants before moving lower over the erection that strained against the fly of his pants.

Brenna gave him a sensual smile while she stroked his full, hard length.

"Brenna," he whispered hoarsely as his hand covered hers. "Don't, unless you want this to end sooner than intended."

No, that wasn't what she wanted at all. She leaned into him, pressing her body to his while her mouth brushed his nipple. She traced it with her tongue until it became pebble hard then playfully nipped at it. "Do you ever fantasize about me, Jabarie?" she whispered.

Jabarie hissed between his clenched teeth. "All the time, baby." Dropping his head, he gazed down at her and she swallowed. The strained look in his eyes emphasized his words. Jabarie was barely holding on. Suddenly, she was anxious to see how far she could push his level of control.

Reaching down, she cupped him again and he pulsed beneath her hand. "Jabarie…" she said in a soft seductive tone.

"Bren, you're playing with fire."

She knew that but right now common sense had no place in this room. She already knew she'd have to deal with the ramifications of her actions later. Tonight was about finding sexual satisfaction. She'd deal with the emotional stuff later. Right now, all she could think about was getting him worked up for the best sex ever.

It's my turn to share one of my fantasies," she cooed then pressed her breasts against his chest.

"I'm listening." Jabarie's large hand took her face and held it gently, while his thumb skimmed her jaw line. Drawing her closer, he lowered his head to hers. His mouth captured hers, demanding this time. Things were about to get out of control.

When his lips left hers, he buried his face at the base of her neck and breathed a kiss there. "Stand back so I can see you," he whispered on a sharp breath.

She did as he asked and stood back and watched his

smoldering gaze as his eyes raked over her lacy thong panties. She hadn't forgotten his love for seeing her in sexy lingerie.

"You are so beautiful."

"I'm glad you noticed." Moving forward, Brenna pushed him down on the bed then with a wanton smile, straddled him. She slid her finger along his stomach muscles. Jabarie growled deep in his throat and squirmed uncomfortably beneath her.

"Can I tell you my fantasy now?" she asked as she lowered her breasts to his chest and wrapped her arms around his neck.

His lips grazed her shoulder. "Baby, I'm all ears."

Brenna rocked her hips against his erection as she whispered near his ear.

"We're here in your condo. Vanilla-scented candles are lit and surrounding us. I'm lying across your bed covered in red rose petals. You're kissing me from head to toe until I am whimpering and begging for you to be inside of me."

Jabarie was growing impatient. His hands were moving along her back, down over her butt where he cupped her round cheeks and squeezed.

"What happens next, baby?" he asked in a tight voice.

"What you always do to me. Your tongue travels and finds my most sensitive spot and you make me so hot that I beg you to make love to me."

He lifted his hands to her shoulders and his fingers slid underneath the straps of her bra. "I like the sound of that," he said while he eased the straps downward. Without the support of the thin material, the cups collapsed under the weight of her breasts, completely exposing her to Jabarie. Desire flashed in his deep dark eyes before he tilted his head and caught a nipple between his teeth.

Brenna gasped and stilled for the briefest moment as pleasure raced from her nipple and coursed through the rest of her body.

Jabarie gave her a split second to react to his contact before his hands cupped her breasts and kneaded them gently. His tongue flicked the other nipple and it puckered to an almost painful point before he drew it into his mouth and sucked hard.

"Yes!" she moaned. Her fingers gripped his hard biceps, her nails pressing into his flesh. She looked down at him as he laved and sucked her breasts, giving equal attention to each one while she fought for a full breath.

Quickly losing control, Brenna released his arms and cupped his head, then arched toward his mouth. She didn't want him to stop. She wanted him to continue. Only he could make her feel this good. His tongue and teeth toyed and teased her sensitive flesh. One hand left her breast and his fingers grazed the damp crotch of her panties.

Brenna started beneath his touch as heat radiated through her.

"Touch me, Jabarie," she whispered against his cheek.

He touched her at the juncture of her thighs with his fingertips. The thin wisp of lace covering her there provided little barrier to the heat he caused. She whimpered her pleasure.

"Baby" he whispered against her throat. "You're so wet."

That she was. She was also hot and restless. Her insides pulsed. "Jabarie," she urged, desperately needing him to touch her. "Please."

"I remember that you like to be on top."

She moaned. "You know exactly how I like it, but take me any way you want me."

Reclaiming her lips, he crushed her to him. His lips and tongue tangled with hers. He deepened their kiss as his fingers pushed aside the material between her legs and brushed over the wet flesh.

Brenna broke the kiss and gasped. Her body became alive with each intimate touch. Her sensitized nipples grazed the hairs on his chest while she fought for a full, steady breath.

Jabarie stroked her folds, causing her to moan in his ear. She rose up a bit off his lap, giving him better access. He found her nub and rubbed it slowly, intensifying the throbbing deep inside her. Brenna closed her eyes and his skillful fingers stroked her until she screamed. When she didn't think she could last a second longer, his fingers slid inside her, stroking her, driving her mad at the sweet intrusion. Her nipples were hard and begged for attention. As if he could read her mind, his mouth latched on while his fingers pumped in and out of her wetness in quick, determined strokes.

The pressure inside her was growing and she was conscious of nothing but what he was doing to her. But she wanted more than this. She wanted all of him.

"I want you inside of me, now," she whispered between breaths.

He released her and she unzipped his pants. He lifted

his hips long enough for her to slide his pants down to his feet and onto the floor. His briefs followed. She then straddled him again and slid her fingers down his stomach and he shivered under her touch. As soon as she gripped him, he covered her hand with his and stilled her.

"Wait, please," he said barely above a groan. "Hand me my wallet."

Brenna retrieved his pants and removed his wallet from the back pocket and handed it to him. Jabarie quickly removed a condom. As soon as he was protected, he eased her over his length. He groaned while she rocked her hips.

She slowly drew him into her body while his thumbs teased her nipples. She took him in farther then eased back toward the tip. She repeated this action, over and over, until he was shifting restlessly beneath her.

"Yes, that's it!" he cried.

Eyes closed, she smiled. She had power over his body and knowing that he was moaning and hard because of what she was doing heightened her arousal. Finally, she drew him completely inside her. She rode him and when she knew they were both close, she increased the tempo, riding him hard and fast. His hands grabbed at her hips and he pressed her down onto him as he arched and thrust himself deeper inside her.

"I'm going to come, baby," he said on a harsh breath.

"Yes, Jabarie. Now!"

She rubbed her hard nipples against his chest while his hands slid around and cupped her buttocks. With their eyes locked, he pushed himself into her and she felt his body shake and convulse from his powerful orgasm.

Seconds later, she cried out his name and sucked in a breath while one wave of ecstasy after another rocked her body. She squeezed her inner muscles tightly around him, wanting desperately to prolong the tremors for as long as possible. She was breathless. Her heart was thundering in her chest and she felt a shiver rock her insides as her muscles continued to contract around him. The moment the tremors stopped and her breathing returned to normal, Brenna rolled over and curled up beside him.

As Brenna drifted off to sleep, Jabarie held her snugly in his arms and listened to her steady breathing that feathered against his chest. Holding her felt warm and comforting, just the way it had always been. Only this time it was different. Tonight he held her almost afraid to go to sleep. Afraid that when he woke up he'd discover the last two weeks had been nothing more than a dream.

Leaning forward he pressed a gentle kiss to her forehead. When Brenna stirred in his arms and his name slipped from between her lips, he knew for a fact he wasn't dreaming. Brenna was really here in his bed.

He pulled her closer. "Shh, I'm right here baby, and I'm not going anywhere."

Chapter 16

Brenna woke to the smell of coffee and bacon. Sitting up straight in the bed, she sniffed again just in case her brain was playing tricks on her, and sure enough someone was in the kitchen cooking breakfast. One thing she knew for sure, that person wasn't Jabarie. That man didn't know a pot from a frying pan.

She stretched luxuriously and rolled over in the bed, opening her eyes. Sunlight poured in through the windows, bathing everything in the room. Outside, the ocean was blue and the day bright and clear. She sighed as her mind quickly recounted what had gone on the night before. They'd made love till dawn. Each time they thought themselves spent, they began to explore each other some more and ended up making love again.

Hearing a timer going off in the kitchen, curiosity

got the better of her and she sat up on the bed. There was no way Jabarie was making breakfast.

"This I've gotta see."

She climbed out of the bed and pulled on one of his T-shirts which was thrown over a chair in the corner. After sliding her feet into a pair of his slippers, she opened the door to the room and headed toward the kitchen. As she walked down the hall, she felt a wave of nerves hit her. Last night they held nothing back sexually, but now they had to face each other, as if it was no big deal, and prepare themselves to let each other go their own separate way.

Brenna stepped into the kitchen. When she finally glanced up, she stopped dead in her tracks.

Jabarie was standing in front of the stove. He was completely naked, apart from a cook's apron. The apron cord hung around his neck and high on his waist, leaving his muscular back and his gorgeous butt on full display. With a hand at her hip, she focused on his nice chocolate behind. She always wondered what all the hype was about a man's butt. Now she understood. Tight. Muscular. Perfect to fit both palms of her hands. The view was so spectacular and amusing that she wished she had a camera handy. She didn't know a woman around who wouldn't be delighted to find a sight like that standing in her kitchen.

"This is a surprise."

Jabarie swung around and the irresistible smile on his face made her heart skip a beat. "Good morning, sleepyhead." He carried eggs over to the table and lowered them onto a plate. "I was getting ready to come up and wake you."

She didn't hear a word he said. Her eyes were focused on the table he had beautifully decorated with a lace tablecloth, napkins, and another beautiful rose bouquet. "The table is beautiful," she began while moving farther into the room. "I…" Her voice began to trail off since she didn't have the foggiest idea what she had been planning to ask him. All she knew was that she was completely touched by his kindness. Tears burned the backs of her eyes that she refused to let go of. Why did she have to love this man so much?

"What's wrong?" he asked and before she could answer, he pulled her into his arms for a slow lingering kiss. The pulse point in the pit of her belly leapt into life. She would have to try to stay focused on rational behaviors at least for some of the time, or she'd start acting like a lovesick teenager every time he touched her. She slipped out of his arms and pretended to be more interested in what he was cooking. She was hungry and her stomach was growling, but still she had to drag her gaze away from him to look at the food.

"I'm starved."

"Good. I've cooked plenty," he answered.

Smiling, she looked down at the delicious meal he'd managed to create. Belgian waffles. Crispy bacon. Fluffy cheese eggs. Fresh fruit. Coffee and orange juice. "Wow!" was all she could say.

"All that hot sex works up quite an appetite," he added with a wink.

She blushed, sat down, and he put a plate down in front of her. She took a mouthful of the omelet and it melted in her mouth.

"When did you learn how to cook like this?" she

asked when he put a plate of toast and a coffee pot on the table and then joined her, settling into the chair opposite her.

He chewed on a piece of bacon while he spoke. "A couple of years ago I discovered that I either learn how to cook or spend the rest of my life eating take-out. I started spending time at the manor in the kitchen learning how to make several simple dishes, including breakfast."

"I would have loved to have seen that," she teased.

Chuckling, Jabarie filled each of their mugs with coffee. "You should have seen my mother's face. I thought she was going to pass out."

"Why? She doesn't believe a man should be in the kitchen?"

"No, when I asked her to come and watch me whip up breakfast I think it was the first time she'd stepped foot in a kitchen in over thirty years," he said with a laugh. Brenna tossed her head back and joined in.

"Next time I'll have to make breakfast for you," she said, and as soon as the words slipped from her lips, she realized she was talking about a future that would never be.

Jabarie looked stunned then pleased by the offer. "Sounds great," he responded. "Speaking of the future…"

"Let's not," Brenna interrupted. She didn't want to ruin what they had now. "Surely we can find something better to do than talk."

For a moment she thought he was going to begin a discussion anyway, but then he seemed to reconsider.

"What else do you have in mind?" he asked, pushing the plate aside.

His intense stare made her feel restless, and she wiggled on her seat, and then set down her knife and fork. She picked up her coffee cup to distract herself then glanced out the window, away from his sexy expression. Leaving him was becoming harder by the second, but talking about them was only going to make matters worse.

"So what else can you cook?" she finally asked, finding food a safe subject.

While they finished eating, Jabarie told her how he had invited his family to his condo Memorial Day weekend for an afternoon barbecue. He wowed the family with his slow-smoked ribs and homemade potato salad.

Brenna brought her orange juice to her lips. "Maybe you should have been a chef?"

"Shh, don't say that too loud. My father might be listening," he chuckled.

After breakfast, Jabarie refused to let her help with the dishes and sent her back to the room to shower and get dressed. He waited until she was down the hall before the smile slipped from his lips.

Brenna was the most stubborn woman he knew. Why couldn't she just admit that she loved him and come back to him?

He reached for their plates and while he rinsed them under the water, he glanced around the room and concluded he was tired of living alone. He had been for a long time but never found a woman he wanted to share his life with except Brenna. He missed spending time quietly on the couch or making love in his bed.

He put another plate in the dishwasher and reminisced over breakfast. The meal had turned out nice, if he said so himself, but the conversation had been uncomfortable and a little stifled for his taste. Brenna didn't want to talk anymore about them, but whether she liked it or not, they needed to talk. He needed to find a way to get her to stay not just as his lover but as his wife.

As soon as he had the dishwasher loaded, he returned to the bedroom. Not finding her, he stepped into the bathroom and she slowly rose from the tub. His mouth went dry. The strands of her hair curled around her breasts, making the chocolate circles of her nipples even more pronounced and beautiful. Water droplets rolled down her skin that he longed to taste. He wanted to lick her dry, then caress her until she was dripping wet again.

She smiled as if she could read his mind. "Want to join me?"

He didn't say a word, just removed his apron as fast as he could then stepped into the water.

As soon as he was seated, Brenna rose on her knees. "I'll wash you," she offered then reached for a towel and straddled his body. As she rubbed the terry cloth across his chin, he reached out and caressed her breasts.

"You're being a bad boy," she groaned. "Let me finish washing you."

"I can't help myself when I'm around you." While her hands continued to move, spending time caressing his nipples, then moving down his stomach, he ran his hand along her back, loving every sensual curve. "I don't think there is one thing about your body I don't love."

"Flattery will get you everywhere," she purred then adjusted her position and began to stroke her fingers along his legs. He stiffened when her fingers closed around his length.

"Now you're being a bad girl," he said with effort.

"Haven't you heard? Naughty is my middle name," she replied as she reached her hand outside the tub and returned with a foil package in her hand.

Jabarie chuckled. "You planned this, didn't you?"

Amusement flickered in the eyes that met his. "Of course. I was just waiting to see how long it took for you to join me." She ripped open the package and with their eyes locked, she slid the condom over his length.

"If I had known you were planning this I could have cleaned the kitchen later."

She rose up and slowly lowered over his length. Jabarie longed to surge all the way inside but held back. She flexed her inner muscles around him, squeezing him until she elicited a frustrated groan from between his teeth.

"You okay?" she asked.

"Hell, yes!" he ground out as she let him slip into her another few, precious inches.

She paused and closed her eyes. Needing to be inside her, Jabarie tilted his hips, sliding even farther inside. Her gasp was a reward, as was the way she latched her legs around his waist.

"You're cheating," she said, voice trembling.

"Haven't you heard…all's fair in love and war," he said then reached around and cupped her rear end. The motion slid her forward and he filled her completely.

"Oh!" Brenna gasped.

He groaned then dipped his head to lap her nipple. Arching her back, she ground against him. Jabarie responded by thrusting upward. The water allowed him leverage and a range of motion he didn't normally have. With his hands firmly at her hips, he guided her up and down as he pressed his mouth to hers.

Brenna controlled the rhythm while he plunged his tongue inside her mouth. He began with slow gentle strokes, but as the excitement grew, his tongue's movements became more erratic. As their desire increased and her breath became labored, he pulled back from the kiss and took her fast and hard, causing the water to slosh around them.

With each stroke, he watched her, loving every whimper, every moan. Loved that she was bringing everything she had to the table in order to bring him pleasure, as well.

He cradled her chin with one hand and tilted her face. Brenna opened her eyes and looked into his. Searching her face, he slowed his rhythm, gentled his pace. Her eyes clouded with tears, but he knew they weren't tears of pain. As much as Brenna wanted to deny it, he had reached her in that most emotional place, the center of her heart.

With a smile Jabarie slid a hand between their wet bodies and found her nub. With a sweep of his finger and thumb, he drove her over the edge. Her legs latched around his waist like a vice and her back arched, lifting her up and against him as she cried out her pleasure and her release.

Jabarie tried to hold back, wanting more than anything to maintain control until she came again and again, but the look of pure pleasure and the joyful tears that cascaded down her cheeks did him in. He held on firmly to her hips and poured himself into her.

As they sat there, locked together for what seemed like a blissful eternity, she looked down into his eyes. Leaning forward, he pressed his lips to her forehead, cheek and lips.

"That was amazing," she whispered as her arms came around his waist and she rested her head against his chest.

Jabarie looked down at her, so comfortable leaning against him, and slowly let his arms come around her waist. It was amazing. And so was this woman.

"I love you," he said as naturally as saying good morning. He loved this woman and he wasn't ashamed to admit it.

Brenna was so quiet, he wondered if she had heard him when she suddenly raised her head to look at him. Tears and rage burned from her eyes. "Why didn't you just ask me?"

He gave her a puzzled look. "Baby, what are you talking about?"

Answering a question with a question appeared to piss her off. "Why didn't you come after me?" she asked, nostrils flaring.

Jabarie gently stroked her arm as he remembered his mother telling him how Brenna had come to the house asking for money, gloating about finally having access to the Beaumont fortune. It had angered him, although, even then he should have known that something wasn't right about what she said. He should have believed in their love.

"Why didn't you come after me?" she repeated.

He had asked himself that same question over and over, time and time again. "I don't know," he finally admitted.

Pushing away from his chest, Brenna rose from the

tub and stepped out onto the mosaic tiled floor. "You know what hurts the most, is that you believed your mother over me. That you didn't love me enough to know I would never squeeze her for money."

Jabarie dragged his leg to his chest and watched as she toweled off her body. "I did love you. I still do. I just…" He wasn't sure what to say.

Her hazel eyes clawed him like talons. "You couldn't have loved me because if you had, you would have trusted me, and that's what hurts."

There was along pregnant silence. "I was a fool…a damn fool."

"Yes. You were." Her words cut him like a razor. He felt it, and knew from the pain on her face she felt it, too. What was it going to take to make this right?

Wrapped in a towel, she stormed into the bedroom. Jabarie hurried out of the tub, reached for a towel and followed. He walked into the room just as she was slipping her dress over her head. "Do you still love me?" he asked while securing the towel around his waist.

Brenna's hand stalled. How could she answer that question, not that it really mattered anymore because it was too late for them. "It doesn't matter because it can never be the same."

His eyes narrowed. "You didn't answer my question."

"And I'm not going to."

Jabarie's lips curled upward. "You don't have to say it. I know you still love me." He closed the distance and pulled her to him then gave her a kiss that was both urgent and exploratory. Easing back, he stared down at her. "Do you know how much I still love you?" he asked between breaths.

"No."

"I never stopped," he whispered then took her mouth again.

She released a soft moan. "It's too late."

"It's never too late," he crooned as he ran kisses up along her cheek and neck.

Brenna pressed a hand against his chest and tried to hold on to her resistance. "We can never go back. That part of my life is over. I have changed."

"So have I."

Somehow, she had to find a way to get through to him. "I'm serious. My life doesn't include you."

Jabarie pulled her tightly into his arms and whispered near her ear. "It can if you let it."

She just wasn't ready to risk her heart again. Brenna pushed against him. "I don't want to."

"Now we're getting somewhere." He stared back at her, challenging her with his eyes. "Why not?"

"Because I've moved on."

He cupped her chin, leaving her no choice but to look at him. "Then tell me you don't love me and I'll leave you alone."

"I can't do that. I love you," she admitted. "Probably always will, but love just isn't enough. It wasn't enough to keep us together and it isn't enough to bring us back."

"I think it's a beautiful start," he replied and she felt his lips touch her like a whisper. "Will you have dinner with me tomorrow?"

Damn, his lips were more persuasive than she cared to admit. "Jabarie, I—"

"I know you're leaving on Sunday and even though

I'm not happy about it, I respect your decision. However, until you leave I want to spend every second I can with you."

"Then what happens?"

He paused then said, "I'll let you decide."

"I'm not changing my mind," she said stubbornly. "I'm still leaving after the parade. When I leave, I'm also closing this chapter of my life."

"Okay," he agreed. "If that's what you want then I won't try to stop you. Now, how about dinner?"

She didn't know what to say because a part of her didn't believe he was accepting defeat that easy. But, in the meantime what was wrong with her also spending every second possible with him? "Okay, I'll have dinner with you."

Chapter 17

The next afternoon, Brenna and Aunt Nellie worked side by side marking down books for the big sidewalk sale on Sunday. She could hardly focus and several times marked down the same book twice.

"Dear, are you okay?" she heard her aunt ask.

Blinking, she focused on her concerned face then nodded and moved to the other side of the store. She hated lying to her aunt, but the truth was too much like putting an ad out in the *Sheraton Beach News*.

Picking up a children's book, she reached for a felt marker and neatly wrote the reduced price on the cover. All day she had barely been able to work. But then how could she with Jabarie constantly running through her mind? Like a merry-go-round, again and again, round and round the last two weeks had been playing through her mind. Every touch, every kiss, every blissful shudder. She was in way over her head and she wasn't sure how she was going to survive losing him a second time. The only consolation was that this time she had made all the rules and it was she who was ending the relationship. Only leaving was going to be harder the second time around.

Shaking her head, she forced her mind back to the present and focused on labeling the last of the books. Sunday's sidewalk sale would also include a parade down Main Street. It was in honor of the first day of summer.

The bell rang over the door and she looked up to see Jabarie walking into the store. Her pulse raced and she tried to bite back a smile. He winked then moved over to where her Aunt Nellie was putting books on the shelves and exchanged a few words with her before making his way over to where she was standing.

As he drew closer with each step, she felt as if the air had been sucked from her lungs. He was wearing navy blue slacks and a white button-down shirt, and his tie hung loose around his neck.

"Hey, sexy."

"Hey, what—"

Before she could get her words out he pulled her against him and met her lips in a searing, toe-curling kiss. "I came to steal you away for lunch."

The kiss had her mind swirling. "But we're having dinner tonight."

Staring down at her, Jabarie lightly stroked her back. "I know, and I want lunch and dinner and breakfast in the morning if you'll let me."

"We're busy."

"Aunt Nellie said it was okay."

Before she could object, he grabbed her hand and led her out the store and down to the sandwich shop on the next block.

They moved to a booth and took a seat and it wasn't long before a waiter came and took their order. Brenna leaned over staring down at the menu. Jabarie noticed the waiter staring down at her breasts that were threatening to spill out of her shirt.

"Are you going to take my order?" he snapped.

Startled, the young boy swung around to meet his angry eyes. "Yes, sir. What would you like to eat?"

"We'll each have the special and two iced teas."

"Yes, sir."

"You can leave now."

"Yes, sir."

Brenna opened her mouth to scold him for being rude but she waited until the young man had scurried off to the kitchen to place their orders.

"Did you have to be so rude?" she hissed.

"He was looking down your shirt."

"Only way you would know that is if you were trying to look yourself."

"Why don't you try wearing more clothes?"

"What's wrong with what I got on?" she said defensively.

"It's not enough."

"I never remember hearing you complain before."

That's because he loved her body, every luscious curve. "Things were different then."

Her arched brow rose. "How were they different?"

"You were my fiancée then. Everyone in this town knew you belonged to me."

"And now they know that is no longer the case."

"I don't want to fight with you."

"Then don't," she challenged.

Reaching across the table, Jabarie placed a hand on hers, tightening his hold. She closed her eyes and shook her head. When she opened them she gave him a direct stare. He eased his grip but did not release her hand.

"You know you're gorgeous when you're angry."

"I'm not sleeping with you tonight."

"Can't I give you a compliment without you thinking I am insinuating something else?" he asked innocently.

"Thank you, Jabarie."

His lips curled upward. "You're welcome."

"But I'm still not sleeping with you."

Tossing his head back he chuckled openly. She was definitely a piece of work. Being around her conjured up feelings and emotions he hadn't felt in years. That's why he was doing everything in his power to show her this was where she belonged.

"You planning to do any shopping on Sunday?"

"If I can get away from the store long enough."

"We have a lot of visitors in town." During Sunday's parade and sidewalk sale, people would litter the streets. There would be snow cones, cotton candy and some of the biggest sales of the year.

He watched as she nibbled nervously on her bottom lip and before he realized what he was doing, Jabarie raised out of the chair, leaned across the table and pressed his lips to hers. As always, their union was explosive, powerful and he wanted more. Reluctantly, he pulled back and returned to his seat and stared across at her moist parted lips, tempted to grab her in his arms and carry her home with him. She was gorgeous, and having her sitting there staring at him innocently had him hard as a rock.

"What was that for?" she asked.

"Just because," he whispered then shifted on the seat as their waiter returned with their iced teas. This time, Jabarie was pleased to see his eyes didn't even stray over in Brenna's direction.

That night she dressed with care. Jabarie was picking her up and they were going to catch a movie and have dinner. She put on a pair of dressy red gauchos, a black halter top and low-heel black sandals. Her hair, she pulled up in a ponytail.

"How about we go ride the Ferris wheel instead?" he said as soon as she opened the door.

Her lips curled with excitement. She hadn't ridden the Ferris wheel in years. "Sounds like fun."

He drove over to the amusement park that was at the edge of the town, back off near the ocean. He climbed out, took her hand, and guided her through the park. The next hour was amazing. They played games and Jabarie won her a stuffed bear. Eating funnel cake, they moved over to the Ferris wheel line and waited their turn. By the time they tossed the plate in the trash, they were instructed to take the next seat. As soon as the bar was safely locked against their waists, the ride began to move.

She giggled.

"Having fun?"

"Yes." Too much fun. In fact she was forgetting her vow not to get too close. She was having so much fun, it would be so nice if she had the courage to take a chance and let herself go back to the way things were, but it was impossible to go backwards. All she could do was move forward with her life. She was too afraid to risk her heart again no matter how badly she wanted to.

"You remember that time we rode this thing and we got trapped at the top?"

How could she forget? It was the first time he had ever kissed her. Staring over at him she saw a look in his eyes that said he planned to kiss her again. Reaching over he cupped her chin and tilted her head back slightly then leaned forward. The kiss sent the pit of her stomach into a wild swirl. She felt like she was flying!

Each kiss. Each touch threatened to weaken her resistance but she had to stay strong and guard her heart. By doing so she could enjoy every second they had left.

After their ride, Jabarie took her back to his condo and carried her to his room where he undressed her and they made slow, passionate love. Hours later, she lay curled in his arms.

Brenna couldn't catch her breath. She felt as if the air had escaped her lungs and had yet to return. Jabarie cradled her close and she clung to him, not wanting this moment to end. But she knew what they had could never last. Or could it?

Jabarie was the perfect man for her and with him she felt everything in her world was so much brighter and though she'd never admit it, she'd spent the last five years hiding from her feelings because she didn't want to love him anymore. She wanted the hurt to go away.

But Jabarie had a way of making her feel things even when she didn't want to. Which was the reason why she'd never wanted to come back to Sheraton Beach. Why she didn't want to start something that she had no intentions of finishing. And why she wasn't ready to take an even bigger risk trusting him again with her heart.

Saturday morning arrived and she felt as if she had just fallen asleep when she felt Jabarie's warm, wet kisses on her face.

"Get up, sleepyhead. You need to get ready for work."

"Not yet," she purred. "Make love to me."

As much as he'd love to spend time twisting in the sheets with her, he needed to settle some things before they went any further. He needed to know if she was going to break his heart again or help him find the land of happiness he'd stopped believing in a long time ago. Before he made love to her again, he needed to try one more time.

Cupping her face with both hands, he lowered his mouth and kissed her. "I want to ask you something."

"What? You want to try something new?" she asked then wagged her eyebrows suggestively. He loved the way her hazel eyes twinkled when she teased him.

"Maybe later."

Brenna trailed kisses down his chest and shoulder and his eyes fluttered closed. He loved her and just couldn't get enough of her.

"Brenna, you're leaving tomorrow and we need to talk," he said and just as he suspected, she shifted away.

"I thought we had come to an understanding."

"The only one who understands is you."

She sighed then rolled over and sat up in the bed with a frustrated look. "Okay, go ahead and talk."

"I don't want you to leave. I want you to be my wife and live with me here."

He expected her to yell and get angry; instead her face became sad and distant. "Why can't you just leave well enough alone? Things were going so well between us."

"Because I love you. I don't understand why it is so hard for you to accept that I want to spend the rest of my life with you." He cursed under his breath then moved abruptly from the bed and reached for his shorts.

"And a part of me will always love you, too, but I'm not ready to go down that same road again," she said as she reached for his shirt on the floor and slipped it on.

"It doesn't have to be today. We can take things as slow as you want. All I need to know is that you're willing to try." He moved around the bed and sank down next to her.

"I can't," she said, facing him.

"You can't or you won't?"

She hesitated. "I won't."

Reaching over he took her hands in his. "Baby, I know you're scared, well so am I, but I'm willing to do whatever it takes for it to work between us this time."

"Can you guarantee me that we'll stay together forever?" she asked and he noticed her bottom lip tremble.

"Brenna, you are my soul mate. Nothing is guaranteed, but I promise you I'll try to do everything I possibly can to see that we have a wonderful life together."

"That's not good enough," she snapped before he

noticed the sheen of tears glistening in her eyes. "I'm not willing to risk my heart again and lose. Love hurts too much. My mother turned her back on me when I needed her most and so did you. I can't go through that again."

"What's it going to take for you to understand how much I love you?"

"If you really love me Jabarie, then, please, let me go." She climbed out of bed, gathered her clothes and hurried off into the bathroom. As soon as the door was closed, she lowered onto the floor and allowed the tears to fall freely. Deep inside, she was dying. She was so tempted to run back into the room and throw herself into his arms and pledge to spend the rest of her life with Jabarie. With him, her world was more vivid and alive and once she left she would return to her dull, restless existence. But at this point in her life, she truly believed that happiness just wasn't meant for her.

Rising from the floor, she moved over to the shower and immediately stepped under the water. She would never forget the look of hurt and pain on Jabarie's face. But hopefully in time he would find someone else. The thought of him being with someone else made her stomach ache but there was no way she could face her fear of being hurt again. She was a prisoner in her own soul.

Large sobs raked her body and she cried freely. Everyday was a game of tug-of-war for her. A struggle not to remember, while also trying not to forget that what she and Jabarie had was special. His love for her touched her deeply and she knew this time he wouldn't be so easy to forget, if at all.

Brenna reached for a washcloth and while she

lathered her body she thought about the cold, lonely life she had waiting for her back in Dallas, and knew that she would always have the memories of Jabarie to keep her warm.

By the time she came out of the bathroom, she was fully dressed. Jabarie was in the kitchen making coffee and English muffins. When she moved into the room, he briefly glanced over his shoulder then turned his head.

"Give me ten minutes to shower and dress and I'll take you home," he replied then brushed past her and headed toward the bathroom.

Brenna stood there for a long moment and when she finally heard the shower, she retrieved her purse and quietly slipped out the door.

As luck would have it, she was able to catch a cab at the corner. She climbed in and gave him directions to her aunt's house. The whole ride she willed herself not to cry. If she was going to get through this again then she was going to have to try to be strong.

The cabdriver pulled up in front of Aunt Nellie's. She paid him and climbed out, hoping she could have a few moments to get herself together before she headed over to the bookstore. She pulled her key out of the purse, turned the lock and stepped in.

"Brenna, sweetheart! Come on in here."

She groaned inwardly. The last thing she wanted was to have to explain her red eyes to Aunt Nellie.

She stepped into the kitchen and stalled when she found her mother, Shaunda Gathers, sitting at the kitchen table.

Chapter 18

"Hello, Bren."

"Hi," she managed to say. Brenna was too surprised to say anything else.

Aunt Nellie rose from her chair. "I'm going to leave the two of you alone so that you can talk. I'll be in my room if you need anything." Panic filled Brenna's lungs and with her eyes she begged her aunt not to leave. Instead Aunt Nellie rose and squeezed her shoulder as she whispered near her ear. "You're a big girl now."

Oh, God. She wanted to scream. *No, please. Don't leave me alone with her*, but instead Brenna watched her aunt leave the room. As soon as she heard her bedroom door shut, her pulse begun to race.

"Brenna, is it possible to get a hug?"

She turned around and looked at the woman who

had abandoned her over a decade ago and faked non-chalance. "Sure."

Her mother rose and wrapped her arms around her shoulders. She loosely hugged her as well and found the scent of her perfume overpowering.

Shaunda pulled back and Brenna stared up with identical hazel eyes that were wet and misty.

"I can't believe how beautiful you are. No, I take that back because you were always a beautiful girl," she replied as she slowly assessed her from head to toe.

"Thank you," Brenna replied and stepped away from her embrace. To put a little distance between them she moved over to the refrigerator and removed a bottle of water.

"Please come and sit at the table so we can talk."

Obediently, she moved over to the kitchen table and lowered in the seat directly across from her mother. Brenna took in her lovely cream dress that complemented her smooth mahogany skin. Shaunda's honey-brown hair was thick and spiral curls framed a small oval face. Diamond earrings were in her ears and a large emerald-cut diamond was on her left hand.

Brenna twisted the cap on the bottle. "I see you're engaged."

Shaunda held her hand out in front of her, smiling as she stared down at the ring. "I got engaged last month."

"Congratulations."

Her eyes came up to study Brenna's face, trying to reach into her thoughts. "Thank you."

There was a long silence while Brenna sat there drinking her water and waiting for whatever it was that she had to say.

Her mother leaned forward in her chair. "You're probably wondering why I'm here."

"That thought did cross my mind especially since I haven't heard from you except for an occasional card."

"I know," she said in a weary voice. "There are a lot of things I've done in my past that I'm ashamed of, but I've changed."

"You mean you're no longer someone's mistress?" Her voice was heavy with sarcasm.

Brenna noticed her mother winced at the remark before she shook her head. "Those days are past me."

Brenna snorted rudely. "Am I supposed to jump up and down because you say you've changed? It's too late now. I'm all grown up." If she thought she was going to forgive her that easily, she was wrong.

"I know that. I'm not trying to jump back into your life. All I wanted to do was talk to you."

She stared down at her water bottle and started painting letters in the condensation. "How did you even know I was here?"

"Nellie told me."

Go figure.

"Brenna, there is no excuse for me walking out on you when you needed me the most, but I wanted to try and get you to understand what I was going through back then," she said, in a small pleading voice.

Brenna wanted so badly to refuse and rush to her room and lock the door, but if she did she would still be left wondering. "I'm listening," she said, ripping out the words impatiently.

Shaunda took a deep breath then folded her hands on the table. "I was an accident baby. My brothers were grown, Nellie was already thirteen and my parents weren't trying to have any more children when my mama discovered she was pregnant with me. From the time I was born I was a disappointment to my parents. I had asthma, didn't start walking until I was almost two and was never much of a student. By the time I was seventeen and found out I was pregnant, my parents had labeled me a screwup and put me out. I had nowhere to go but to Nellie's."

Brenna took another drink. She didn't remember her grandfather because he had died when she was barely three, but she did have vague memories of Grandma Pearl reading her bedtime stories while she curled up on her lap.

"Your father loved me so much, but I refused to marry him. Instead, I was determined to find a man who would impress my parents. So I told another man you were his child, hoping he would marry me, only he didn't. It wasn't until I saw your father with another woman that I realized what a fool I was. I really did love that man, and he loved you and me so much he was willing to look past everything I had done and marry me." Shaunda paused and reached into her purse for a tissue and used it to wipe her eyes. "After your father died, I was so hurt I blamed myself because if I hadn't been playing games, he would have married me years ago and he wouldn't have died coming home from the jewelry store. Losing him hurt so much I vowed to never fall in love again. I went back to dating rich men, but after all these years I couldn't do it anymore. Money did not fill the empty hole in my heart. I wanted to love again," Shaunda said between sniffs. "And then I met Tim."

Brenna met her teary-eyed gaze. "Is that your fiancé?" she asked softly.

Her mother nodded and couldn't hide the sparkle in her eyes. "I fell in love with him from the first moment I spotted him walking down the hall at the hospital. I was working there as an administrative assistant."

"What does he do?"

"He's a food service supervisor." She chuckled. "Can you believe it?"

Brenna frowned then shook her head. Her mother was marrying a hospital worker. "No, I can't."

She gave a laugh that lacked humor. "That's how I knew I really loved him. It wasn't about what kind of car he drove, or if he was buying or renting. All I knew was that I loved this man. And I thanked God for giving me a second chance. He and I attend church every Sunday and I have realized I've made a lot of mistakes in my life, my biggest being you. I thought you would be better off with Nellie, not with me jumping from one man to the next, but one thing I realized was that not once did I ever think about what you might have wanted and what you might have been feeling all these years, and I'm sorry."

She stared across at the woman who had given birth to her and tried to put her feet in her shoes. Brenna didn't know why, but she actually felt sorry for her.

"Can you ever forgive me?"

"I already have. It's the forgetting I'm having a problem with. But I'm sure that will come in time, as well."

Her mother looked relieved by her answer. "That's all I ask. I left Tim at the hotel so we could have a chance to talk but I would really like for you to meet him this evening."

Her mother had come all this way, the least she could do was make an effort. "Okay."

Reaching across the table, Shaunda cupped her hand. "Do me a favor Brenna, and don't let your life turn out like mine filled with pain and regret. If you find love, grab onto it because there is no telling if it will ever come your way again."

The store was busy that afternoon and she was happy for the distraction. She and Aunt Nellie got the carts ready for the sidewalk sale. For almost a week, the banners had been posted up and down Main Street. Tomorrow was going to be one big party.

While working, every time the bell over the door rang, she jumped expecting to see Jabarie coming through the door, but he never did. She told herself that it was a good thing, but deep down she was dying for him to hold her in his arms and tell her everything was going to be all right.

By the close of business, she began to believe that maybe he had finally accepted their time together for what it really was and had stepped back from her life.

Her mother arrived at dinner with Timothy, a tall, dark-skinned man in his mid-fifties. Surprisingly, she instantly liked him. He seemed to genuinely care a great deal for her mother, and the way her mother was looking one could tell she adored him, as well. Brenna was happy for them. All during the meal, she thought about what her mother had said, and she couldn't help but wonder if she was making a mistake.

Hours later, the couple had gone back to the hotel, and she was out on the porch enjoying the breeze when she heard the doorbell. Padding on bare feet she moved across the hardwood floor to the door and found Jabarie standing on the other side.

"Hey," she said, moving back enough for him to enter.

"Hey, yourself." He tucked his hands deep inside his pockets. "Where's Ms. Nellie?"

"She went next door to play bridge."

He sniffed. "Do I smell her apple pie?"

Brenna laughed. "Yep. I just took it out of the oven. You want some?"

Jabarie had never been able to say no to apple pie. "You got vanilla ice cream?"

"You know I do." She signaled for him to follow her into the small kitchen that smelled of cinnamon and apples. At the center of a table covered with a red table-cloth was a beautiful Dutch apple pie.

"Have a seat." She moved over to the cabinet and removed two bowls and carried them over to the table. She then retrieved two spoons and a knife and took a seat across from him.

"You want to wait until Ms. Nellie gets back?"

"Nope," she said as she carved into the piece. "She made this pie for you."

"For me?"

She nodded. "She knows how much you love her pie, so since she knew you'd be dropping by to say goodbye, she decided to make one for you."

He swallowed in response.

Brenna moved over to the refrigerator and removed a carton of ice cream then scooped a large spoonful and dropped it on top of his pie.

"Thanks," he said as she handed it to him.

She put some on her plate then returned the ice cream to the freezer before returning to her seat. "Now dig in."

He smiled then looked down at his bowl and reached for his spoon. As he ate he watched her dig in, as well.

"What's so funny?" she asked defensively.

He shook his head. "Nothing. I just love the way you put away some food. That shows how different you are."

Leaning back in her chair she gave him a long hard look. "Is that a bad thing?"

"No, baby. It's a wonderful thing. I wouldn't have it any other way." Leaning across the table he kissed her cheek.

She brought her ice cream to her lips then said, "My mother's in town."

His eyes snapped to hers. "And how do you feel about that?"

Her stomach tied in knots. That was one thing about Jabarie. His immediate concern was her welfare. *That's why I love him so much.*

Brenna shrugged. "I'm not sure yet how I feel. She brought her fiancé down so that we could meet him and I have to admit that he seems to be a really nice guy."

"Another sugar daddy?"

"Not this time. She has actually fallen in love," she added with a frown.

"What's wrong with that?" he said and she didn't miss the note of irritation.

"Nothing. I guess whatever works."

Her statement brought silence to the room. She dropped her eyes to her bowl and finished her pie. A minute later, Jabarie pushed his chair away from the table. She looked up.

"Thanks for the pie. I'll drop by the store tomorrow and say goodbye before you leave."

She simply nodded and watched him leave.

Chapter 19

Brenna packed her bags and loaded them into Aunt Nellie's car. She was scheduled to take an airport shuttle at seven.

She straightened the room and put fresh linen on the bed. As she stepped out of the room, she turned around and gazed at it one last time. Tonight, she would be back in her apartment in Dallas.

She pushed back feelings of despair. Last night she spent most of the night thinking about what her mother had said, and also her relationship with Jabarie, and wondered if maybe she was making a mistake. Loving him wasn't even a factor. She loved him with every breath she took. It was her fear that oversaw every decision in her life, and that's what scared her.

She and Aunt Nellie arrived at the bookstore an hour

later. People were already flooding Main Street, visiting the sidewalk sale. They moved inside and as soon as she put her things away, Brenna retrieved the rolling cart of books and pushed them outside the store. It wasn't long before the two students arrived and they stood outside serving the customers, while she and her aunt handled the crowd that had moved inside.

For the rest of the afternoon they were busy, but Brenna still had time to think about Jabarie. She was going to miss him. Walking away wasn't going to be as easy as she had originally imagined. The second time around was going to be three times harder than before.

The parade started and from the storefront window she had an excellent view as she watched the Sheraton Beach Marching Band parade past the store. As soon as they moved to the next street, Brenna glanced over at her mother standing at the window at the far right with her fiancé beside her. The looks they gave each other told her that the two were definitely in love. It was the same way Jabarie always looked at her. Dear God, was she making a mistake?

Her mother looked so happy, but it had taken her twenty-seven years to find love a second time. This time she had sense enough not to let it slip through her fingers.

Is that going to be me in twenty years?

Fear took over and Brenna started hyperventilating. Quickly before anyone noticed she dashed off to the office and closed the door behind her. As soon as she was in the chair, she lowered her eyelids.

Was she behaving just like her mother? Would she

have a life filled with regret? Oh, boy, she hoped not. But could she just walk away from her new life?

Her heart began pounding rapidly because the answer was as clear as the nose on the end of her face. Yes, she could. Without Jabarie in her life, the success of her bookstore and her life in Dallas had no meaning if she couldn't share her world with the man she loved. What good was anything anymore if she felt empty inside?

A small sob slipped from between her lips that she choked back. "Now what do I do?" she asked. One thing for sure, she had to talk to Jabarie before she left.

"Brenna!"

She jumped at the sound of Sheyna's voice and swiped tears from her cheeks just as her friend came barging through the door, eyes wide with excitement.

"You have got to get out here now!"

"Why?" she asked.

"Just come and see."

Forehead bunched with confusion, she allowed Sheyna to drag her through the store and outside. It took her a few moments before she realized the crowd was cheering her name. "Brenna!"

She stood against the building stunned as the drill team danced down the street and a float drew near with a miniature replica of the Beaumont Hotel. Her heart dropped straight to her toes. Jabarie was on the top, dressed in a robe with a crown on his head, holding a microphone.

"Brenna! Brenna Gathers!" he shouted.

She waved so that he could see her. As soon as he did, the float stopped and he came off, still holding the microphone.

"What are you doing?" she said with her hand at her hip so she wouldn't throw herself into his arms.

"I came for my princess."

"Your princess?" She couldn't resist a smirk. "Oh really?"

"Yes. We all have."

"We?"

He pointed to the float and she looked up and spotted Jace, Bianca and his parents all waving down at her.

"I can't believe this," she murmured under her breath.

"Believe it, baby."

She glanced over and watched her mother and Aunt Nellie both coming out of the store. She felt so embarrassed with everyone watching. "Please don't do this," she whispered. "I'm getting ready to leave for my plane."

Jabarie moved and stood in front of her. "And if you do, I'm going to follow and bring you back."

Brenna wrapped her arms around herself. "Please, just go away."

He shook his head slowly. "Not without you."

She couldn't believe this was happening to her.

"I love you, Brenna. I've loved you for as long as I've known you. It was with you I learned what love was."

"Please, you've already turned my life upside down. Can you just let me go?"

He stepped closer and she caught his masculine scent. His eyes were dark and his lashes long. He was gorgeous. "I can't do that, baby. I love you and want you in my life."

Her heart was about to bust wide open. "And what the prince wants the prince gets, right?" she asked.

"No, what I want, I fight for. I am fighting for us and am willing to do whatever it takes."

Her knees wobbled. "It'll never work."

"It'll work if we want it badly enough," he said as he caressed her cheek. "You've fought for what you wanted all your life. Tell me you're willing to fight for us, too."

"Oh, Jabarie." It was then that she realized all this time he had been talking into the microphone.

"Brenna, I don't want anyone but you. I admire your strength."

Oh, God, how could he say that when she was a coward?

"The things that make you different are the things that I admire the most. You are smart and funny, sexy, and so damn stubborn. But I wouldn't have you any other way. I love everything about you and am honored that you've even allowed me to be a part of your life. Now Brenna I want you to become a part of mine."

Glancing around she noticed all the people standing around, watching. She backed up slightly and started crying. She was starting to become a big cry baby.

Jabarie reached up and gently wiped the tears away. "Go ahead, baby, let it all out and when you're done I want you to be ready to put the past behind us and get ready to share your future with me."

"I'm such a coward," she said between sobs.

"Coward? Brenna you are the bravest woman I know. I love you baby and need you in my life—that's why I am willing to confess my love for the whole town to see." He cupped her chin. "Now please tell me you love me, too. I need to hear that."

She scrubbed her wet face. "I've never loved anyone but you. But love hurts."

He kissed her cheek. "Being without you hurts even more."

She couldn't help it, she flung herself at him and wrapped her arms around him. It felt so good to let go of her fears, to trust someone again.

Jabarie pulled back slightly and gazed down at her. "Now we can do this one of two ways. You can come back to Sheraton Beach and be with me, or I can move to Dallas."

"What would you do in Dallas?"

He kissed her lips. "It doesn't matter as long as we're together."

Rearing back, she stared up at him. "You would do that for me?"

"Anything, baby."

She started shaking her head. "I could never make you leave. You love this place as much as I do." She pulled him close. "I love you so much, Jabarie."

"And I love you, but now I need to make this official." He released her and dropped to his knee in front of her. Her pulse raced as she watched him reach into his pocket and pull out the four-carat diamond and sapphire ring he had given her over five years ago.

She gasped. "Oh my, you kept it."

"That's because in the back of my mind, I always hoped that you'd come back." He took her hand in his. "Brenna Gathers, will you marry me?"

She glanced over at her mother and aunt who were holding each other with tears in their eyes. Her eyes traveled to the Beaumonts, who were holding hands, staring down at them, anticipating her answer. Her gaze swept the crowd, as well. By the time she looked down at Jabarie, her eyes were flooded with tears of her own.

"Yes, I'll marry you."

The crowd cheered and clapped while Jabarie slipped the ring on her finger. As soon as he rose, she threw her arms around his neck and rained kisses all over his face.

"I love you," he murmured then lifted her in his arms and carried her over to the float. His father and Jace helped her up onto the platform.

She was pleasantly surprised and immediately put at ease at the warm, friendly smile on his mother's face. She pulled Brenna into a big hug and whispered close to her ear, "Welcome to the family."

"Yes, dear, we're glad to have you," Mr. Beaumont said when it was his turn to embrace her. "I hope you can find it in your heart to forgive two old fools."

Mrs. Beaumont rolled her eyes. "Who'd you call old?"

Brenna was laughing and crying at the same time. "Thank you both. That truly means a lot."

By the time Jabarie climbed onboard, the motor started and the float proceeded down Main Street with all of them waving to the crowd. Brenna took her place beside her prince, who lowered a crown onto her head. "Now you are officially a member of the Beaumont family. You sure you can handle the jokes about us being descendants of royalty?" he asked with a twinkle in his eyes.

"As long as I'm with you, nothing else matters."

Jabarie leaned down and kissed her. Brenna wasn't sure when she'd ever been this happy, but one thing for sure, love was even better the second time around.

His TEMPEST

Favorite author

Candice Poarch

To gain her birthright, Noelle Greenwood assumes
a false identity and plays a risky game of seduction
with Colin Mayes. But when her feelings become
too real, the affair spirals out of control.
Then Colin discovers the truth....

*Available the first week of June
wherever books are sold.*

KIMANI™
ROMANCE

ALWAYS
Means
FOREVER

DEBORAH FLETCHER MELLO

Despite her longtime attraction to Darwin Tollins,
Bridget Hinton rejects a casual fling with the notorious
playboy. But when Darwin seeks her legal advice,
he discovers a longing he's never known.
How can he revise Bridget's opinion of him?

*Available the first week of June
wherever books are sold.*

KIMANI™
ROMANCE

KPDFM0210607

Can she handle the risk...?

daring
devotion

ELAINE OVERTON

Author of FEVER

Andrea Chenault has always believed she could live
with the fear every firefighter's wife knows. But as her
wedding to Calvin Brown approaches, she's tormented
by doubts as several deadly fires seem to be targeting
the man she loves.

*Available the first week of June
wherever books are sold.*

KIMANI™
ROMANCE

Acclaimed author

Adrianne Byrd

Blue Skies

Part of Arabesque's At Your Service military miniseries.

Fighter pilot Sydney Garret was born to fly.
No other thrill came close—until Captain James Colton
ignited in her a reckless passion that led to their short-
lived marriage. When they parted, Sydney knew fate
would somehow reunite them. But no one imagined it
would be a matter of life or death....

"Byrd proves once again that she's
a wonderful storyteller."
—*Romantic Times BOOKreviews* on
THE BEAUTIFUL ONES

Coming the first week of June
wherever books are sold.

ARABESQUE®

www.kimanipress.com

KPAB0120607

"Like fine wine, Gwynne Forster's storytelling skills get better over time. Drama, family struggles, passion and true-to-life characters make Forster's latest her best yet."
—Donna Hill, author of GETTING HERS

BESTSELLING AUTHOR

GWYNNE
Forster

HOT
Entertainment
SERIES

Just the Man She Needs

Felicia Parker is a successful New York columnist with a Rolodex full of celebrity connections—but zero social contacts. So when a glitzy event requires bringing a date, she hires stunningly handsome, high-powered CEO John Ashton Underwood. Their worlds clash, but the scorching attraction between them could burn up the pages....

Coming the first week of June wherever books are sold.

ARABESQUE®

www.kimanipress.com

KPGF0130607

A brand-new Kendra Clayton mystery
from acclaimed author…

ANGELA
HENRY

Diva's Last Curtain Call

Amateur sleuth Kendra Clayton finds herself immersed in
mayhem once again when a cunning killer rolls credits on a
fading movie star. Kendra's publicity-seeking sister is pegged
as the prime suspect, but Kendra knows her sister is no
murderer. She soon uncovers some surprising Hollywood
secrets, putting herself in danger of becoming the killer's
encore performance….

"A tightly woven mystery."
—*Ebony* magazine on *The Company You Keep*

sepia™

Coming the first
week of June
wherever books
are sold.

KPAH0440607

tangled
ROOTS

A Kendra Clayton Novel

ANGELA HENRY

Nothing's going right these days for part-time
English teacher and reluctant sleuth Kendra Clayton.
Now her favorite student is the number one suspect in a local
murder. When he begs Kendra for help, she's soon on the road
to trouble again—trying to find the real killer, stepping into
danger...and getting tangled in the deadly roots of desire.

"This debut mystery features an exciting new
African-American heroine.... Highly recommended."
—*Library Journal* on *The Company You Keep*

*Available the first week of May
wherever books are sold.*

KIMANI PRESS™

www.kimanipress.com

KPAH0680507